GEOFF NICHOLSON

Geoff Nicholson has been hailed as a witty and acute writer for his novels STREET SLEEPER, THE KNOT GARDEN, WHAT WE DID ON OUR HOLIDAYS, HUNTERS AND GATHERERS, THE FOOD CHAIN and THE ERROL FLYNN NOVEL. The sequel to STREET SLEEPER, STILL LIFE WITH VOLKSWAGENS, will be published in paperback by Sceptre in 1995. Geoff Nicholson is also the author of two works of non-fiction, BIG NOISES and DAY TRIPS TO THE DESERT. He lives in London.

sceptre

Also by Geoff Nicholson and available from Sceptre Books:

DAY TRIPS TO THE DESERT:
A sort of travel book
THE FOOD CHAIN
HUNTERS AND GATHERERS
STREET SLEEPER

Geoff Nicholson

THE ERROL FLYNN NOVEL

sceptre

First published in Great Britain in 1993 by Hodder and Stoughton

First published in paperback in 1994 by Hodder and Stoughton, a division of Hodder Headline PLC

A Sceptre paperback

British Library C.I.P.

Nicholson, Geoff
The Errol Flynn Novel
I. Title
823.914 [F]

ISBN 0 340 599197

10 9 8 7 6 5 4 3 2 1

Printed and bound in Great Britain for Hodder and Stoughton Ltd, a division of Hodder Headline PLC, 338 Euston Road London NW1 3BH by Cox & Wyman Ltd.

THE ERROL FLYNN NOVEL

1

Dan Ryan said to me, "It starts like this. Exterior establishing shot; a big, green, English landscape with a huge castle up on a hill. The guy who owns the castle, the Lord of the Manor, is returning from a hunting party with his band of men. They're on horseback, they've got a pack of dogs, swords, bows and arrows, all that stuff. Camera zooms in on a window in the tower of the castle. Interior shows a bedroom, coats of arms on the wall, suits of armour, and a big four-poster bed with animal skins and furs for blankets; and in the bed there's Errol Flynn and a woman, the lady of the castle, the wife of the guy we've seen returning from the hunt. At first I thought he could be in bed with two women, the wife and the daughter, but I decided that's maybe going too far too soon.

"So Flynn wakes up, hears the sound of horses' hoofs, realises the guy's returning, knows he's got to get out of there and fast, so he leaps out of bed, swigs back a goblet of mead or real ale, or whatever, and starts getting dressed. The wife wakes up, doesn't want him to go, says something corny like, 'Don't leave. I'll die without you.' And he says something like, 'Madam, I shall die if I stay,' though I'm sure we can come up with something snappier than that. So he gives her a long, final embrace, and, you know, this is an Errol Flynn for the nineties, and it could be quite an explicit embrace, definitely bare breasts, maybe more. Then he leaps out the window, and it just so happens there's a rope hanging out the window so he starts to climb down it.

"But the Lord of the Manor is getting pretty close to the castle by now, and he sees Flynn up on the tower, and realises what's been going on. He's mad as hell and they've been out hunting, right, and they're still in the mood for blood so he blows his hunting horn and a real manhunt starts, with Flynn as the prey.

"Flynn's climbed to the bottom of the rope, but it's too short so he does a spectacular dive into the moat, comes out the other side and starts to run. Now it's got to be made clear that he isn't the kind of guy who would normally run from a fight, but hell, he's got a dozen big English guys and a pack of hounds after him, what else is the guy going to do?

"So there's a chase scene and we see him leaping over ravines and swimming across rivers and swinging through trees. This goes on for quite a while, intercut with shots of baying hounds, horses' hoofs and the Lord of the Manor foaming at the mouth and swearing vengeance. Then we see Flynn disappear into a clump of forest, hotly pursued by two of the hunters. They ride into a clearing and there's no sign of Flynn. They look around. They know he's here somewhere. Suddenly he drops down out of the trees above their heads, knocks them off their horses, runs them through with his sword and takes off on one of their horses. Now he's in with a chance.

"More chase, with Flynn's horse leaping over fences and hedges and riding up and down rock faces, maybe through waterfalls. Anyway, it looks like he's finally escaping, and the horse gallops away, right to the edge of a two-hundred-foot cliff. There's no way down, and there's no way back. He has to stay and fight. So the hunters start to arrive, not all at once, in ones and twos, and he fights with them. Some he stabs, some he throws over the cliff. Lots of slow motion shots of bodies falling and twisting through the air; really balletic. Flynn's doing pretty good. He gets rid of them all until at last it's just him and the Lord of the Manor, the guy he's cuckolded. The guy laughs and says, 'I wanted this pleasure all to myself.' So they fight – long fight – swords, knives, fists – some of it pretty dirty, a lot of kicking in the balls and that kind of thing. Finally they're on the ground wrestling, edging closer and closer to the big drop over the cliff. And Flynn's getting the worse of it, he's being strangled and as he struggles it looks for a moment as though they're both going to go over the edge. And Flynn looks the other guy right in the eyes and then he plants a big wet French kiss on him. And the other guy returns it, really gets into it, so instead of being a fight scene, it's now a smoochy homo love scene. Big shock for the audience.

"Then somebody shouts 'Cut' and they both get up laughing and the camera pulls back and we see the director and the sound crew and the continuity girl and the catering truck. And Flynn walks back to his trailer and goes inside, and there's a cute little blonde sixteen-year-old dressed in Nazi regalia, you know, maybe like Charlotte Rampling in *Night Porter*, just waiting for him to return. He slumps down in a chair. He's tired, exhausted. He's getting far too old for this stuff. He knocks back half a bottle of vodka and shoots up some morphine, and suddenly there's a knock on the door and a guy says, 'Mr Flynn, I'm from the IRS. You owe us three-quarters of a million dollars.' And Flynn just starts laughing and the sixteen-year-old takes her clothes off and Flynn starts fucking her. And basically, that's the end of the pre-title sequence. What do you think, Jake?"

"It sounds good," I said.

"What do you *really* think?"

"I think it sounds expensive."

"Jake," he said, "you've got to stop thinking of money as a problem."

But I never quite did.

I think two things need to be said before we start this whole thing.

The first is, and I know this is completely obvious, that life is nothing if not changeable. Out of the blue things happen that change our lives completely and for ever. The old lives we had simply disappear. You say to yourself, "Where did my life go?" And someone might answer, "Your life's right here." And you might say in return, "No, no, I don't mean this life, I mean the old one, the one I used to have. I liked it more. It suited me better. I was more secure, I was happier. That's the life I want. Surely it must be around somewhere, if only I knew where to look." But, of course, you don't know where to look.

I realise that in the end this probably comes down to some kind of Christmas cracker motto bullshit, like there's no going back, pleasures are fleeting, all things must pass.

I was ready for change, but inevitably I was not ready for the specific change that occurred. I wanted excitement, drama, money, love, and I got the lot, but, of course, it wasn't the kind of excitement, drama, money and love I'd had in mind. I was left, as I guess people often are, asking what was that all about, and wondering where my life went. Well, you say, what's so unusual about that?

The other thing that needs to be said is that I did, unfortunately, used to look quite a lot like Errol Flynn.

2

I was twenty-five years old and I was making such a success of my career as an actor that I'd had to take a full-time job working in a photocopying shop. I had been out of drama school for four years and I'd got my Equity card without too much trouble, though admittedly only by doing a dodgy collection of children's theatre. Then I had a couple of seasons in provincial Rep, I'd played a taxi driver in one episode of a television sitcom, and I'd appeared on a commercial for "golden turkey nuggets". I knew that this did not add up to a substantial body of work. In the spirit that it was better to be doing something than nothing I had found myself acting in plays on the fringe of the London fringe, working for no money to no audience. But I'd stopped doing that. I'd decided it was a waste of time. It wasn't "real acting".

To say I was disillusioned only tells half the story. I wasn't disillusioned with acting. I was disillusioned with *not* acting. I knew I was at least as good as some of my contemporaries who were now "doing well". It didn't particularly surprise me that they were doing well while I wasn't. I knew that was how things were in the acting biz. I knew it was unfair. I knew it was a game. I didn't mind that. My only objection was that I wasn't in the game, and I couldn't work out how to get in.

I thought I was a pretty good actor but I never thought I was a star. That, I reckoned, was something well worth knowing. A lot of actors end up frustrated and suicidal because they don't get to be Laurence Olivier or Warren Beatty. I thought I wasn't cut out to be the leading man, but I thought I could do a damned good job as the leading man's best friend. But that required somebody to give me a part, and lately I hadn't even summoned up enough enthusiasm to go to auditions. The doting parents had subsidised me for a while, but when my self-respect got too much for me I started working in a photocopying shop. It wasn't glamorous but at least it was paid and nobody ever told me I was wrong for the part.

I had never spent much time analysing my motives for becoming or wanting to be an actor. I wouldn't have objected to being rich and famous and loved by millions, but that was never my main aim. I think I became an actor for no better reason than that I was quite good at it, and I've not been good at many things in my life.

Like a lot of actors I would say I was essentially shy. I was never an extrovert. I was never the life and soul of the party. I didn't like showing off. It seems to me that half the actors in the world want to bombard the audience with what they take to be their wonderful personalities, and the other half gets into acting precisely as a way to avoid doing that. I was definitely in the latter category.

When Sacha Henderson turned up at the shop I wanted to run away and hide, I was so embarrassed. Sacha and I had been at drama school together. I hadn't seen her in the four years since I'd left. She was one of the ones doing well. Oddly enough I didn't feel so bad about that. It had been so obvious from the outset that Sacha was going to be a success that it was hard to resent it. If I'd had to guess I'd have said she'd go straight from drama school into an American mini-series. She had the voice, the bone-structure, the body-language. She was Hollywood's idea of an English actress. I had thought she would turn into another Jane Seymour or Jacqueline Bissett, but I was quite wrong.

Despite her saleable looks, and despite a couple of good offers, Sacha hadn't gone into a mini-series at all. She had become, in her own mind at least, a serious actress. On stage and on screen Sacha had a very compelling, enigmatic quality. She could be still and silent, and an aura of mystery would settle itself around her. If you wanted to buy-in some enigma, Sacha was your woman. It was great for playing femmes fatales, murderesses, trauma victims, and, of course, Ophelia. Sacha was also not averse to taking her clothes off.

Immediately after drama school she had gone to Krakow to work with some great Polish theatre director who was dying of cancer and was staging one vast, final, avant-garde production of *Hamlet*. The production, which, of course, I only read about, was set outdoors in various locations all over Krakow. There was a cast of hundreds, if not thousands. There were twenty actors all playing Hamlet, and Sacha was one of a dozen or so actresses playing Ophelia. There was a lot of shouting, lots of masks, lasers, electronic music, banks of video screens, cars set on fire, and, of course, nudity. It sounded like a good one to have on your c.v.

After that, Sacha had done a lot of quirky but high-profile stage plays, and a few highbrow, low-budget movies; always being enigmatic. You could have said it was all a bit artsy fartsy and pretentious, and that was precisely what some of us who had known Sacha at drama school *did* say. Nevertheless it all sounded a million times more interesting and satisfying than what I was doing with my own life.

Sacha was profoundly, wonderfully sexy. Her face and her body could, and did, make you ache. But I couldn't say I ever really "fancied" her. You don't fancy someone who is totally unobtainable. You may lust after sex-goddesses but you don't "fancy" them exactly. When you fancy someone you ask them out for a drink or to go to the pictures. You wouldn't have asked Greta Garbo out to the pictures and similarly I wouldn't have done so with Sacha. I knew my place. Sacha may not have been a sex-goddess in the true sense of the word, but she was the nearest thing to it that I'd ever encountered. Women like Sacha didn't have affairs with men like me, and frankly I couldn't blame them.

When she came into the photocopying shop I thought at first she wasn't going to recognise me. That would have suited me fine. But, of course, she *did* recognise me. She appeared to be pleased to see me. She was very friendly, very warm, and above all very genuine. There wasn't any hint of "Oh, you poor boy, reduced to having to do a real job for a living", which I was half expecting.

I felt the need to explain myself to her, even though I couldn't. I muttered some nonsense about being broke, being bored not acting, about feeling the need to get out in the real world. Sacha was good enough to say that sounded very sensible. We did some standard actors' chat about which of our mutual acquaintances were working and which weren't, what jobs were coming up, what plays and movies were new and good. She was much better informed than I was. She finally got around to saying she needed some photocopying done. She got a mound of books and papers out of her bag. There were some loose pages of script, some handwritten notes, newspaper cuttings, a c.v. (not hers), and two or three books about Errol Flynn. I copied the documents and then some pages from the books, and I said, "Errol Flynn?"

"Yes," she said. "I'm doing some pre-production work on a movie about Errol Flynn."

"Who's doing it?"

"A guy called Dan Ryan."

I tried to look as though I'd heard of him, but she could tell I hadn't.

"He's not very well known. Not here, anyway. He's American. He's interesting. He's got some good ideas. And he's got some money."

"Are you going to be acting in it?"

"Who knows? Probably it won't ever get made. But it's all experience."

"Sure," I said.

"You should meet Dan Ryan," she said.

"Yes?"

"Well, it's all about contacts, isn't it?"

This surprised me slightly. I'd read a couple of newspaper interviews with Sacha and in those she had suggested acting wasn't so much about contacts as about discovering essences and plumbing the dark caverns of the human spirit, but maybe I was being too cynical.

"There might be some work in it, who knows?" she said.

"Yes," I said. "I could always play Errol Flynn's best friend."

"That was David Niven. Or maybe Tyrone Power."

"Well, I like a challenge."

She laughed. "I'll tell Dan Ryan about you," she said.

I didn't think she knew enough to be able to tell an American film producer about me, although, let's face it, there wasn't much to know. I didn't expect to hear from Sacha for another four years. I was touched that she'd even made the effort to pretend. Two days later, however, I was being "interviewed" by Dan Ryan.

We were in the bar of the Savoy. It was crowded. I was there with Ryan and Sacha. I was wearing a jacket and tie because they wouldn't have served me otherwise. It was not my usual costume. It was not my usual territory.

Ryan was a big man. He had big hands and a big head, a lot of carefully arranged hair and a very trim beard. He wasn't fat as yet but you could tell he had to work hard in order to stay thin. He was American-looking, handsome I suppose, aged about fifty. He looked like he had money, yet he didn't look like my idea of a film producer, not that I'd met many film producers at that stage in my life. I still haven't. Also, there was no denying that he bore some resemblance to Errol Flynn. He wasn't a dead ringer, he wasn't a lookalike, but I thought there was something definitely Flynn-like about him. At the time I thought there was nothing at all Flynn-like about me, but then again, I knew almost nothing about anything.

I wasn't really sure what I was doing there. I had no idea what we were going to discuss, but I assumed it would all be very polite, very general, very non-committal on both sides. I was wrong. The first thing Dan Ryan said to me as he shook my hand, was, "Hello, Jake, would you like to suck my cock?"

I wasn't so much offended as deeply, deeply embarrassed. I could tell it was some kind of test, some kind of in-joke, and a part of the audition process, but basically it struck me as a really stupid thing to say. He said it with a dead straight face, and Sacha who was sitting right beside me didn't show any surprise. I didn't say anything at first but it soon became clear that nothing else was going to happen until I made some sort of reply. So I said, "Well, no, actually I wouldn't," at which point Ryan cracked up laughing, and Sacha laughed too, and, not wanting to be left out, I thought I'd better laugh as well.

"It's okay, Jake," Ryan said. "That's not me speaking. That's Errol Flynn speaking. He used to say that to guys when he first met them. It had a kind of disarming effect. As you saw."

Then we laughed some more. My laughter was a little forced. Ryan and Sacha's was conspiratorial. They were in this together, "this" being something more than just the movie business. They looked to me like two people who were having an affair, one that had started very recently and was still new and exciting and pretty hot stuff. I didn't know why but I found that depressing.

We ordered drinks and Ryan said, "So the deal is this, Jake; I'm going to make a great movie about Errol Flynn. I'm producing and directing and I need some help, some collaborators. At some point I'm going to need experience, professional expertise, some old hands, but right now what I need are some new faces and some fresh input. I need new talent. You've obviously got talent. Do you want in?"

"Well, I'm certainly interested," I said stiffly.

"You want to play Errol Flynn?"

"Er . . . I don't know."

"He wants to play David Niven," Sacha said.

"Oh yeah?" said Ryan.

"Not really," I said. "But I'm not sure that I really see myself playing the lead role in a movie about Errol Flynn."

"No? You wanted a small part maybe? A walk on? You wanted to be an extra? You wanted a non-speaking part in a crowd scene? You want something that demands nothing of you?"

I shrugged. I guessed I was supposed to say that when he put it like that I did indeed, desperately, passionately, want a major role in this project. But I wasn't going to play that game. So I said, "I'd like a part in your movie if there's one for me. I want to work. I'm not afraid of doing things that are difficult. But I still don't think I'm an obvious choice for Errol Flynn."

"You said it, Jake. I'm not going to be doing anything obvious in this movie. I don't want an Errol Flynn lookalike. I don't want an Errol Flynn impersonator. Have you heard of Bertolt Brecht?"

"Just once or twice," I said.

"Good. So you know all about the alienation effect?"

I nodded.

"So maybe in this movie of mine Errol Flynn could be played by an old man of eighty, or by a black teenager, or by a woman, or by a different actor in every scene."

"I suppose so," I said.

I looked over at Sacha and she was taking this all very seriously. Maybe, I thought, he'd got her into bed by promising to let her play Errol Flynn. But no, Sacha may have been artsy fartsy but she wasn't plain stupid.

"This is what's so great about starting a project," Ryan said. "Don't you think? This sense of endless possibility, of open vistas, of great opportunities just waiting to be grasped."

"Yes," I said, and I actually meant it, although it seemed to me that however broad the range of possibilities, you might decide to abandon the option of a black teenage Errol Flynn quite early on.

"Look," Ryan continued, "this is not going to be an expensive movie. We're only talking about a few million dollars or so. Okay, that means we won't be hiring Robert Redford, but it also means we can be free in a way Hollywood never dreamed of. We can be outrageous. We have the freedom to be weird. It's important that you know what kind of director I am, Jake. I'm not a David Lean. I'm sure as hell no Dickie Attenborough. I'm more Andy Warhol meets David Lynch meets Peter Greenaway. Is that okay by you?"

"That's fine by me," I said.

"And look, in the end it may not be a movie about Errol Flynn at all, not the Errol Flynn who actually lived. It may be about ontology and iconography, and sensuality, and fame, and myth, and, of course, death. And you know what it's going to be called? *The Errol Flynn Movie.*"

He paused to give me time to appreciate the greatness of the title.

"Is there a script?" I asked.

Even as I said it I suspected that was the wrong thing to ask. I imagined Ryan might think I was being terminally pedantic and unhip. Who needed a silly old thing like a script? I was pleasantly surprised when he said, "Sure. My wife and I are writing a script. She's back in the office working on the rewrites while we're sitting here. My wife is Tina Ryan, you may have heard of her."

I hadn't but I found it reassuring to know that someone else other than Ryan was involved with this project even if it was only the man's wife. I was still naïve enough to believe that the existence of a script was an encouraging sign. Anyone can sit in a bar and talk about the wonderful film they're going to make. To actually sit down and write a script, I thought, showed serious intentions.

"Can I read it?" I asked.

"Well, of course, but you know, I'm hot to make this movie. I want to get it rolling, and if the script isn't one hundred per cent perfect on the first day of shooting, I hope you'll bear with me."

"Well, sure," I said.

"Jake," Ryan said, "I can't promise you that this movie is going to make you a star, and at this stage I can't even promise you that you'll be playing Errol Flynn, but if you give me the kind of commitment I'm looking for, I can absolutely promise you, it'll be the experience of a lifetime."

"Are you offering me a part?" I asked.

"Maybe. How much do you know about Errol Flynn?"

"Very little," I confessed. "I think I've seen a couple of his movies on television. I know he was a swashbuckler. I know he was supposed to be a great womaniser. I know he was supposed to have a big penis."

"Scholars differ on that one," said Ryan. "Not that size means anything."

He and Sacha did some more of that conspiratorial laughter.

"How about this for a deal?" said Ryan. "I want to see if you can get an angle on Errol Flynn. I want you to do some research, read some books, see some movies, see if you can get a feel of the man and the issues, and we can take it from there."

This didn't make a terrible amount of sense to me, not if the film wasn't actually going to be about the Errol Flynn who actually lived, but I didn't protest, especially not when he said, "And, of course, I'll pay you for your time and trouble. I'm not going to rip you off, Jake, which in itself makes me one of the more unusual people you're ever going to meet in the movie business."

He took a thick calfskin wallet out of his jacket pocket and slid out a cheque, already made out in my name, and for an amount which I suppose wasn't massive by movie standards but which still looked pretty juicy to a guy who was working in a photocopying shop.

"Think of it as a retainer," he said.

Then he handed me a copy of Flynn's autobiography, *My Wicked, Wicked Ways*, dropped a couple of notes to pay for the drinks, and said he'd be in touch again soon. I gave him my phone number. He conspicuously didn't give me his. Then he and Sacha said they had to go to the movies and they went, and I was left alone in the unfamiliar splendours of the Savoy. I looked at the cheque he had given me. On the strength of it I ordered myself another drink.

3

The next ten days were a little strange. I read Errol Flynn's autobiography. It read like a Hollywood screenplay, not a very good one. It had pace and punch and it was easy to read, but it didn't sound very credible. I had no idea how much, if any, was true, but I'd have guessed very little. However I soon had much more to do than read the autobiography. Each day the postman delivered another package of research materials sent by Ryan. Some of it might well have been what I'd copied for Sacha, but there were also bundles of film stills, videos of Flynn's movies, an audio cassette of film music by Erich Korngold who'd done the soundtracks for some of Flynn's best movies, some recordings of Flynn acting in early radio plays, a copy of a gossip magazine from the 1940s containing a salacious article about Flynn. There were some costume drawings, photographs of 1930s Hollywood architecture, photographs of a New Guinea copra plantation dated 1929. There was nothing resembling a script.

There were also phone calls from Ryan. They must have averaged two a day. In some of the calls he simply asked me if I'd got the latest batch of stuff he'd sent, and then told me to read and enjoy it. Sometimes he'd be more inquisitive, asking me, for instance, if I'd got to the part in the autobiography where Flynn gets into a fight with a Hindu rickshaw-puller who slashes his (Flynn's) stomach open with a knife. I had. According to Flynn, the slash was so deep that his intestines started to fall out, so he stuffed them back inside and went to a hospital where they gave him sixteen stitches. He was supposed to stay in bed for two weeks, but two days later he was on his feet again, chasing the nurses and so on. The wound then exploded again.

"Do you believe a word of that?" Ryan asked

"Well, maybe some of it," I said. "I think Flynn probably did get into a fight with a rickshaw man and maybe the guy even pulled a knife on him, but I guess he probably made up the stuff about the sixteen stitches and the guts falling out."

"I like it," said Ryan.

Then the next day he'd ring up again and say he'd been thinking about what I'd said and he'd thought of a way to use it in the film.

"So what happens is this," he said. "First of all we see Flynn being pulled along in the rickshaw. He gets where he's going, there's an argument about the fare, the driver curses him and then runs away. Then we show the scene again, but now it's the way it's told in the autobiography; the slashed stomach, the stitches and so forth. Then we go for it one more time, but now it's as though we're watching an Errol Flynn movie. This time the rickshaw man is a huge foreign devil carrying a sabre. He and Flynn have a sword fight, in a bazaar, or whatever they have in India, and it's a great duel and finally Flynn gets the guy down on his knees and makes him beg for mercy. Then he lets him go to show what a noble fellow he is. What do you think?"

"It sounds interesting," I said.

He said he'd get back to me on it. Occasionally it got a little embarrassing when Ryan rang me at work and asked me, say, what were my views on underage sex or statutory rape. I couldn't give a very considered answer when I was standing there in the shop with a queue of people waiting to get photocopies. Very politely I'd offer to ring him back later, but he didn't want that, so I'd ask him to ring me at home in the evening, which he would do, but by then he'd have some other bee in his bonnet, and the issue of underage sex or statutory rape would have been forgotten. Sometimes he'd ring me up and ask if I could ride a horse or if I'd ever sailed a boat, and all he would want was a simple yes or no answer then he'd hang up.

I, in turn, was trying to phone Sacha. I wanted to know more about Ryan. How had she met him? What movies had he done in the past? Where did he get his money from? I knew I could, and probably should, have asked Ryan all these questions to his face but I was too inhibited.

I wanted Sacha to say that Ryan wasn't a fake and that I wasn't completely wasting my time on this project. Of course I knew that however bona fide Ryan turned out to be, there was still a strong possibility that his movie would never get made, that's how it is with movies. But I wanted some confirmation that I wasn't involved with a complete charlatan, that he wasn't deceiving himself and me into the bargain.

But Sacha remained elusive. She wasn't in the phone book, though that was hardly surprising. I tried friends of friends but nobody could come up with a phone number for her. Her agent, understandably, wouldn't give out her number either, nor her address, and wouldn't admit to knowing anything about Ryan or about any Errol Flynn movie. I felt very much on my own. I realised too that, even if I had spoken to Sacha, her views on Ryan were likely to be decidedly unobjective, if, as I suspected, she was having an affair with him.

To the limited extent that I allowed myself to have an opinion about Ryan at all, I thought he was probably a raving eccentric, though probably not a raving madman. Most of his ideas sounded like bullshit, but even he admitted they were only ideas. They could all be edited, transformed, tidied up, before they became part of this mysterious script that he and his wife were supposedly writing.

I thought it was a little strange that he hadn't asked me to read or do a screen test for him, but I didn't really know how these things worked. Maybe that would all come later. I suppose the thing that encouraged me most was Ryan's money. Even in the world of movies people surely didn't throw away money for no good reason. However eccentric he was, his money was perfectly concrete. His cheque had not bounced, and I took that as an extremely clear sign that he was serious about the film.

As more and more packages arrived from Ryan, my evenings became extremely busy. Now there were production sketches and CDs of music he was considering using for the film, and there were more videos of Flynn's films. I was determined to keep my day job, but getting through each new batch of material in a single night was hard going. Fortunately I was a social disaster anyway. There are some people who get invited out all the time and some who would never get invited out at all if they didn't work pretty hard at it. I was in the latter category. If I chose to stay in my flat for ten consecutive evenings nobody was going to beg me to come out to play. And in the same way that actors "rest" between parts, I was resting between girlfriends. There were no social or romantic demands on me. There was, therefore, absolutely nothing stopping me from devoting my evenings, and most of my tea breaks and lunch hours, in fact most of my spare waking hours, to Errol Flynn.

The strange thing was, or maybe it wasn't so very strange, the more work I did the more I was able to convince myself that I might just possibly be right for the leading role.

It came as no surprise when Ryan rang me about nine o'clock one Wednesday evening. This was some ten days after our first meeting.

"Hi, how you doing?" he said.

"Fine," I said. "I'm actually re-reading Charles Higham's book on Flynn."

"Are you gripped?"

"Well, I'm very interested."

"Could you use a beer?"

"Sure," I said.

I still haven't worked out whether that was the right or the wrong thing to have said. Ten minutes later Ryan turned up. He was wearing full evening dress, driving a Rolls-Royce, and already looking very drunk. He came into my flat, made some unconvincing remarks about how pleasant it was, and helped himself to my Scotch.

"Where are we going for this beer?" he asked.

"I was thinking of the local pub," I said, "but I don't know about dressed like that."

"They'll learn to love it," said Ryan.

So we went to the Railway Tavern. It was my local, a very ordinary London pub, big, brightly lit, small tables placed well away from each other, a young crowd. Rock bands sometimes played in the back room. We got some strange looks from the other customers as we ordered our drinks, but Ryan was completely unembarrassed. He looked perfectly at home in evening dress. Probably he wore it all the time. Besides, this was London, this supposedly great cosmopolitan city. People surely walked the streets and entered pubs wearing infinitely stranger outfits than this.

"So how's Errol Flynn?" he asked me.

"Errol Flynn's pretty good," I said, and I meant it.

"You still want a bit part?"

"No, I want more than that."

"Good. Are you ready to play Errol Flynn?"

"Yes, I think I could be."

"Let me know when you're sure."

"I'm sure. I was just being understated."

"Very English."

"Not very Errol Flynn, eh?" I said.

Ryan smiled at me. It wasn't something he did very often. I felt I'd made some kind of breakthrough.

"Do you get bored easily?" he asked.

"No," I said.

"I do," he said. "This pub's boring me already."

He looked around the place restlessly, searching for something to interest him. His eyes fell on a couple at a table in a corner of the pub. They were sitting in silence, barely acknowledging each other's existence. The man was broad, beefy, tattooed. He looked like a nasty piece of work, a yob, but he was just sitting there minding his own business. His girlfriend was fat and plain and completely unremarkable. Ryan walked over to their table. The yob looked up, giving a kind of snigger when he saw how Ryan was dressed.

Ryan said to him, "You know, I've been looking at you, and I think you look like a faggot. And you know what else? I think your girlfriend looks like a faggot too."

He gave a slight bow of his head, turned his back to them and came to rejoin me. He must have seen the panic in my eyes. I was already preparing myself for a quick exit.

The yob was soon on his feet and had an empty lager bottle in his hand, just right for smashing on the edge of a table and jamming into somebody's face. He was advancing very quickly on Ryan's back. Ryan turned round.

"Put the bottle down," he said.

The yob hesitated.

"I said put the fucking bottle down."

I don't know if it was the American accent, or Ryan's age, or simply the evening dress, but the bottle was duly put down. I was amazed. Ryan squared up to the yob. The yob threw a punch. It missed by a long way. Ryan caught the fist, and the arm attached to it, and started to twist it. I guess it was some kind of karate grip and Ryan was attacking some pressure points. The guy was in agony. His free arm and his legs flailed trying to make contact with Ryan, but somehow they got nowhere near. The guy fell to his knees. He started to plead. Then he started to weep.

"You see how it is?" Ryan said to me. "You see how easy it is to make your life more interesting? And especially how easy it is to take control. This fellah here, the one down by my feet, he's done everything I wanted him to. I can make him attack me. I can make him put down the bottle. Now I can make him lick the soles of my shoes if I want to. That's how it is when you're a Hollywood director!"

The landlord of the pub was now out from behind the bar. He was obviously accustomed to breaking up the occasional fight, but I guess he wasn't that accustomed to protecting yobs from middle-aged Americans.

Ryan said to him, "I don't think you'll have any more trouble from this one," and let go of his victim.

The landlord stood between the two of them in case hostilities were going to break out again, but the yob had had enough. The landlord turned to Ryan, and I really couldn't believe this, he said, "Thanks, mate."

Ryan made a "think nothing of it" sort of shrug and we left the Railway Tavern. My heart was still beating too fast, even after we'd been in the car and driving for a while. That's the effect violence has on me, even just watching it. I don't like it. It upsets me. Ryan could see I was shaken. He gave me a drink from his hip flask.

"Not scared by a little violence, are we?" he said.

"Well, yes," I said.

"Errol Flynn wasn't."

"I'm not Errol Flynn, okay?"

"Not yet, anyway. There was a time when Errol Flynn couldn't walk into any bar in America without someone taking a swing at him, someone wanting to prove they were more of a man than Errol Flynn."

"It was you who started that fight," I said. "Why? Am I supposed to be impressed?"

"Oh, Jake, don't be such a wimp. A good fist fight never hurt anybody. A few beers, a half-hearted attempt to get laid, and then a good old brawl. For thousands of years that's what it's meant to be a man. That's the kind of man Errol Flynn was."

I must have looked unconvinced by this.

"Look, in 1940, say, Errol Flynn represented just about every ideal of what a man should be. He was a hard-fighting, hard-drinking, womanising son of a bitch; and that's what all men wanted to be like. What's more, that's what women wanted men to be like. In 1940 all men wanted to be Errol Flynn, and all women wanted to get laid by Errol Flynn.

"Okay, so times change. These days Errol Flynn represents to you liberals just about everything that a man shouldn't be. Hard-fighting, hard-drinking womanisers aren't in fashion this season. Is this a good thing or a bad thing? Discuss."

"How can it be anything other than a good thing," I said.

"Well," said Ryan, "at the very least it might be the basis for a movie, right?"

We went to a wine bar in St John's Wood. It was dark and low-ceilinged and full of ersatz-looking sawdust and wine barrels. Ryan ordered a bottle of champagne and asked for four glasses. He sat down at a table already occupied by a couple of office girls. At first I thought he knew them but it soon became clear that he didn't. They were busy showing each other their holiday snapshots.

"All right!" Ryan said. "Dirty pictures! These I have to see."

I thought this was a remarkably crass opening line. I'm no expert on picking up strange girls in wine bars, but something told me this was not the way. I was wrong. Ryan could get away with it. The girls accepted some of his champagne. They were obviously intrigued by him. They weren't at all intrigued by me, and frankly I wasn't very intrigued by them. They looked like very boring girls to me. I couldn't see why Ryan was bothering with them, certainly not when he had Sacha, not to say a wife, back home. After a while he brought the conversation round to movies.

"So who's your favourite male sex symbol?" he asked the girls. "Don't tell me, it's Mel Gibson, isn't it?"

I began to think perhaps he was just carrying out some market research.

"Mel Gibson's all right," one of the girls said.

"Tom Cruise," said the other.

"How about Robert Redford?" Ryan asked.

"He's too old."

"Hell," said Ryan, "I thought you looked like the kind of girls who preferred older men."

The girls thought that was quite funny.

"How about Dustin Hoffman?"

"No, he's not sexy. He's a brilliant actor but he's not sexy."

"So how about Arnold Schwarzenegger?"

"Well, I wouldn't kick him out of bed."

"Now here's something I've been thinking," Ryan said. "Old Arnie is a big boy, right? Every muscle on him has been worked on and pumped up to twice its normal size. But you know, there aren't any muscles in a cock, so it seems to me his cock can't possibly have kept pace with the rest of his body. It must be this tiny little thing sitting in a vast sea of muscle."

They liked that. They laughed.

"How about Errol Flynn?" Ryan said.

"Well, yes," one of them said, "he filled a nice pair of trousers in his day. But I don't think he's sexy."

"Why not?" Ryan asked.

"Well, he's dead for one thing."

"That's true," said Ryan. "Aren't people sexy when they're dead?"

There was a lot of joking around then about "stiffs". I was getting very bored. The bottle of champagne was soon empty. The girls were eating out of Ryan's hand by now. They even offered to buy another bottle. Ryan wouldn't hear of it.

"Okay," he said to them, "this is how it is. I could buy another bottle of bubbly, and then another, and then we could go get something to eat. We'd go in my car, you'd be impressed by my car. Then we'd go on to a night-club, then to my place, and at some point I'd get to fuck one or both of you. And you know what? I don't want to do that. And you know why not? Because I think you both look like lousy lays."

The girls looked even more threatening than the yob had. We left rapidly. As we drove away Ryan said to nobody in particular, "Plain girls are swell, they don't tell; and they're grateful as hell. That's not me speaking, that's Errol Flynn."

I didn't understand what Ryan was up to. And I didn't really understand why I couldn't just say I'd had enough and go home. Maybe I was finding Ryan as charismatic as everyone else seemed to. Maybe I thought that only wimps went home, and I knew Ryan wouldn't want a wimp playing the part of Errol Flynn.

He took me to some kind of drinking club in Soho. He knocked on a featureless, unmarked door and in we went. He left the Rolls parked on the pavement outside. I felt sure it was going to get towed away. I had never been to a Soho drinking club before, and I was a little disappointed. It looked pretty much like an ordinary bar. It wasn't at all sleazy and it wasn't full of the exotic Bohemian types I'd been expecting. On the other hand, fortunately, it didn't look like the sort of place you were likely either to get into a fight or pick up girls.

We drank a lot of expensive fancy lager though Ryan drank two to every one of mine, and he said, "Look at these people. Not just these people, any people. If you offered them enough money they'd do anything. You could buy them, any of them. They all have their price, and it's not so high. It's like actresses who say they'll only appear naked in your movie if it's artistically valid. What they mean is they want extra money. People will strip off for money. They'll fuck for money. They'll commit murder. They'll do anything if the price is right. They'll even play the part of Errol Flynn."

I wondered if I was supposed to be offended.

"My agent does all my negotiating for me," I said.

He seemed to like that. He got up and crossed the room, went to a table where three young men were sitting. They looked very hip, like perhaps they worked for a record company or something. At first I thought he might be picking another fight, but the conversation looked amicable enough. After a while he got out his wallet and handed over some money. I didn't see how much. Then he came back. Nothing happened for a while, then the three guys stood up, took down their trousers and underpants and exposed themselves to the entire clientele of the bar. A few people clapped and jeered. Ryan hardly even bothered to look. He had proved his point.

We had some more to drink. It was late by now. Ryan still wanted to party. We got in his car again. It hadn't been towed away. His driving was dangerously erratic but I was too drunk to care. He said he knew of a party happening somewhere in Chiswick. I said I wasn't that keen to go to Chiswick and that I had to work the next day, but I was pretty unconvincing about it.

"Flynn's real problem was he got bored very easily," said Ryan. "His whole life was an attempt to stave off a terrible boredom. He used whatever he could to break up the monotony; sex, drink, drugs, sailing, riding, even making movies. Although I think making movies bored him more than most things."

"Is that the story of your life too?" I asked drunkenly. It was most definitely not a question I'd have asked when sober.

"Maybe," he said. "Except that making movies doesn't bore me."

"So tell me about these movies of yours," I said.

Ryan stopped the car. At first I thought I'd said the wrong thing and angered him. But he said, "Police," and I looked round to see that a patrol car was following us.

We were in some godawful, anonymous part of London, nowhere that I recognised. We were on the edge of a council estate. There was a timber yard on one side of us, a used car lot on the other. The road was empty. It looked nowhere like Chiswick.

The police car duly pulled in behind us. There were two officers in the car. One got out and walked up to the Rolls. He was young and very thin. He didn't have much natural authority, but fortunately he wasn't making up for it by being an obnoxious bastard. We went through all the usual "Is this your car, sir?" routine and I discovered the car was only rented. I wasn't sure whether that was a significant discovery or not. Ryan answered the questions politely and with some charm. Nevertheless anyone with half a brain could tell that he was drunk as a skunk and I didn't see how they could fail to arrest him, and maybe me too for being some kind of drunken accomplice.

Eventually the policeman produced a breathaliser bag and Ryan said, "Don't even bother with that thing. There's no point. I'm drunk, okay? I shouldn't have been driving, I know it, I've been a damned fool. Do what you have to do."

"Are you American, sir?"

"That's right."

"Over here on holiday?"

"Well, kind of a working holiday."

"What line of work are you in, sir?"

"The movies."

"Really?"

"Afraid so."

"What kind of movies?"

This guy was far better at asking Ryan questions than I'd ever been.

"I've always been an independent," said Ryan. "With a capital I. You might call it avant-garde. You might once have called it underground. Non-mainstream. Anti-studio. Anti-Hollywood. Good stuff. Personal cinema. You know?"

The policeman nodded as though this meant something.

"But," said Ryan, "I'm over here setting up a major project that I can really believe in, a movie about Errol Flynn."

"That's a bit strange isn't it?" said the policeman. "I thought all the money was in America."

"Well you're absolutely right. All the money's in America, but all the talent's in England."

"I see," said the policeman.

From then on it was as if they were old pals. The policeman turned out to be a movie buff. He certainly knew a thing or two about movies, far more than I did. He and Ryan got talking about the power of agents, and how the major studios were all run by accountants these days rather than by real film-makers, and about "pay or play" contracts. They soon lost me.

Finally the policeman said, "Look, the film industry in this country is in a bad enough state without me making it any worse. I tell you what, I'll do you a favour. Give me your car keys."

Ryan handed them over. The policeman took them and lobbed them high over the wall of the timber yard. It was quite a throw. The wall was a good twenty feet high. There was no way we were going to be able to climb over and retrieve the keys.

"If you get here about eight o'clock tomorrow morning you can get your keys back," said our friend the film buff. "Now get a taxi home and make sure I never see you again except in the movies."

He got back in the patrol car and drove away. We were stranded in what certainly wasn't the best part of town to be looking for a taxi, but I still thought we'd been incredibly lucky. Ryan didn't say anything. Then, when he was sure the police weren't coming back, he reached into his trouser pocket and produced a duplicate set of car keys.

He drove me home. We were both laughing like maniacs but I was petrified we might meet the same, or indeed another, patrol car on the way. We didn't. Ryan said he'd talk to me soon then drove off. I stumbled into my flat. I lay on the bed. Both my mind and the room were spinning around. It had been one hell of a night for me, yet I expected it was all pretty routine for Ryan. I was drunk and tired and I should have been able to fall into a deep sleep straight away, but I was still barely dozing an hour later, when the phone rang and I heard Ryan's voice on the other end, and at first I thought he might have been arrested on the way home and wanted me to come and bail him out, but in fact he said, "Okay Jake, you convinced me. You've got the part. You're my Errol Flynn." After that I couldn't sleep at all.

I felt surprisingly good when I got up in the morning. I didn't even have a hangover. I suspected that Ryan, wherever he was, had a bad one. Maybe it was so bad that he wouldn't even remember that he'd offered me the part of Errol Flynn. Strangely enough I didn't think that would be the case. Drunk as he was, I somehow knew that when he sobered up he would still want me in his film. I wondered if he had been trying to prove something to me, show me something. It briefly crossed my mind that perhaps he had been trying to show me what a night out with Errol Flynn might have been like.

I went to work as usual. I hoped that Ryan would phone me in the course of the day to talk about contracts and dates but I'd made up my mind not to panic if he didn't. I carried on as normal, as though nothing had happened, but inside I felt pretty damned good. My big break (let's face it, my first and only break) had arrived.

I didn't get a phone call from Ryan that day, but as the photocopying shop was closing Sacha turned up carrying a bottle of champagne and some flowers for me. I was a little embarrassed. We shared the booze with the other people who worked in the shop and Sacha told them rather grandly that I wouldn't be going back to work, and then it all came out that I'd got this part in this film, etc., etc. I thought Sacha was exceeding her brief here, but for some reason I didn't protest. Carrying on with the day job would have been impossible. All my co-workers wished me well, and there was a fair amount of joking about the size of my penis when they learned I was going to play Errol Flynn.

Then Sacha announced that she was taking me out to dinner to celebrate. I walked down Baker Street with Sacha on my arm. It felt pretty good. A lot of people stared at me. They thought I must be somebody famous, but I suspected that was because I had Sacha on my arm and was carrying a bunch of flowers, not because I had suddenly developed monstrous amounts of movie-star charisma. It was a good dinner. I even learned a little about Ryan.

"So tell me about his movies," I said to Sacha.

"I've only seen one, actually," she said. "It was rather good. It was strange. It was sexy. Very unconventional."

"What was it about?"

"It wasn't about anything. I'm not sure great art ever is."

"Who was in it?"

"Mostly unknowns. He likes to work with unknowns."

"So I gather," I said. "And where does Ryan get his money?"

"I think he has a group of backers, some people who own a chain of hotels, something like that."

I must have looked dubious.

"His money is perfectly real," said Sacha.

"Good," I said.

And then I asked a question that I should certainly have asked before. "Are you going to be in this film?"

"Well, of course," she said.

I found that strangely reassuring.

"What part?"

"We're still not sure," she said. "When we last discussed it Ryan was talking about having the same actress playing all the female parts; Flynn's mother, Lili Damita, the whores he went with, the girls he raped, and so on."

I must have looked more than dubious this time.

"I can see how it would work," she said, the implication clearly being that if I couldn't see how it would work then I was some kind of terrible Philistine.

I nodded. I did not want to appear to be a terrible Philistine.

"Have you seen a script yet?" I asked.

"No."

"Doesn't that worry you?"

"No. Should it? Ryan's not that kind of film-maker, and frankly I'm not that kind of actress."

I must have been feeling drunk or high or something because I then said, "Are you having an affair with Ryan?"

"No," she said, casually. "We've slept together but we're not sleeping together if you know what I mean."

"What about his wife?" I said.

"It's not a problem. She knows. Of course."

"Have you met her?"

"Of course. It's not a problem."

"This wife really sounds like one in a million," I said. "She writes scripts, she let's her husband sleep around. Where can I get one of those?"

"Don't be so suburban," she said.

She was joking, of course. Even in Sacha's world you couldn't use suburban as an entirely unironic term of abuse. But I knew what she meant and she was right. The world I came from and belonged to was very straight indeed, very boring if you like. It was not a world full of money or art or adultery. I got the distinct feeling that thanks to Ryan I was about to step into a quite different world from the one I was used to, and I could hardly wait.

4

This, more or less, is what I learned about Errol Flynn from my researches. Even then I realised it was only what you might call a beginner's guide.

He was born in Hobart, Tasmania in 1909. His father was a Professor of Biology and his mother was a distant descendant of Fletcher Christian. It wasn't a very happy marriage and both parents had affairs, although hers seem to have been more frequent, exotic and successful than his. They were an unlikely couple, and as a boy Flynn used to fantasise that he was really the illegitimate son of an Irish sailor.

Flynn described his relationship with his mother as a "war". It's said that she beat the young Errol frequently and mercilessly, but when she wasn't beating him she ignored him completely. She caught him playing doctors and nurses with the little girl next door and gave him such a thrashing that he ran away from home. And once when she discovered he'd been playing truant from school she locked him in a back room for two days.

In later life he would refer to "My mother, that cunt", which I still find an incredibly shocking thing for anybody to say. You have to feel that his relationship with his mother must explain a lot about his subsequent attitudes towards women. He wanted to impress them and conquer them, but he also wanted to dismiss and reject them. But maybe that's being too ingenious too soon. There are an awful lot of men in the world who want to conquer and then dismiss women, and it surely can't all be blamed on their relationships with their mothers.

At school Flynn was good at sports, especially football, tennis and boxing, and he enjoyed reading, but he was a bad and difficult pupil and was expelled from several schools, usually for petty stealing.

In 1921 the family moved to Sydney and Errol went to yet another new school, but shortly thereafter his mother left his father and went to Paris, taking Flynn's sister Rosemary with her. Flynn was expelled from school once again but he still managed to get a place at the University of Tasmania, where he studied biology, presumably to please his father. He gave up after one year.

In 1928 he went to New Guinea, attracted by the gold rush there. He did a variety of jobs, including mining, but he seems to have been most successful as a recruiter of native labour.

He returned briefly to Sydney and bought a boat called the *Sirocco*, in which he eventually sailed back to New Guinea. To pay for the trip he did some work as a photographic model, showing off suits. This was his first paid work in front of a camera.

Once back in New Guinea he wrote some articles which he submitted to an Australian newspaper, the *Bulletin*. In fact he wrote throughout his life and he seems to have thought that writing was a far more honest and worthwhile occupation than acting. He even wrote a couple of books and got them published. However, when he eventually came to write his autobiography he employed a ghost writer.

In 1931 he leased a tobacco plantation but couldn't make a success of it. The next year, back again in Sydney, he landed his first part in a movie. It was an Australian production of *Mutiny on the Bounty*. Possibly his distant family link to Fletcher Christian helped to get him the part. The film was not well received, but Flynn had embarked on an acting career, even if only in a half-hearted sort of way. He doesn't appear to have taken it very seriously. He was soon back in New Guinea recruiting more native labour. Quite what the difference was between legal recruiting and illegal recruiting I don't know. I suspect it must have been a fine line. But Flynn overstepped it. In 1933 a warrant was put out for his arrest. He left rapidly for the neighbouring island of New Britain.

There he met the man he refers to in his autobiography as Dr Gerrit Koets, and who may have been in reality one Dr Hermann Erben, a known Nazi spy. They travelled together to Hong Kong, French Indo-China, India, and eventually to France where they went their separate ways. Flynn's autobiography makes a lot of their adventures together; the seductions, the brawls, the cockfighting, the visits to whore houses, etc., etc. The rickshaw driver story comes from this period. It's the section of the autobiography that is least convincing, though I realise that doesn't necessarily mean it was untrue.

From France Flynn went to London, where he began to make serious moves towards becoming an actor. He got a walk-on part in a movie called *I Adore You* but he couldn't break into the West End, which was what he really wanted. Instead he went to work in Rep in Northampton. Flynn was still comparatively young but he was quite a man of the world. He was tall, handsome, tanned, athletically built. He had travelled extensively, had pursued several careers. He was by no means a typical young English actor. I can't imagine what Northampton made of him, nor what he made of Northampton.

He did a lot of work in his eighteen months in Rep. He played Prince Donzil in *Jack and the Beanstalk* and the title role in *Othello*. I would guess he made a better job of Prince Donzil. Eventually two of the Northampton productions transferred to the West End and although they didn't run, Flynn was spotted by Irving Asher, the head of Warner Brothers in England. He hired Flynn to play the lead in *Murder in Monte Carlo*, a low-budget thriller, and on the strength of that Flynn was given a contract to go to Hollywood. It all sounds depressingly easy. I'm sure it must have been harder than it sounds, but maybe the ease with which Flynn became a movie actor was the reason why he never thought much of movie acting.

His first Hollywood role was as a corpse in *The Case of the Curious Bride*, and he had a couple of scenes in a B picture called *Don't Bet on Blondes*. This was not the big time and he wasn't very happy. On the other hand he was doing pretty well for a beginner, and at least he was working. By *my* professional standards he was already a fantastic, raging success.

By now he had met and, in some sense or other, fallen in love with the French actress Lili Damita. Lili was vain, temperamental and madly possessive. Some sources say she was bisexual, but we assume that wouldn't have bothered Flynn too much. She was part of Marlene Dietrich's circle. She had been acting much longer than Flynn had, and in fact her career was past its peak, but she knew her way around Hollywood and she had an air of European sophistication, breeding and good manners that Hollywood still found very appealing. She taught Errol a lot. They got married. It was a stormy and painful relationship, and Flynn was, of course, utterly incapable of being a faithful husband, yet they stayed married for six years. By some standards that would have to be called a success.

They also had children, including Sean, Flynn's only son, the one who became the wild, reckless war photographer and died mysteriously in Vietnam. Flynn used to send his teenage son money "for condoms and/or flowers". It must have been at least as tough being Errol Flynn's son as it was being Errol Flynn. His children, like many of his friends, called him The Baron.

Lili may have been at least partly responsible for Flynn's landing the all-important role of Captain Blood. She was a good friend of Jack Warner's fiancée and it's said she talked the fiancée into pleading Flynn's case. Robert Donat was to have played the part but had withdrawn. Giving the role to a complete unknown was undoubtedly a risk, but I'm sure Jack Warner didn't do it merely on his fiancée's say so. Flynn is said to have done a great screen test, and I'm sure he wouldn't have got the part if Warner hadn't detected some star quality in him.

Captain Blood, only his third film, remember, made Flynn's name and completely defined his image. This was the archetypal Flynn role, the archetypal Flynn movie. There were sword fights and duels, and sea battles and plenty of love interest. It was directed by Michael Curtiz, co-starred Olivia de Havilland, had music by Erich Korngold; all the classic ingredients. It opened in December 1935 and was a big, big hit.

Flynn was immediately established as a movie star, and unlike today's stars, he consequently made a *lot* of movies, not all of them typical Flynn pictures. For example he made quite a few cowboy movies. Now, I'm no great fan or expert when it comes to cowboy movies, but it seems to me Flynn is far too smooth and suave, maybe just too "English", to be a very convincing cowboy. But chiefly the next six or seven years were the peak of his career, the swashbuckling days, the period when he made *The Charge of the Light Brigade, The Prince and the Pauper, The Adventures of Robin Hood, The Private Lives of Elizabeth and Essex* and *The Sea Hawk*. If you love Errol Flynn, these pictures are the reason why you love him. Right from the start Flynn had a reputation for being professionally difficult, and a hell-raiser in his private life. His arguments with director Michael Curtiz were legendary, and off screen he spent his time drinking, brawling and womanising. David Niven, who was Flynn's best friend at this time, is quoted as saying, "You could always rely on Flynn. You knew he'd always let you down."

Olivia de Havilland co-starred in quite of few of the early movies. Flynn seems to have been in love with her but he was pathetically bad at showing it. It's said that on one occasion he put a dead snake in her underpants. I don't entirely understand this story but I guess they were in a drawer at the time, rather than on her body. It was not the way to her heart.

His marriage to Lili Damita was pretty sour by now. He continued to sleep with lots of women, and if you believe the stories he also made frequent trips to Mexico where he could have sex with men without fear of being caught.

It seems perfectly likely to me that Flynn was bisexual. He was very highly sexed and wasn't very choosy about who he had sex with. He might have had sex with men out of curiosity, as an interesting variation, or simply because they were there. However, it seems to me not to have been a case of polymorphous perversity, more a case of any port in a storm. There are those who say that he had an affair with Tyrone Power but that their sexual tastes were incompatible. I don't see how you can ever prove this stuff one way or the other.

In 1937 Koets/Erben reappeared, and he and Flynn went to Spain together to take a look at the Spanish Civil War. Flynn wrote some articles about the trip, but he was there as an adventurer rather than as a serious journalist. Some newspapers reported that Flynn was killed by an exploding shell, and certainly he was injured, but he lived to tell the tale, which I suppose was the point of the exercise.

Those who think that Flynn was a Nazi spy, of course, assume that he was in Spain up to no good. I'm afraid I can't really believe in Flynn as a Nazi spy. This Koets character may well have been a Nazi sympathiser and even a recruiter and agent provocateur, and Flynn probably wouldn't have held that against him so long as he was entertaining company; but that doesn't make Flynn a spy.

He was certainly no sort of good liberal. He didn't have much respect for women, Jews or blacks. He saw himself as an outlaw. He didn't kowtow to laws or governments or movie studios. He genuinely doesn't seem to have given a damn about most things, and breaking laws was one of the ways he asserted his existence as a free spirit and adventurer. I can see the argument that says a man who lives his life as a sexual and social maverick might be a political maverick too. but that makes Flynn sound like Guy Burgess or Anthony Blunt.

Flynn was no sort of political sophisticate, and although that could cut both ways, in the end I just don't believe he would have wanted to help Nazi Germany to rule the world. I am also prepared to admit that I'm not a political sophisticate either, and I could be wrong about this.

When the Second World War started he certainly wanted to enlist, the way David Niven had. However, he failed the medical. He was classified 4F. At the time he was suffering from emphysema and recurrent malaria, the latter having been picked up in New Guinea. I think Flynn was hurt badly by this rejection. I think he genuinely did want to join the war effort. In all sorts of ways he was a very brave man. He genuinely thought of himself as a hero. He wasn't just playing a part. And heroes aren't supposed to be too sick to go to war.

Instead he made war pictures, like *Dive Bomber*, *Desperate Journey* and *Objective Burma*. The last of these is an interesting one. Flynn plays Major Nelson, and I think he's very good. There are none of the flamboyant, swashbuckling heroics that you might have expected. However it does look as though the Americans, and Flynn in particular, won the war in Burma without any help from the British. In 1942, when the film was released, this did not go down very well in Britain. The film had to be withdrawn after a few showings in London.

No, Flynn did not have a very good war. In 1942 Lili Damita divorced him. The settlement was fantastically generous to Lili; ruinous to Flynn. Also in 1942 Flynn was charged with two counts of statutory rape. Flynn did not even know there was any such thing as statutory rape. At the time California law stated, and for all I know still does, that sex with a girl below the age of consent is an act of rape even if the girl is willing.

The prosecution produced a couple of girls who claimed to be under eighteen and to have had sex with Flynn. Their names were Peggy Satterlee and Betty Hansen. The girls were not exactly delicate flowers and it was thought the case would never get to court but it did, giving rise to the perfectly reasonable theory that Flynn was being made the scapegoat for Hollywood's real and imagined "decadence" in a time of war.

Flynn claimed never to have had sex with Hansen. He *had*

had sex with Satterlee, but her true age was a matter of serious doubt and debate throughout the case. The trial was a farce, and that probably helped Flynn. Betty Hansen came to court dressed as a schoolgirl. A lot was made of the fact that Flynn supposedly kept his socks on while in the act, and Peggy Satterlee lost a great deal of credibility by saying she stared out of a porthole and watched the moon while Flynn had sex with her. She was trying too hard. Flynn was acquitted. The jury, in fact probably the whole country, simply couldn't believe that Flynn needed to rape anybody in order to get laid. Girls were queuing up to have sex with him. On the other hand he hadn't denied that he knew and had hung around with Hansen and Satterlee, and it must have seemed strange that when he could have had his pick of women he should have picked these two.

My guess is that Flynn was not in any ordinary sense of the word a rapist. But if you found yourself alone on a boat with him there wasn't much point saying you just wanted to be friends. If you didn't want to have sex what were you doing hanging around with Errol Flynn? I know that this isn't entirely a "good thing". It tells us that Flynn was not a model of restraint and nonsexism, but I think we knew that already.

Like many womanisers Flynn felt far happier in the company of men than of women. He was, to use an archaic phrase, a man's man. He liked drinking, brawling and gambling with the boys; and women were peripheral to that. Flynn and his cronies certainly chased and caught women, but after they'd caught them they'd have sex with them while the other guys watched. I think this is sometimes known as "male bonding".

Flynn also installed two-way mirrors in his house, and in one case a two-way ceiling, so that he could watch his guests in the act. I don't think this necessarily makes him a bad person, but it doesn't sound like evidence of a happy, healthy, well-adjusted libido either.

You might think the trial would have done at least some damage to Flynn's popularity. It didn't. Flynn was far more popular after the trial than he'd been before it. Suddenly he was mobbed everywhere he went. The public loved this "bad publicity".

In that sense the episode didn't do Flynn's career much harm, but it did mean that Flynn's name would always thereafter be associated with sexual scandal and sexual high jinks. "In like Flynn" became a catch-phrase, and his movie titles all suddenly seemed to contain double entendres, like *They Died With Their Boots On* or *Desperate Journey* or *The Perfect Specimen*. There were now lots of jokes about Flynn, his sexual endowment and his sexual prowess, which had the ultimate effect of turning Flynn himself into a kind of joke. None of this was very helpful to a man who now wanted to have his acting taken seriously.

While in court facing the rape charges Flynn had met the woman who was to be his second wife, Nora Eddington. She was the daughter of the sheriff's secretary and she was eighteen years old. It was another bad marriage. By now Flynn was drinking very heavily indeed and had started dabbling in cocaine and morphine. But he was so seriously, so continuously ill by this time that I think he probably used the drugs mainly as painkillers. He remained pathologically unfaithful. The relationship was stormy and on several occasions he beat up Nora. This marriage also lasted six years, and this time there were two daughters.

In 1947 Flynn starred in *The Adventures of Don Juan* for Warner Brothers. It was an expensive movie, and was a perfect vehicle for Flynn, at least it would have been for the young Flynn. He was thirty-eight, hardly ancient, but his various illnesses and his abuse of drink and drugs were taking a toll on him. The movie was a nightmare to make. According to some sources Flynn walked off the picture and went on a binge for several weeks at one stage, although other sources say he was absent because of his recurring malaria. However, even when he showed up he still drank a lot too much and by the afternoon of any given day he was far too drunk to do any acting. Even when he was sober he lacked the concentration to carry off long scenes or long exchanges of dialogue.

Warner Brothers were prepared to put up with it, I suppose because drunk or sober there was only one Errol Flynn, and because they knew they could make money out of him. And in the final analysis the movie is very good. Flynn doesn't look particularly old or drunk or past it. He looks okay in the duelling and action sequences, although we know that great use had to be made of stand-ins, and he certainly looks the part in the love scenes. If Flynn could turn in a performance as good as that without even trying, while in fact doing just about everything he could to sabotage the film and himself, then I think you have to admire the guy even more.

Flynn's relationship with Jack Warner had always been bad and he finally left Warner Brothers in 1952. He immediately began work on his own Cinemascope production of *William Tell*. He wrote an outline, budgeted for $860,000, and went into a fifty-fifty partnership with a bunch of dodgy Italians. Flynn put up his half of the money in cash and production started. When that was spent he asked the Italians to come up with their half. They never did. Flynn fought for a couple of years to find some other way of financing the film, but never succeeded. It's said that there's some wonderful footage of *William Tell* locked in a vault somewhere.

At more or less this time Flynn received a tax demand for $840,000 and discovered that his business manager had been helping himself to the money that should have been put aside to pay tax. There were other debts too, and there was the continuing alimony. Flynn, by his own account, was now broke.

All his life Flynn had owned and sailed boats, and he does seem to have had a deep and genuine love of the sea. However, this wasn't just messing about in boats. He liked to be in the middle of storms and high seas, battling with the elements, living dangerously and testing himself to the limit. Earl Conrad tells the story of being in a rowing boat when Flynn deliberately capsized it because the afternoon was getting too predictable. In order to save money he lived for most of the next few years aboard his boat the *Zaca*, although he also spent time in Jamaica where he still owned an estate, which suggests to me that Flynn's idea of being broke was a little different from your or my idea of being broke.

But he still had to work in order to stay solvent and in order to pay off some of his more persistent creditors. This last phase of his movie career was, at best, patchy. He made some mediocre movies like *Istanbul* or *Crossed Swords*, and some absolute horrors like *Cuban Rebel Girls*. But he did make *The Sun Also Rises* in which his portrayal of the disintegrating drunk Mike Campbell is not at all bad and looks very much like a meditation on his own life. And he made *Too Much Too Soon* in which he played John Barrymore, a role he might have been rehearsing all his life.

Barrymore had been one of his drinking buddies. They both shared the same self-destructive urges and maybe the part was too close to home for Flynn to give a really great performance. It isn't a great film. Flynn was drunk most of the time he was filming the movie, which can't have helped. But things were made worse by a lousy script and some lame directing, both by someone who rejoiced in the name of Art Napoleon.

Acting was not the only scheme Flynn had for making money. I find this hard to believe but apparently he went on quiz shows as a contestant and won thirty thousand dollars answering questions about sailing. He also realised that suing people could bring in the bucks. With some justification he sued *Confidential* magazine for printing some sleazy lies about him. He sued for a million dollars and settled for fifteen thousand. He successfully sued an Italian vermouth company for using his picture without permission, and a judge awarded him damages from a Canadian millionaire called Duncan McMartin after the two of them had got into a fight in a bar.

At the same time others were suing him in return. Flynn claimed to have written the screenplay for a terrible movie called *The Adventures of Captain Fabian*, but in fact it was written by Charles Gross. Gross sued him. Then Vincent Price, the movie's co-star, also sued for non-payment of wages. Lawyers chased him for alimony and maintenance. He still owed tax. Creditors who were often owed only trifling amounts had to take legal action before Flynn would pay them. There was even another rape case. The parents of seventeen-year-old Denise Duvivier wanted damages of two thousand eight hundred dollars because of what they claimed Flynn had done to their daughter aboard his yacht. It seems to me they placed an insultingly low value on their daughter's virtue, and perhaps they'd have got further if they'd demanded more. Flynn denied everything and the case was thrown out.

In fact that charge of rape was brought on the day of Flynn's third wedding, to an actress called Patrice Wymark. After divorcing Nora Eddington, Flynn had been briefly engaged to a nineteen-year-old Romanian princess whom he referred to as "The Geek". He ditched her for Patrice. The most remarkable thing about her, according to press reports at the time, was that she wore spectacles. In the popular imagination this was synonymous with braininess, and therefore an unexpected choice for Flynn.

In some curious way Flynn does seem to have been the marrying kind. Certainly he gave the impression of being serious about marriage this time. He said Patrice was one of the few intelligent women he'd ever been involved with, and he talked about raising a large family and settling down on his farm in Jamaica, and for a couple of years he seems seriously to have tried to lead a more sane and ordered life.

It didn't last, and inevitably Flynn didn't settle down in Jamaica. He continued to work in Hollywood and returned to his old womanising ways. Patrice never accepted that the marriage was completely over, but Flynn certainly behaved as though it was. Now aged forty-eight, he started dating young girls again. One of the youngest was Beverly Aadland. She was only fifteen when Flynn met her, and you might have thought that at his age he would have known better than to pursue underage girls. But perhaps he was past caring.

Flynn spent the last few years of his life with Beverly, and by all accounts she appears to have made him very happy. He was sick for much of that time and the rumours are that he was sexually impotent too, although he said several times that he and Beverley were planning to have children.

Flynn died on October 14th, 1959 of a heart attack. His heart was the least of his problems. He was only fifty but the coroner was amazed he'd lasted so long. His body was that of a man many years older. As well as the continuing emphysema and malaria, Flynn was also having serious trouble with tuberculosis and hepatitis. His liver and lungs were badly damaged. His gut was infected. There were cancerous lesions on his tongue and throat. His back had been severely damaged in a fall years earlier and was causing him a lot of pain by the end. He was suffering terribly from piles. He had smoked heavily all his life. He was an alcoholic and a morphine addict. It's often said that Flynn packed enough into his life for two lifetimes. He may have lived fast and died (comparatively) young but he certainly didn't leave a beautiful corpse.

There was still drama after his death. Nora and Beverly both said he had always wanted to be buried in Jamaica, which was true. But Patrice Wymark was still his wife and she arranged for him to be buried in Forest Lawns in Hollywood. The director Raoul Walsh is said to have put a dozen bottles of whisky in the coffin, but that sounds like a Hollywood story to me. And for reasons I've never been able to discover the grave was left without a marker for twenty years until 1979.

That was as much as I "knew" about Errol Flynn, and most of that came second- or third-hand, from memoirs or biographies where the authors frequently had axes to grind. It seemed there was no "objective" view on Flynn.

I found it hard to see Flynn's life as tragic exactly. He was a successful actor by almost any standards. He made good films.

He made and lost a great deal of money. He was well-loved. He lived the way he wanted to live. He had more sex, more pleasure, more fun than most of us are ever going to have, and yet his desperate need to fill up his life with incident doesn't suggest to me a very happy man. Ryan said it was because he got bored easily, but I didn't think it was as simple as that. His desire for massive amounts of sex, drink and drugs might indicate a powerful, devil-may-care appetite for life, but it actually suggested to me that he was constantly trying to blot out some terrible and uncomprehended psychological pain.

Flynn had a square question mark as his personal monogram and symbol, and that might well suggest that Flynn was a mystery to himself as well as to everyone else. Many of his acquaintances said they never knew the real Flynn, but I would guess that's true of most movie stars. For entirely obvious reasons they don't reveal their real selves to every Tom, Dick and Harry they meet.

In his *Biographical Dictionary of the Cinema* David Thomson writes: "The real Flynn was a proof of the wounding journey between myth and actuality – a man who could hardly take a drink or look at a woman without wondering who he was."

I could see why someone might think that of Flynn, but I wasn't sure it was the whole story. I don't think Flynn was nearly so unaware of himself as Thomson implies. There's a lovely quote from Flynn, something he said very late in his career: "When I open a film script and it explains there's a man who's a shadow of his former self, once handsome now decadent, then I know that's my part. Oddly enough I make more money today being a shadow of my former self than when I *was* my former self." Now I'm sure some of that is bravado, but it doesn't strike me as the remark of someone who genuinely didn't know who or what he was.

Flynn used to complain that he wasn't taken seriously as an actor. It's true he got stuck doing swashbuckling roles, and I suppose a lot of people aren't going to take you all that seriously if you spend most of your acting life wearing tights.

However, it seems to me that he brought an enormous amount of charm, wit, conviction and a certain lightness of touch to the things he did, and in my book that is perfectly serious, and very good, acting. He didn't have a fantastic range, but he was always utterly believable, and it's easy to think of dozens of star actors who would fail to be convincing in the kind of parts Flynn played.

If I had a problem with Flynn, it was this: when I came to describe his qualities as an actor I found myself using a vocabulary that could equally well be used to describe a penis. So that Flynn was always upright, straight, erect. He was strong and sleek, but also delicate and sensitive. Sometimes however he could seem rather stiff, rigid, wooden almost. I wondered if he wasn't in fact a sort of walking phallus in his films. I thought this was probably not a compliment to an actor. Nevertheless, however you looked at it, the part of Errol Flynn was one that any decent actor would love to play. It was a great challenge and a great opportunity, and not one to miss. I still wasn't sure I had the build or the looks for the part and I didn't know how Ryan saw Flynn, and I certainly didn't have any idea of what kind of movie he intended to make. But I thought that given half a chance I could do a hell of a good job playing Errol Flynn for him. I was very, very happy to have got the part. I had come a long way in a very short time from the actor who thought he was only cut out to play best friend parts.

5

Six weeks later I was standing in a converted barn somewhere in the Suffolk countryside wearing a swashbuckler's costume, complete with sword and tights, and I was shooting my very first scene of *The Errol Flynn Movie*. Frankly I was surprised ever to have made it that far. The period between getting the part and starting the shooting had been rough, a peculiar mixture of activity and inertia.

Ryan had phoned me the day after I'd been out to celebrate with Sacha. He had done all the talking, of course. He talked about getting me a personal trainer, about getting my body into shape, making it more athletic. I had no objections to that. There was also talk of my taking lessons in fencing, boxing, sailing and horse riding. Most of these never materialised, although he did organise for a friend of his to give me a couple of sessions on how to use a bow and arrow. "Imagine you're crushing a grape between your shoulder blades," was the one thing I remembered. On my own initiative I did a lot of running and swimming, and worked out a little at the gym, and by the time filming started I felt extremely fit.

Ryan told me to go along to my local hairdresser and get my hair cut into a style like Flynn's. This wasn't very easy since Flynn's hair changed considerably over the years and depending on what part he was playing, but I did my best. I grew a pencil moustache. I thought it made me look like a weasel, but I was prepared to go around looking weasel-like for the sake of my art.

Ryan also talked about sending me a contract that I could show to my agent, and on the basis of which we might negotiate my fee. Ryan assured me that if money was the problem there was no problem. I still considered myself to have an agent at that time, although I wasn't sure that my agent considered himself to have me. He had not got me any work in the last six months and I had not earned him any commission and therefore I suspected I might be in his dead files. I also felt reluctant to give him ten per cent of what I earned from Ryan since he'd had no hand in getting me the job. I knew better than to sign any sort of contract without taking some professional advice; on the other hand I didn't have much faith in my agent's ability to work his way round the small print of a movie contract. I told myself I'd worry about it when it came. In some ways I suspected it never would. I would probably have done the film without one, but in fact the contract did duly arrive and I did show it to my agent and he assured me it was a perfectly good document, we agreed on a more than generous fee, and I willingly signed.

The calls kept coming too. Ryan's enthusiasm knew no bounds. Things were always going very well. He had always just had a brilliant idea or met a composer who would be just the man to write incidental music, or he'd just had a meeting with someone who wanted to distribute the film in Hungary. Ideas for scenes continued to flow from him, or possibly from his wife. Some sounded completely mad, like having me play Flynn as a vampire, for instance, but others sounded very interesting and perfectly workable.

My own confidence waxed and waned depending on how long it was since I had last spoken to Ryan. I came to think of him as a plate-spinner with me as the plate. Any time I started to wobble and lose momentum, Ryan was there to set me in motion again.

I wondered at first whether he would expect me to do a lot of partying with him, whether there'd be lots of strange nights out like that first one. But there weren't. I didn't see him at all in those intervening six weeks, and all his plate-spinning was done by phone. I thought this was a strange way of doing things, but then everything about film-making was strange to me. I thought this probably wasn't how Spielberg worked, but so what? Every director had his own way of working. As an actor I had to work around that.

I kept reading about Flynn and thinking about him and wondering how I was going to portray him. Ryan wasn't very much help. He was fine on the theory and the principles, what he called "the big picture", but he wasn't so hot on details like trying to get the voice right. I found Flynn's voice peculiarly thin and clipped, not quite English, not quite American, and despite his background, not at all Australian. I hoped I could make something out of that, out of the fact that his voice, like his personality, was rootless, and charming but indefinite. Apparently he had a habit of addressing people as "sport".

But I decided the real problem was one of style. Flynn had style by the bucketload. When he entered a room, according to Ava Gardner, it was like somebody had turned on a light. Everyone knew he was there. Everyone noticed him. When he talked to a woman it was as though he worshipped her, as though no other woman on the planet existed. When he knocked back a drink, he wasn't just boozing, it was as if he was drinking a health unto Her Majesty. When he sailed he was the archetypal seadog. And when he fenced, even though he was apparently no great fencer, he did it with such panache and aplomb, you believed he was the greatest swordsman who ever lived.

This triumph of style applied as much to Flynn's private life as it did to his public career. Now, in my real life, I am someone who never made any claims to be dashing or charming. I never had any style. But that was okay because I was an actor and I could portray character traits that I didn't personally possess; a thing that Errol Flynn, for all his success, probably couldn't do. That didn't make me any "better" than Flynn, but it did demonstrate the difference between a good actor like me, and a great star like Flynn. Actors act. Stars simply are. I could act the part of Errol Flynn but Flynn could never have acted the part of someone like me. Flynn was always, in some sense, more or less playing "himself".

It was strange and interesting to be acting the part of someone who didn't do much acting, and I was starting to enjoy myself a lot. I relished the problems, I liked the contradictions, and increasingly I liked Flynn too. On a good day I had the distinct feeling that I was going to give a very good performance in this movie, maybe the performance of my life.

Although I never saw Ryan, I started to see a lot of Sacha. My celebratory dinner with her had proved to be the first of a series. We met about once a week, and had a couple of drinks and a meal out, and talked a lot. It wasn't clear whether she was doing this under instructions from Ryan as part of the rehearsal process, or whether it was her own idea. Either way nobody could object to spending evenings with Sacha. She said the better we knew each other the better our performances would be. I was not convinced of the essential truth of this, but I didn't argue. I was enjoying myself too much.

Sacha's conversation, of course, was intelligent, cosmopolitan and intense. She talked about books and art and film, and even about politics and love and acting. She might have been a bright undergraduate. She made me feel like a dull schoolboy. I tried to get through by smiling and using what little charm and wit I possessed, you know, the way Errol Flynn might have, but I'm not sure that she was charmed. I suspected that she thought I was a lightweight, both as an actor and as a human being, but she was far too polite to say so. She treated me as though I was an equal but I think both of us suspected I wasn't.

Having Sacha as a dining companion opened a certain number of doors. Waiters gave us wonderfully good service. Taxi drivers went out of their way to be helpful. People in wine bars tried to fall into conversation with us. I don't think this was necessarily because they recognised Sacha as an actress, although some did. I think it was more because she had a kind of glow, a kind of sparkle that people wanted to be close to. And I was no different from them. It felt good going around with her. It felt especially good when people sometimes assumed I was her boyfriend, even if it seemed an absurd assumption to me. I didn't see how you could possibly think that someone like her would be attached to someone like me.

As I got to know her better, her status as sex-goddess inevitably changed. She didn't seem quite so distant or enigmatic, although she certainly seemed every bit as unattainable. But, strange as it may seem, I really had no desire to "attain" her, whatever that might mean. As a result of our evenings out together we were becoming quite good acquaintances, but we were not becoming good friends. We found each other easy enough to talk to, but we were not becoming close. There was no intimacy, and I much preferred it that way. In the past I had fallen in love with a couple of my leading ladies, most recently and disastrously while in a production of *Peer Gynt* in Leicester. It had not helped my performance, and I had made up my mind not to do it again. This was my version of being a serious actor.

I knew that Sacha saw Ryan from time to time, and she assured me he was in great form and all was going well with the film. If I'd wanted to be paranoid I might have found scope for it here, in the fact that Ryan ignored me, his leading actor, while he had various meetings with Sacha; but then his reasons for wanting to see Sacha might not be entirely connected with film-making.

I tried hard not to worry, but there were two occasions when I couldn't help it. The first was when there was a ring at my doorbell at six in the morning while I was still asleep. The ringing was frantic and relentless, and immediately told me that something was wrong. I pulled on some clothes and went down to answer it. The person I opened the door to was a stranger and yet I had no doubt who it was. It was Ryan's wife.

I had tried to picture her before, to imagine who would be married to a man like Ryan, and I'd come up with a blank, but now that I saw her she was somehow very much as I'd expected. She was younger than Ryan, although probably not very much. She was elegantly thin, but it looked like the sort of thinness brought on by neurosis rather than by dieting or exercise, and although she did not look old exactly, she somehow looked well-preserved rather than actually young. Her clothes were youthful: a high fashion black leather jacket, loose silk trousers, red with black spots. Her hair was jet black and cut into a bob, and despite the time of day she was perfectly made up; dark, heavy eyes and vermilion lips. I noticed her hands. They were long and elegant but the nails were short and square although expertly manicured and painted to match her lips. They did not look like the nails of someone who spent long hours at a keyboard hammering out a movie script.

"Hello, Jake," she said.

"Hello. You must be . . ."

"Yeah, yeah. Is he here?"

"You mean Dan?"

"No, I'm tracking down the Maltese Falcon."

The voice was American, and although she was cracking wise it wasn't that harsh, brash, smart kind of American accent that Ryan had. I don't know my American accents all that well but it sounded California old hippie rather than New York wheeler-dealer.

"Well, he's not here," I said. "It's six o'clock in the morning."

"Thanks for the time check."

"I haven't seen him for weeks," I said.

And the truth was, of course, that despite the strangely central role he now occupied in my life, I'd only actually met the man twice since this whole business started.

"Mind if I take a look?"

The idea that I might be hiding Ryan from his own wife struck me as so absurd that I didn't even feel insulted. I let her into my flat. She made a brief but thorough search, and confirmed that Ryan wasn't hiding in the kitchen cupboards, the shower or under the bed.

"No, he's not here," she said.

"Has he gone missing?" I asked.

She gave me a look of considerable contempt, which I probably deserved for asking such a stupid question. She said nothing. So I tried again.

"When did you last see him?"

That seemed a reasonable question to me but she wasn't going to answer that either.

"What do you know about my husband?" she asked.

"Very little," I admitted.

"You know he's an alcoholic?" she asked.

I hadn't known, and yet now that she said it I wasn't entirely surprised.

"There's a reasonable chance that he's lying in a gutter somewhere," she said. "One of the many things I do for my husband is try to find which gutter."

"Oh," I said lamely.

"Not your gutter, obviously."

"No," I said, but that didn't feel like enough of a response. "Look, when we went out together he took me to a Soho drinking club. I don't know, maybe he's there."

"Okay, what was its name?"

I thought for a moment and realised I had no idea. I wasn't even sure it had a name. I certainly couldn't have found my way back to it. I admitted my ignorance.

"You're doing great, Jake."

"I'm sorry. Can I do anything else?"

"Doesn't sound like it, does it?"

"I'm sorry."

"It isn't your fault."

"Have you tried Sacha's place?" I asked.

I didn't know if that was the right thing to say or not. Sacha said she and Ryan weren't having an affair but I didn't really believe her. She said there was no problem with his wife, and I wasn't sure I believed that either. But Sacha's place was the best suggestion I could come up with.

"He wouldn't be there," she said.

She said it with sufficient authority that I believed her. She stood in the centre of my living-room, staring around as if still looking for clues. I didn't know what I was supposed to say. There was nothing more I could do to be of help and she knew that, yet she showed no sign of leaving. Out of embarrassment I offered her a cup of coffee. She said no. Then we stood in silence.

"How about calling the police?" I said in desperation.

"Don't be a fuck-wit, Jake."

I didn't respond. Living with Ryan could surely make you tensed up and brittle at the best of times. If he kept disappearing and being found in gutters, that might well make you impatient with lame brains like me who made "helpful suggestions". I instantly forgave her for calling me a fuck-wit. Then she was staring at me rather than at my flat, inspecting my face as though still in search of clues. She took her time.

"Yes," she said. "I can just about see it. I can just about see you in the part."

This, by a very long way, was the pleasantest thing she'd said to me. I thought I'd try to encourage her.

"How are you getting along with the script?" I asked.

There was a long, spiralling silence.

"Look," she said, "this is pretty hard for me, you understand. This script, it takes a lot out of me, really a very great deal. This isn't my form. Christ, I'm trained as a choreographer, you know. I'm no Dostoevsky but I'm trying. I'm working every hour God sends. There will be a script, all right? It may not be a work of genius, it may not be *Citizen Kane*, but it will be the best I can dredge out of myself. It'll have my nerves and bowels and guts in it. Okay? Will that be enough for everyone?

Will it? And what I really don't need at this particular time is a missing husband."

"I'm sorry," I said again.

"It's still not your fault."

Now she wanted to go. She headed for the door.

"If he turns up?" I said.

"He won't turn up."

"Should I call you?"

"No point."

"Then you call me if you find him."

"No," she said, "but I'll call you if I don't."

And then she left. I went with her to the door to see her out but she moved faster than I did. She was soon out of the door, in the street, in her car and gone. She didn't call me later, and a couple of days later Ryan did, so I drew the obvious conclusion. I didn't tell Ryan that his wife had been to my flat looking for him. I was too embarrassed. It would have been as good as telling him that I knew he was an alcoholic who passed out in strange gutters. I didn't think that would be good for our professional relationship.

My professional relationship with my screenwriter had not got off to an auspicious start but I had always known that writers were an awkward and difficult tribe. That didn't bother me, at least it didn't bother me nearly as much as having a director who was likely to disappear in an alcoholic haze worried me.

The second time I got worried was when Ryan "raped" Sacha. It seems to me that rape should not be an equivocal word, not one that you can put in inverted commas like that. Someone is raped or they are not, just as someone is murdered or they are not, and yet it wasn't that simple. I suppose I shouldn't have found it surprising that between them Ryan and Sacha could turn even rape into an equivocal activity.

Most of what I know about men I've learned from women. It's women who are in a position to generalise about these things. They say this is how men are, this is how they think, this is what they say, this is what they do. Men don't know much about how other men behave with women, especially not in bed.

Women have told me there are certain men to whom they can't and don't say no. They may not particularly want to sleep with these men, but they find themselves in a certain situation where it would be too much trouble, too much hassle, or even too dangerous to say no. So they say yes. They have sex. The man's happy enough. The woman probably isn't as happy as the man is but at least it's soon over and she's saved herself a lot of grief. This is not an ideal, and certainly not a very right-on or politically correct, way for the sexes to deal with each other, but my sources tell me it goes on.

Errol Flynn I'm sure was such a man, and it wouldn't have surprised me to find out that Dan Ryan was as well. The moment such men ask a woman out a whole set of implications and expectations fall into place. The man will insist on buying dinner. He will attempt to get the woman drunk. He will take her back to his place, to his hotel room or his boat, and there will be no point in her saying she only came to see his etchings.

The corollary of this is that there are certain men to whom women have no problem at all saying no. Women actually say they like this kind of man. They can talk to him, laugh with him, have fun with him, but at the end of the evening they don't want to sleep with him. They may say he's too nice for that. They may even say they like him too much for that. I should know. This, alas, is the man kind of man I seem to be.

Now, don't get me wrong. I'm not some sort of sexual inadequate. I have had my share of sexual partners, although you could debate whether or not it was a *fair* share. I am not one of those men who feels he has to make a lot of conquests, and I certainly don't see why you would want to have sex with someone who didn't want to have sex with you, and I'm definitely liberal enough to believe that women are entitled to say no and be believed. On the other hand I do wish that rather fewer women had felt free to say no to me over the years than actually have.

So, it was one in the morning. I was at home. I hadn't gone to bed. The phone rang and it was Sacha. At first she simply asked was it all right if she came round. I thought that was a slightly odd request at that hour and I hesitated for a moment, and as I hesitated she said, "This is very important. I really am very distraught." So of course I said she must come round at once. I even offered to go to her place, but she didn't want that.

While I waited for her to arrive I put on some coffee and got the whisky bottle ready. I had no idea why Sacha should be distraught, and even less why she should choose me as a shoulder to cry on. When she arrived she didn't look distraught at all. Her hair may perhaps have been the slightest bit bedraggled, but otherwise nothing was out of place. When she said, "I think I've been raped," I somehow didn't quite make sense of it. And even as it sank in, I still had in mind the old characterisation of the rapist as some ferocious stranger who leaps on you in the dark and drags you into some alleyway and violates you there. I couldn't understand why Sacha looked so neat.

"Do you want me to phone the police?" I asked.

"It was Dan," she said.

"Dan Ryan?"

She nodded.

"Oh no," I muttered. "When? Can you talk about it? I mean, do you want to? I mean . . ."

"It's all right. Yes. I do want to talk about it."

I poured two whiskies and waited to hear the worst.

"I told you Ryan and I weren't having an affair, and that was more or less true. From the beginning I found him very attractive and he felt the same way about me. The second night I ever met him we finished up in bed together. It was good, spectacularly good. But afterwards both of us said it had probably been a mistake and that we wouldn't be doing it again, at least not till the film was finished, and by then everything would be different in any case. And we meant it.

"I carried on working for him, making contacts, setting up meetings, doing some casting, and we both realised that knowing a thing is a mistake doesn't necessarily negate it. We'd started something, and just pretending that it wasn't happening wasn't going to be enough. And Dan said, and I agreed with him, that an affair would be a very banal arrangement. We both deserved more, something more difficult, more special. How much do you know about sadomasochism?"

I almost dropped my glass. I thought it best to say I knew nothing at all about sadomasochism, which was in fact the truth.

"I think it's probably true to say that sadomasochism is about power rather than about sex," said Sacha. "There is a top and a bottom, a dominant partner and a submissive one, although these roles can be confusing and you could argue that the submissive is ultimately the empowered one in such a partnership. And frankly in a perfect world I would have chosen to be the top rather than the bottom, but Ryan wasn't having any of that. I'd dabbled with this stuff before, but I hadn't found anyone to go the whole way with. So we tried it. We've been trying it. And it worked.

"And of course there's a certain amount of acting involved in sadomasochism, a lot of role playing. And obviously there's a fine line between acting out a fantasy and merely playing silly charades. Ryan is rather adept at staying on the right side of the line.

"Now, I know a lot of this will sound a little trite to you, a little bit naff, but we used all the normal paraphernalia, the usual props; the handcuffs, the dog lead, the whips, the leather thongs. We had some very good sex."

For a moment I thought she wanted me to congratulate her. I resisted.

"And there have to be rules in all this, you see," she said. "If you're the bottom you submit. You're a victim. It can get scary, and of course that's the best part, that's the turn on, that's why you're there. But it *is* only a fantasy and so you have a codeword, a safety valve that both partners agree will stop everything and bring you back to reality. You can cry out, 'Please stop, don't hurt me, let me go,' or any other lines suitable for a victim, and that's just fine, the top will just carry on because that's not the codeword. He knows you want more. But when you say the codeword, that really does mean stop. He knows then that you mean it and he has to stop. That's a rule of the game. Our codeword was 'Errol Flynn'. Guess whose idea. So earlier tonight we were doing our usual routines and at first it was fine, it contained the right amount of edge, of risk. And then suddenly, for no very good reason, it started to get too scary. I panicked. I looked at Ryan and I was terrified, absolutely terrified, and I wanted it to stop. So I said 'Errol Flynn' and I kept saying it, screaming it, and guess what. Ryan wouldn't stop."

She was not crying as she said any of this. She wasn't upset. She was cool, almost icy. She might have been reading a script. I was horrified yet fascinated. I wanted to know more.

"Did he hurt you? I mean physically?"

"A little. You know, bruises but no blood."

"How could he do that?"

"He didn't really do anything to me that he hadn't done a dozen times before, but the point is, I was begging him to stop."

"By crying out Errol Flynn," I said ruefully.

"And again," she said, "it wasn't just that he frightened me, because he'd done that before too. It was the fact that he suddenly frightened me too much. So you see why going to the police doesn't seem like such a great idea."

"Yes," I admitted. "But I think something ought to be done."

"Like what?"

"Maybe I should talk to him."

"And say what? That he did wrong? He knows he did wrong. That he can't get away with it? He can get away with it."

"But you can't just let it go."

"I don't know," she said. "At least it's over. I just need to be with someone. I just need to feel safe."

"Is there someone I should call, a female friend or someone?"

"No, you idiot. I want to be with you. I feel safe with you."

I put my arm around her. I suppose I was flattered. I was glad to be there when someone needed me. I was glad that she felt safe with me. I knew, however, that this wasn't entirely flattering. Safety is not something that every woman craves in a man. Ryan was okay for wild sex. I was okay for chaste, brotherly affection. I wasn't sure how many steps above eunuch this put me.

She stayed the night. She even slept in my bed. But I slept on my couch. I woke very early and wasted a lot of energy wondering what to do about Ryan. I had no desire to involve myself in anybody else's sex life, especially not the kind of sex life as described by Sacha. And yet I *was* involved. She had involved me. Maybe I should simply have confronted Ryan and threatened to give him a good horse-whipping, challenged him to a fist fight, something macho and old-fashioned and masculine. But, of course, I didn't.

I had seen all along that Ryan was strange and potentially dangerous, and nothing Sacha had told me had come as an absolute surprise. Ryan a sadist; well sure, why not? Ryan, a man with a taste for weird sex; well, where was the big shock in that? Ryan a man who cheated and broke the rules of any game he was playing; you don't say?

Nevertheless I felt that something had changed. I could no longer feel the same about Ryan as I once had. Until then it might just have been possible to believe that he was some kind of cherishable eccentric. But by the time filming started I had to accept that he was something darker and more dangerous and potentially destructive than that. I didn't like it one bit, but perhaps I was being suburban again.

Ultimately I did nothing because I didn't see what there was to be done. Sacha didn't even want me to do anything. At best I could have told Ryan that I disapproved of him. That sounded pathetic. So we carried on. The first day of shooting wasn't far away. Ryan had rocked the boat but the likes of me, Sacha and even his wife, saw that it was our job to make sure the boat didn't capsize.

I didn't see either of the Ryans again until I went down to Suffolk to start shooting. I was staying, and we were filming, in a country house not far from Southwold. Ryan had rented or possibly even bought the place (he was vague on this as on much else) and he was using it both as a headquarters and a location. The house was constructed mostly of red brick, and Ryan called it the Red Visitation, an allusion that I never quite worked out. It had been much extended and partially rebuilt over the years and it now contained a variety of architectural styles. You could see how from certain angles it might, with a little work, be made to resemble a medieval castle, while from others it could do service as the home of a Hollywood movie star. That was how Ryan intended to use it. It had wooded grounds that he assured me would be transformed into Sherwood Forest by the magic of cinema.

The whole area around the house was littered with trucks and equipment, cranes and dollies, and all sorts of stuff I didn't even know the name of, much less the function. People often talk of film crews being like small armies. The atmosphere here was more that of a boisterous and extremely complicated party game. I was welcome enough at this party, and in a way was the guest of honour, but the party had already started without me. I was a latecomer and everybody was too busy to make a fuss of me or explain the rules by which they were playing. I felt like what I was: a very green and inexperienced actor.

Ryan and his wife, Sacha, myself, and some selected members of the crew had rooms in the house. The rest of the crew were camping in some rather spartan outbuildings.

Inevitably this was not a full-scale union production and Ryan was certainly not paying union rates, but I was still amazed when I heard how much some of the team were being paid, and he had managed to round up some extremely reputable and experienced technical people. Their credentials were all infinitely more impressive than mine.

There was a large sitting-room in the house which had been converted into the production office. Ryan called it the Gag Room, some ironic reference to the days of silent film when Max Sennett kept a roomful of comedy writers and expected them to be able to provide sure-fire gags to order and at a second's notice. Our modern Gag Room was appropriately rigged out with a word processor, telephone, video, fax and Xerox machines. It was an office and a meeting place, but it was also a sort of shrine to Errol Flynn. There were literally hundreds of posters, film stills and portraits of Flynn all over the room, acres and acres of his image, and there were mountains of books and magazines on Flynn, piles of videos of his movies. I thought Ryan had sent me a lot of material, but it was apparent I'd received only the tip of the iceberg.

The room was always dimly lit. The blinds remained drawn. There were baggy old couches and rugs and bottles of wine all over the place. It looked as much like a hippie pad as it did a nerve centre. And in one corner of it all Tina Ryan sat at a keyboard bringing words very slowly into life on a monitor screen. The first time I saw her there she was wearing camouflage pants and a sleeveless vest that revealed little sproutings of under-arm hair. She had on sun-glasses and was smoking relentlessly. I thought she looked faintly absurd. Ryan introduced us. Naturally neither she nor I admitted that we'd met before.

"So you're my mouthpiece," she said.

"That's right," I replied.

Then she pointed towards the wall above her head. Someone had taken a portrait of Errol Flynn and made twenty or so identical black and white photocopies of it. Then they'd done the same with a photograph of me. The photocopies had then been stuck around the walls of the room at frieze level, images of Flynn and me alternating. I can bear looking at my own face as much as the next actor but this was disturbing. There was no doubt which of the two faces looked more convincingly like a movie star, like a leading man. My own face looked irredeemably inert, dead and lumpen when put next to Flynn's.

"How are you getting along with the script?" I asked, perhaps a little cantankerously.

"Just fine," she said.

We smiled at each other. I wouldn't say they were false smiles exactly, but they were smiles with an unusual amount of subtext.

And so, eventually, I found myself standing in a converted barn somewhere in the Suffolk countryside, wearing swashbuckler's gear, and trying with increasing desperation to act my first scene from *The Errol Flynn Movie*.

I was holding Sacha in my arms and we were standing on the "balcony of a moonlit medieval castle". This balcony was mocked up extremely unconvincingly out of some hardboard and two by four. The "night sky" behind us was painted a preposterous shade of navy blue and the moon was a crescent of aluminium suspended from above by all too visible wires. The set would have done justice to a school production of *Romeo and Juliet*. Ryan and his production designer (a winsome girl who dressed in lycra and looked about fifteen) told me that was precisely the effect they were striving for.

A complete script had still not materialised, although to be fair I had been given the pages of half a dozen self-contained scenes. Ryan said he couldn't wait for a final script. He was eager to start shooting and besides, he said, movies were made in the editing suite not at the typewriter. I was sure that was true, but I still didn't quite see how we could work without a full script. I didn't see how he could draw up a budget. I didn't see how he could build sets or get costumes made if he had no idea of what would be required. And I wasn't at all sure how I was going to turn in a good performance when I didn't know what sort of performance I was supposed to be giving. Basically I couldn't see film as such an entirely ad hoc and improvisatory form as Ryan did. But what did I know? And it must be said I was the only person who seemed to be worried by this. The camera crew, the lighting and sound men, the make up girls, the costume designers and electricians, and all the many flunkies and go-fors were perfectly happy to go along with Ryan's methods of working just so long as they got paid.

The absence of other actors concerned me every bit as much as the absence of a script. The few scenes I'd been given all involved Flynn and one other female character. I was always Flynn and Sacha was always the female character, though never the same female character twice. Ryan was sticking to his idea of one woman playing all the female parts. He had explained his reasons for this, that Flynn wasn't interested in women as people, that they were all interchangeable for him, and that in any case the only woman in his life was his mother, and I could see that might well be true, but I wasn't sure it was going to work in a film. I just hoped some other actors were going to turn up one of these days. Ryan assured me they were but he never got round to naming names, nor even to telling me what parts they'd be playing. Perhaps he didn't know.

The balcony scene consisted of the following lines of dialogue:

FLYNN
I have loved you since time began.
WOMAN
But you've only known me since yesterday.
FLYNN
Yes. That was when time began.
WOMAN
But you've made love to so many women.

FLYNN
My dear, an artist may paint a thousand pictures before achieving one masterpiece. Would you deny a lover the same opportunity to practise his art?

Errol Flynn scholars will recognise that as a paraphrase of a scene from *The Adventures of Don Juan*. Tina Ryan had changed some words here and there in order to avoid copyright problems. Ryan told me the copyright was probably vague since there had been twenty or more writers used on *Don Juan* including William Faulkner. Ryan was very good at coming out with these little bits of information. What he wasn't so good at, I soon discovered, was directing actors.

We spent the best part of three days on and around that fake balcony. The first day I didn't get to do any acting at all. We just fiddled around with camera angles, lights and microphones. I didn't complain. Everyone always says that making movies is a painfully slow and boring business for actors. I was somehow reassured to find that was true.

Ryan did a lot of shouting. That was his most noticeable mannerism as a director, but he wasn't shouting at anyone in particular and he never sounded particularly angry. I guess it was done in order to establish himself as a large, loud, powerful figure of authority. It appeared to be working.

I didn't feel entirely comfortable in my costume. I feared that I looked pretty silly. Sacha, naturally, looked fantastic. She was wearing a trailing burgundy velvet gown with a deeply swooping neckline. Her face was perfect. All she had to do was stand there, look into the camera and ravish the audience. I wished I had been able to do the same. By now I looked passably like Errol Flynn, or at least passably like an actor trying to look like Errol Flynn. The moustache and the hair were fine. The accent was not unlike Flynn's. It was just the words I had trouble with.

When I finally got to act the scene I began by playing it much as I remembered Flynn playing it in *The Adventures of Don Juan*, while trying to bear in mind that Ryan didn't want me to give a mere impersonation. I thought I was doing all right but Ryan wasn't happy. He wanted it some other way, and so I embarked on a series of "alternative readings". He asked me to try it with varying degrees of irony, although it seemed to me I'd been doing it with irony all along. Then he asked me to take a risk or two, and he had me doing it as broad farce, as high tragedy, as a Noël Coward play, as Marlon Brando, as John Wayne. There was one hysterical moment when I even played it "as myself". When he asked me to play it as a mincing queen I thought he'd taken leave of his senses, but I still went along with it.

If nothing else, I managed to impress the crew with my versatility, though frankly I thought my mincing queen lacked conviction. Whether I'd uttered a single word that would actually be usable in the finished film I doubted. Whether Ryan had got what he wanted from me I had no idea. He seemed neither pleased nor displeased by what I'd done. After each take he said. "That's great, Jake," but if they were all so great why did we have to keep finding new ways for me to do the scene?

A part of me thought he was testing me again, maybe wanting me to turn on him and tell him to stop fucking me about. But I wasn't ready for that yet. It was my first film, my first days of shooting. I also thought it was far more likely that Ryan, this confident, loud, dangerous egomaniac, probably wasn't quite sure what he wanted. After three days on or around that balcony I was praying that he found out soon.

We didn't so much finish the scene as abandon it. It didn't feel like a very good start, but the lighting cameraman, an unflappable and avuncular man called Charlie Webb, told me not to worry, that the best films always started out as badly as this. I was glad to hear it. I found Charlie a wonderfully reassuring presence. He was middle-aged, grey-haired, stocky, thoroughly untrendy, and somehow you felt he wouldn't be involved in anything dodgy or specious. Of course that knowledge was based on nothing at all except possibly wishful thinking, but if he told me there was nothing to worry about I was only too keen to believe him.

The next day we were supposed to be shooting a scene at a Hollywood party. Quite how we were going to do that with only two actors remained to be seen. I could hardly wait. Fortunately I had no dialogue. All I had to do was kiss Olivia de Havilland (Sacha) on the back of the neck. It wasn't a scene that was going to require a lot of preparation but I needed an early night. I went to bed feeling that this whole business of film acting was a thousand times more difficult and demanding than I had ever imagined. And I had the distinct and uneasy feeling that I might prove not to be so very good at it. I had a miserable, sleepless night. This, I knew, was not at all the way Errol Flynn would have handled things.

6

Things did indeed get better after those first few days of shooting. They could hardly have got worse. First we shot the Hollywood party scene. This was actually one of the scenes in which I had some faith. Flynn is now getting quite old. He's not wearing well. He's at the party and he sees Olivia de Havilland, an old friend from way back. He crosses the crowded room, comes up behind her, and plants a kiss on the back of her neck. She turns round in a fury. She's not accustomed to being kissed on the back of the neck by strangers. She wants to know who's had the audacity to do that, so she looks at the culprit but she doesn't recognise it as Flynn. All she sees is some old man, some old lecher. And she sneers at him, "Do I know you?" And then she does recognise him, and she's appalled at herself. And we see how hurt Flynn is and how sad she is that she's hurt him, but we also see the pity she feels because Flynn's in such bad shape and has deteriorated so much. It was a good actor's scene: a lot of acting and very few words.

Ryan, I was pleased to discover, had rounded up some extras for the scene and dressed them in dinner jackets and ball gowns. They weren't the cream of the acting profession and I wasn't sure that they looked convincingly like 1950s Hollywood celebrities, but at least they were there. One room of the Red Visitation had been decked out for the party. My page of script had described it as a ballroom, but it was far too small for that. The make-up people had done a reasonable job of making me look old and past it, and an even better job of making Sacha look exquisitely beautiful again.

In retrospect I think this was as good as it ever got shooting *The Errol Flynn Movie*. The camera followed me as I crossed the room and planted the kiss. Sacha turned and delivered her line. Then we did close ups and reaction shots and it all went very well indeed. Ryan didn't give me any direction to speak of, which in this case happened to suit me fine. I did my job and didn't get asked to perform it in any idiotic styles. It took all day to shoot the scene but it felt like a day well spent.

Next day I was playing the younger Errol Flynn again. He is in a hotel room with a very young girl (Sacha absurdly dressed in a school uniform). He gives her some lines of chat and then invites her to sit down on a chair. She does so, and as her bottom lands on the seat there's a twanging sound and a giant dildo snaps out from a secret compartment in the chair and pops up between her legs.

Ryan had assured me this was a true incident. Flynn really did own such a chair and did invite his guests, both male and female, to sit down on it. Tina Ryan explained to me, just in case I was a moron, that this scene demonstrated Flynn's stunted, adolescent, unhealthy attitude towards sex. It seemed to me that the wife of Dan Ryan probably knew a lot about unhealthy sex, but I kept quiet.

Dan and Tina Ryan worked very strangely together. Much as he liked to shout at the other members of the team, he was peculiarly gentle, almost protective towards his wife. He was a buffer between her and the real world. She could always be found in the Gag Room working (rather too conspicuously, I thought) on the script. Obviously that was the script we eventually shot, so she was hardly unconnected with what was going on, yet she remained well apart from the practical business of making the movie. Of course you wouldn't necessarily expect the screenwriter to be deeply involved with every member of cast and crew on a daily basis, but Tina Ryan was more distant than I could have imagined. She was an almost spectral presence. At first I thought it was a pose designed to reinforce some misguided idea about the sanctity and separateness of the creative artist, but gradually I came to the conclusion that it was thoroughly authentic. She couldn't help it, and certainly it didn't make her very happy.

We shot the scene with me and Sacha and the dildo and the chair. It went well enough, but I could have done without the school uniform. I could have done even better without Howard Hughes.

There are those who believe that Howard Hughes was gay, a lot gayer than Errol Flynn. Hughes kept women in apartments all over America but this was supposedly just a smokescreen and, if you believe the stories, he actually preferred men. He would sit in his suite in the Desert Inn and Casino in Las Vegas (he owned the place, of course) and his people would send in male prostitutes. Naturally he never knew exactly who he was getting until they arrived and on one occasion Flynn, whose sense of humour ran along these lines, is supposed to have turned up posing as the male prostitute. Our scene purported to show what happened next.

I could see there was something in this: the great swashbuckling heart-throb meets the great millionaire recluse, and they discover that neither of them is what the public thinks they are at all. It obviously had possibilities, in fact I thought there was probably a whole play in it. As a two-hander with a couple of big name actors it might have run and run. As one scene in a movie about Flynn I thought it was more of a problem. You might well wonder what Flynn and Hughes would find to say to each other, but the two pages of script I'd been given didn't enlighten you much.

When Ryan handed them to me he said Tina had been up all night working on the scene but she wanted me to know that if I had the slightest trouble with any of the dialogue I should feel free to go and talk to her about it.

The script ran like this:

*

HUGHES

So, Errol, you old son of a gun, how are you finding Las Vegas?

FLYNN

I'm finding Vegas fine, old sport, but for your information, I'm not a son of a gun, I'm a son of a bitch, the son of a whore.

HUGHES

Hey, Errol, that's no way to talk about your mother.

Errol crosses the room, picks up a bottle of vodka and pours himself a huge drink. We see that his hands are shaking.

FLYNN

I'll talk about her any way I damn well please.

HUGHES

Say, Errol, did you ever fuck Jane Russell?

FLYNN

No. Did you?

HUGHES

Nah.

FLYNN

How about Ava Gardner?

HUGHES

No, but I sure tried. Did you?

FLYNN

No. I didn't even try.

HUGHES

How about Olivia de Havilland?

FLYNN

Only in my dreams.

HUGHES

How about Marlene Dietrich?

FLYNN

No, but my first wife did.

HUGHES

Ah yes, Lili Damita. She was a little Spitfire wasn't she?

FLYNN

She was a whole squadron of Focke-Wulfs.

They laugh heartily but crudely.

HUGHES

How about Tyrone Power?

FLYNN

Well sure. Everyone's fucked Tyrone Power. Haven't you?

HUGHES

Well sure. Everyone's fucked Tyrone Power.

They laugh crudely again.

HUGHES

You like a nice piece of ass, eh Errol?

FLYNN

I sure do, Howard, and frankly I don't care what sex that ass is.

HUGHES

They tell me you've got a big piece of meat in your pants.

FLYNN

Well, you know, Howard, size is in the eye of the beholder.

HUGHES

In the eye, say, that's a new one. Tell me, Errol, did you ever take it up the ass?

FLYNN

Not me, Howard. That's for fags. (And then thoughtfully:) How would you like a blow job, Howard?

HUGHES

No, thanks. I think I'll go down to my casino, maybe risk a few bucks on the roulette wheel.

FLYNN

Hope you get lucky, sport.

HUGHES

I'm always lucky.

Camera moves in very tight on Flynn's face. His features show pain and uncertainty. He knows he has never been lucky.

I wanted to go along to Tina Ryan and protest that the scene was crass, absurd and unplayable, but I didn't do that because I didn't think it would help. I thought she might go hysterical on me. All the same, I didn't see how I could accept this scene without at least hinting, in the gentlest, most futile way possible, that it wasn't the very best scene in the history of the cinema, and wasn't there, please, some little way we might improve it? I went to her and said as humbly as possible that I wasn't quite sure how to play the scene.

"You just say the words, Jake," she snarled, hardly the sympathetic screenwriter Ryan had promised.

"But, I mean, did this conversation ever really take place?"

"Who gives a shit?"

"But am I supposed to play it naturalistically? It doesn't exactly read like naturalism."

"Why don't you ask the director?"

"He told me to ask you."

"The bastard. Why don't you both just say the scene stinks?"

"It doesn't," I lied. "I like the scene, I like it a lot. I just want to be clear what your intentions are so I can be faithful to them."

I knew I was talking bullshit, and I suspected she must know it too, because she went very, very quiet. I was ready for her to explode in rage. But she didn't.

"Did you really like the scene?" she asked.

She said it as though my opinion really mattered to her, as though it was all that mattered, as though nobody in the world had ever given her any approval and that her whole happiness, her whole being, depended on my liking the scene. So, of course, I said, "Of course," and felt myself sinking deeper into the mire.

"What I'm trying to do in this scene," she said carefully, "and I'm not even sure that my husband entirely understands it, is suggest that male sexuality is essentially independent of its object, that the male libido is pretty constant, whether it's heterosexual or homosexual. It's the same whorehouse/bathhouse mentality. Men will stick it anywhere if they're desperate enough, right?"

"I think I know what you mean," I said.

"What lines would you like me to change?"

I couldn't bring myself to say every last one of them, so I said something about it not being a problem with the words but with my own acting style. I said I'd sort it out for myself.

"What if I cut the line where you offer to give Hughes a blow job?"

"Well, okay Tina, if you like, that might work, yes."

"You got it," she said triumphantly.

I didn't know what I'd got.

"Who's playing Hughes?" I asked Ryan.

It had occurred to me that he might be going to stick a false beard and a grey wig on Sacha and have her do this part as well. But he said he'd got an actor called Bill de Vere. I'd never heard of him but Ryan assured me he'd done lots of good work. When I met him he looked as though he might have been born to play the part of Howard Hughes. There was no need for wigs or false beards with Bill de Vere. He looked like an authentic maniac recluse, though he didn't look much like a millionaire.

We shot the scene. I thought it was terrible. I was probably terrible too, but Bill de Vere was the worst. He couldn't act at all so far as I could see, which meant that he kept acting all the time, and far far too much. It was as if he thought he was in a Benny Hill Show, although given the script that was probably forgivable. Ryan, to his limited credit, could see that the scene wasn't working. He kept telling the guy to tone it down but it did no good. In desperation Ryan acted the scene himself to show how he wanted it done. He made a fair job of it and I was interested to see that the camera kept rolling as he did it. The actor appeared to be watching closely as Ryan did the scene. They then talked. The actor appeared to be listening, even understanding. Then we did the scene again and it was as bad as ever. Ryan called off shooting for the day. He said everything was all right. He said he was sure he'd got something usable. I thought he was wrong. For the first time I almost considered feeling sorry for Dan Ryan.

We worked long hours and in the evenings we would watch the rushes from the previous day's shooting. I had read that certain actors never watch their own rushes because it makes them too self-conscious. I could see the logic of that but I had to watch them anyway. I watched with what I liked to think was a grim, hypercritical fascination, and I concluded that on balance I didn't look too bad. I didn't bump into the furniture. I didn't fluff my lines. Perhaps I didn't look too much like Errol Flynn either, but that problem had been with us from the beginning and frankly I didn't think it was *my* problem. I was conscious, however, that I was being regularly acted off the screen by Sacha. She was so good at doing nothing. Doing nothing gave her a kind of power, whereas when I did nothing I seemed to disappear. I knew I would have to work on this. But for the moment at least, I thought I was doing okay, and most importantly, I wasn't letting anybody down. Ryan, in an act of generous and welcome plate-spinning, regularly told me I was fantastic.

After the dailies there was often a communal meal followed by a drinking session. I went for the meals but stayed well out of the drinking. It wasn't because I wanted to keep my distance and/or some bogus star status (although unlike a lot of actors I've never had any desire to be thought of as "one of the lads") but because I wanted to be compos mentis for the next day's shooting. The crew thought I was being very strange. They couldn't deal with the fact that an actor who played Errol Flynn all day didn't want to behave like Errol Flynn all night too.

After one of the screenings Tina Ryan told me she wanted

to speak to me. We sat outside the Red Visitation drinking espresso. It was dark and I could barely see her face, but I could hear the creak of her black leather jacket and I could smell her perfume. I think it was Chanel, one of those perfumes that smells of itself and of its wearer.

"I have a lot to thank you for," she said.

"Do you?" I said.

"For not telling Ryan that I came looking for him that night."

"No problem," I said.

"And I guess I should say thank you for being Errol Flynn."

"Well, it was your husband who gave me the part."

"But thanks for giving a good performance."

I wondered if this was a mutual admiration society and I was now supposed to thank her for writing me such a wonderful script. I couldn't quite go for that.

"This film means a lot to him," she said. "More than you might imagine."

In fact I was starting to have trouble seeing exactly what this film did mean to Ryan. He did appear to be deeply, passionately committed to this movie but what exactly did that involve? What did it mean to be committed to spending a lot of money filming a series of disconnected, wacko, avant-garde scenes from the life of Errol Flynn? Maybe it would all be salvaged in the editing but maybe it would end up as a series of disconnected, wacko, avant-garde scenes. I had known all along we weren't working on a well-made movie for all the family here, but still . . .

Sometimes I thought I was caring too much. Sometimes I thought I should just coast, not care too much about my performance, just take the money and run like a lot of others working on the film. But, call me a fool, I still had too much self-respect for that. My respect for Ryan was far less solid.

Right from the beginning Ryan had taken the occasional drink while working. He made no attempt to hide it. There was always an open bottle of wine or a litre of whisky to be seen when Ryan was in the vicinity. I didn't think that was so terrible, though personally I found it virtually impossible to work at all if I'd had as much as a small sherry. My timing and my critical faculties got blurred the moment a drop of alcohol entered my bloodstream. Ryan never appeared to be seriously drunk, but then he never appeared to be entirely sober either. I wasn't surprised, of course. The guy's wife had told me he was an alcoholic. What else could you expect? When shooting finished for the day he carried on drinking long into the night with the hardiest members of the crew, and on a couple of mornings he appeared for work obviously suffering from monstrous hangovers. On one occasion he didn't turn up at all. Tina said he was in his room making some absolutely vital and urgent phone calls to his American backers, but we didn't really believe her.

Another time he went missing in the middle of the afternoon and was eventually found in the back of one of the trucks, having it off with the winsome production designer. You could tell he wanted to be found. He thought it was funny and made him appear quite a guy. What Tina Ryan thought I had no idea.

Then there was the time he got into a terrible fight with an electrician. I never knew what they were arguing about, but it started out as a loud exchange of views and before anybody knew what was happening, Ryan had punched the guy in the face, knocked him down and was kicking the hell out of him. It took three men to pull him off.

None of these events endeared Ryan to me. I considered that I had worked with some strange and awkward directors in the theatre, but I was now in a different league of strange and awkward.

On another occasion, apropos of nothing, he asked, "So, Jake, are you good in bed or not?"

We were in the Gag Room. Tina was there too. I laughed. I assumed it was a joke.

"Well, are you?"

He was serious. He wanted an answer.

"It depends on who I'm with," I said.

"Good answer. Good English answer; polite, restrained, evasive, jokey. So, sometimes you're good in bed, but not always."

"I said it depends who I'm with."

"Sometimes you're bad in bed."

"I suppose."

"You only suppose. Nobody's ever told you you're a lousy lay?"

"No."

"You're lucky. And sometimes you're a real stud, right?"

I laughed again with embarrassment.

"Sometimes you're a real Errol Flynn, aren't you?"

"That's right, Dan. Sometimes I'm an absolute sex machine," I said irritably.

"You see how easy it is to cut through all that English politeness, restraint and evasion?"

"Yes," I said sulkily. "I know. We did exercises in it at drama school."

"So," he continued, "sometimes you're good in bed and sometimes, even though nobody's ever told you so to your face, you're lousy in bed. And according to you it only depends on the person you're with. You are constant. You are always equally skilful and adept. It's only your partner's failings that bring out any failings in you. It's the woman's fault if you're not always the stud you know you can be."

"You're taking me too literally," I said.

"Am I?"

"Or maybe you're just trying to piss me off."

"Could be," he said. "How old are you again?"

"Twenty-five."

"Plenty of time. You'll learn."

I hoped that was the end of the conversation. It wasn't.

"So," he continued, "what do you do when you're being good in bed?"

"The same as everyone else, I suppose."

"What? You kiss and cuddle and stroke and bite and nuzzle and lick?"

I nodded helplessly.

"And then you eat pussy? And put your tongue in her ass? And then you put your cock in her and you keep going for a very long time and then you both have long, powerful, simultaneous orgasms? Is that it?"

"Something like that."

"And what do you do when you're being lousy in bed?"

"Much the same," I said. "But without the orgasms."

"Good answer," he said, and then he swanned out of the room.

Tina had been watching and listening to all this, from her position at the word processor. I looked over at her. I smiled with embarrassment. She didn't smile back.

"He's right," she said. "It *was* a good answer. Maybe I can use it in the script."

She never did. Would that the screenplay had ever contained anything so comprehensible. The next bunch of gibberish masquerading as a scene from a movie involved Flynn pursuing a nameless female (Sacha, who else?) through a sylvan glade (i.e, the woods at the bottom of the garden). Flynn is in modern clothes, carrying a rapier. The woman is dressed but not overdressed. Flynn never lays a hand on her but he uses the sword to strip off her clothing; a slash here, a cut there, and her clothes fall away until she's completely naked. At which point the still fully-dressed Flynn completely loses interest in her. There was no dialogue. Ryan told me he'd be using some Philip Glass music as accompaniment. The scene took a long time to shoot. Ryan kept telling me to "stylise" my performance. Most of the time I wasn't aware of giving a performance at all, just trying to remember the rudiments of fencing that I'd learned at drama school, and trying not to poke Sacha's eye out with the rapier. Of course we had to fake all the swordplay. Undressing a woman using only a rapier is, should you ever need to know, totally impossible.

After I'd inadvertently pursued Sacha through a clump of stinging nettles, much worse for her than for me, I said, jokingly, "Do you really think this is a sensible way for two adults to be making a living?"

And she replied quite seriously, "You know what your problem is, Jake, you don't know how to give yourself to a director. You don't know how to submit."

Given some of her dealings with Ryan I thought that was a bit rich, but I let it go. I didn't want to have another conversation that showed how little I knew about sadomasochism.

There were other scenes to be filmed: Flynn is in bed with some bimbo. Amazingly enough the bimbo wasn't played by Sacha. She was a plump, pretty, ordinary-looking extra that Ryan had drummed up from somewhere. She was Spanish and had no lines to deliver, which was fortunate since she spoke no English. Flynn is in bed with her. He hears the sound of his wife returning but doesn't stir. His wife (Sacha, of course, playing the part of Lili Damita) comes into the bedroom, says "My turn," takes off all her clothes and swaps places with Flynn. I found this utterly ludicrous.

I wasn't at all sure that all this female nudity was politically correct. I wouldn't have expected political correctness from Ryan, and let's be honest, there were occasions when I didn't strictly demand it from myself, but sometimes the repeated baring of female flesh, usually Sacha's but not always, was just too gloating for anybody's good. I even said so to Sacha.

"It's all right," she said.

"Is it?" I asked.

"It's just skin. It's just flesh. I know my body's worth looking at. It's an asset, like having expressive eyes or a deep, husky voice."

"You don't worry about Joe Pervert sitting there in the dark drooling over your body and playing with himself?"

"He's not drooling over my body. He's drooling over my image."

"You don't mind him drooling over your image?"

"There are worse things going on in the world, you know."

I did know that, and who was I to give lectures on feminism to Sacha? But it did make me feel awkward, especially since Ryan was keen that I keep most of my clothes on most of the time. It wasn't that I had any burning urge to strip off, quite the reverse. I just thought it would have evened up the score a little. Ryan had no desire to even up the score.

Another scene: Flynn is at a café table discussing a film project with a young, enthusiastic film producer. Flynn appears to be interested. He says, "And now the question of money." He reaches into his pocket and takes out a cheque book. "I can write a cheque for half a million dollars and it will be honoured," he says. "And you?" And the young film producer crumples because obviously he is all talk and hot air and has no money at all.

And another: Flynn walks into a bedroom. On the bed is what appears to be a big pile of photographs, nude photographs showing rather arty sections of women's breasts and legs and buttocks. Flynn starts to sift through them. As he does so we realise there's a real, living nude woman under the pile. As he picks up the photographs her real naked body is gradually revealed. Flynn shows more interest in the photographs than in the real body.

I could usually appreciate the point the script was trying to make, but did this sound like the kind of movie anyone would want to see? Not to me it didn't.

Like a lot of actors I have the basic desire to please, to entertain, to give people what they want. I wanted to please Ryan, to do good work for him. Increasingly, however, I didn't know if I was succeeding or not. He seemed happy enough with what I was doing. He said everything was great, but that wasn't exactly what I wanted to hear. I didn't want praise so much as guidance, but Ryan wasn't prepared to do any guiding. Okay, so maybe I was asking too much. Maybe he wanted to make me stand on my own two feet, but if so he might have told me that. My relationship with Ryan wasn't deteriorating exactly, it was simply dribbling away, and at times that got me very angry.

We'd been shooting for about two weeks and I was feeling worn out by it all. I was sitting on a couch in the Gag Room and Ryan was talking long and hard to me, though inevitably not in a way that was going to help me with my performance.

"Supposing Errol Flynn came into this room right now," he said. "What could he possibly make of it all? These objects, these machines, they'd look like magical instruments to him. Okay so he may have seen a phone and a television but he wouldn't have seen a *portable* phone or a *colour* television. And he wouldn't have seen a computer or a Xerox machine or even a pocket calculator. He'd think we were demons or wizards or something.

"And clothes, man, he'd think we were all in fancy dress. There are guys working on this movie who wear flowered shirts and red pants: a guy would have been arrested in Flynn's time for walking down the street in a flowered shirt. And the women. They'd all have looked like whores, not wearing bras, not shaving their armpits.

"And out there, man, cars like spaceships, Concorde, compact discs, video arcades, Japanese restaurants. Flynn would have thought he was on another planet.

"But that's what twentieth-century history is like. Every generation is completely incomprehensible to every other generation, and maybe that's what this movie is about too, that some things wear well and other things don't. Heroes don't wear well, that's for sure. Look at John Wayne. And sex symbols don't always wear so well either. Is any modern, healthy adolescent going to get turned on by looking at old pictures of Clara Bow? I don't think so. It's partly style, partly fashion. Certain types of look just don't cut it after a while. Betty Grable's legs, Jane Russell's cleavage, who can see what all the fuss was about any more? With men it's a little easier, but you know, would an actor like Flynn have any chance in movies today? Would a man like Flynn get laid? And you know, Flynn mostly did costume parts. He wasn't so hot in contemporary roles. So I think what we're talking about here is the need for a historical perspective. You like that idea?"

"Sure," I said. "It's an interesting idea."

"But I hear you, Jake. You're saying that ideas don't make movies, images make movies, and you're dead right. And between us Tina and I have found the right image."

"Good," I said.

But of course they hadn't found the right image. What they had found was an idea so dumb, so embarrassing and so completely insulting that I walked off the picture, though it didn't start out like that.

The idea that carried all this massive weight of history with it was that Errol Flynn should walk down a crowded, modern English street, a street in Lowestoft to be specific, on a busy Saturday afternoon, dressed in swashbuckler's costume, closely followed by a cameraman. The Saturday afternoon shoppers would stare at him (i.e, me), maybe laugh, maybe jeer, maybe engage in conversation. Maybe, Ryan suggested, I would even run into a bunch of skinheads and get into a fight. The camera would keep filming whatever happened. Wasn't that a great idea, huh? I had to think about it for a while. I took a long, slow walk round the outside of the Red Visitation. Yes, it sounded like crap, but a lot of the scenes I'd already done sounded like crap too. Why couldn't I just grit my teeth and get on with it? I didn't know why but I couldn't. Essentially, I concluded, it was because I didn't want to be humiliated. It was possible, of course, that this whole film would be a humiliation but I thought my part in it so far wasn't too blameworthy. So far I was reasonably sure I hadn't made a fool of myself. Now Ryan wanted me to make a fool of myself, and I couldn't stand for that. I had to say something, and something quite strong.

I went to talk to him. He was still in his Gag Room, talking intensely to a production assistant. Tina was still in the corner processing words. I didn't particularly want the others to hear the argument I knew I was about to have with Ryan, but if they did they did.

"Dan, I need to talk to you," I said.

"Not now, Jake, gimme an hour."

It would have been easy to say okay, but I knew that if I waited I might lose the courage of my convictions.

"No," I said, "I can't give you an hour."

Ryan looked surprised.

"Okay," he said, "tell me about it."

"I can't do that scene," I said. "It's nonsense. It's stupid. It's a waste of everyone's time. I can't do it."

"You mean you won't."

"If it has to come to that, yes."

"You're doing the scene," said Ryan, trying to come over all tough and commanding.

"Oh really?" I snapped back.

"I'm directing this movie and I'm telling you that you're doing this scene."

I could feel myself getting angry, and I knew that getting angry was the wrong thing to do but I couldn't help it.

I said, "Well I'm the one doing the acting, and I'm not getting any help from you, and I still haven't seen anything resembling a complete script and I'm getting sick of all this bullshit."

"What bullshit is that exactly?"

"How long have you got?"

Even as I said it I realised that things were going further and faster than I'd intended. All Ryan really needed to have done was take me aside, have a quiet, persuasive word with me, and he could probably have coaxed me into doing the damn scene. As it was, he was pushing me into a corner and for once I happened to be in the mood to want to push back.

"I've got long enough," he said. "Tell me what's on your mind."

"Look," I said, "I don't know what the fuck I'm doing in this film. The scenes make no sense, the script makes no sense and your direction makes no sense. And I could maybe put up with not knowing what I'm doing if I thought you did, but I don't think you know what the fuck you're doing either."

I was shocked by my own words. I hadn't intended to say any of that. My mouth had run away with itself. I was regretting it even before I'd finished saying it, but I still thought it was true, and there was no backing down now.

"You're doing the scene, Jake," Ryan said again.

"No I'm not. I'm not even doing the film."

I walked out of the room, out of the house, got in my car, spun my wheels a bit on the gravel drive and headed back to London. Nobody tried to stop me. Nobody appeared to be coming after me. All the way home I felt a weird mixture of liberation and guilt. It felt good to have stood up for myself, but I felt a little ashamed to have flounced off the picture like that. Until now I had had a reputation (if you could use so grand a word) for being the most reasonable, unflappable and untemperamental of actors. Of course it hadn't got me anywhere, but that wasn't the point. But I hadn't walked off *The Errol Flynn Movie* because I was suddenly some sort of tragedy queen. I was protesting about this scene because I thought it was garbage. If I hadn't given a damn I'd have just done it. I was a professional. I had my pride. Ryan had pushed me too far. I thought my actions were completely defensible but I also had a sense that I had done the wrong thing.

Errol Flynn, of course, never had any such qualms. He was always telling producers and directors to get stuffed. He was happy to turn up drunk, or late or not at all. He was happy to take off for a few days and go sailing when he'd had enough. That was his charm, his technique. His greatest strength was that he really didn't appear to give a damn. His directors and producers and his fellow actors would always care more about the picture than he did. They would always have to come running after him. More proof. I thought, if more proof were needed, and personally I didn't think it was, that I was no Errol Flynn.

7

The moment I got home I phoned the Suffolk number. My plan by then was a simple one. I intended to speak to Ryan, apologise profusely, say I had been completely wrong about everything and offer to do any damn scene he wanted. But I couldn't get any reply. That was strange in itself and it weighed heavily on me because it denied me the opportunity to grovel and debase myself. My need for grovelling and self-debasement was considerable.

I needn't have fretted. I hadn't been home more than fifteen minutes when Ryan's Rolls-Royce pulled up outside my flat. Why had he decided to come looking for me here? Was I so predictable? Mightn't I have driven to some lonely spot on the Suffolk coast to be alone with my thoughts? Ryan obviously knew better. I looked through my window, down at the car and I could see there were two people in it, Ryan and his wife. They both got out and came to the front door of the house. Ryan rang the bell. I could see he was carrying a black briefcase. I opened the door.

"I'm sorry," I said immediately. "I'm really sorry. Please come in."

Above all else, I expected Ryan to be angry. I thought I would be on the receiving end of some loud verbal abuse. I could take it. I could almost welcome it. I was even ready for him to take a swing at me. I was determined to turn the other cheek. But they both sat down on my sofa and it slowly became apparent that Ryan looked more sorrowful than angry. Tina Ryan, whose emotional state had never been an open book to me, looked close to tears. Neither of them would say a damn thing. I assumed it was a tactic to get me to do all the talking.

"I was out of line," I said. "I spoke out of turn. I was upset. It was childish of me, very unprofessional, I don't know what came over me. Forgive me."

They listened carefully. I guessed they wanted to be sure my apologies were fulsome enough before they accepted them. I did what I could.

At last Ryan said, "That's very big of you, Jake."

I thought perhaps he was being sarcastic, but then Tina said, "Thank you, Jake. Thank you for that."

Then Ryan said, "It takes a big man to say that he was wrong."

I was glad he was starting so quietly but I still assumed this was the calm before the storm. But he said, "However, Jake, you weren't wrong."

That threw me completely. That I hadn't been expecting.

"You were right," Ryan said. "I've been doing a lousy job. I haven't had my act together. I want to make this film so badly that my eagerness has been getting in the way. I've been doing a lousy job of directing. I haven't been giving my actors what they want and need, and I realise that now."

"And the script," Tina said, "I know, we both know that it isn't good enough. We know that you deserve better."

"And we only realise it because of you," Ryan said. "I've been fucking up on this film. I guess I kind of knew it all along but I was too scared to admit it. And none of those sons of bitches I employ to tell me where and when I'm going wrong had the guts to tell me. But you did, Jake. And that makes you a hell of a guy."

I didn't know whether any of this was sincerely meant, or whether it was just another tactic, but either way I could already see it was probably going to give me a lot of trouble.

"You're not exactly fucking up," I said.

"You said I didn't know what the fuck I was doing," Ryan

replied. "You're telling me now you didn't really mean it?"

"Okay, I guess I meant it."

"Sure you did," Ryan said. "Maybe you should have said it a lot earlier."

"Maybe," I said.

"And the script," said Tina. "When we discussed that Howard Hughes scene, I see now you were just being English, polite, understated. I think we all realise now that we're not going to get anywhere by being polite. And it's you who made us realise that."

"We came to the conclusion," said Ryan, "and again I guess we knew it all along, that you're a pretty smart guy: talented, sensitive, intuitive. Let's face it, you're precisely what we need in this movie. There, I said it. We need you, Jake. Now tell us what *you* need."

I suddenly wasn't all that sure what I needed, and of course I was aware that by putting me on the spot like this the Ryans could well be playing a very simple power game. On the other hand it did occur to me that maybe this was how directors always treated their stars, as though they were important, as though they were Errol Flynn or somebody. I knew I wasn't a star to anyone except maybe Ryan, and maybe not even to him, but it did strike home that if I sat there and insisted that I didn't want to be in this picture, then Ryan was seriously in the shit. I didn't particularly want him to remain in the shit but he didn't know that. I could see that there were powerful reasons why he should be nice to me. It was all a bit of a game, but why shouldn't I play the game too? Now, in order to be taken seriously as a player, I knew I had to make some attempt to tell him what I wanted.

I probably talked a lot of nonsense about needing more support, about needing clearer direction. I remember saying that less was sometimes more. I said I wanted a clearer idea of the overall shape of the movie and where my performance fitted into it. Essentially, I said, I didn't want to feel I was making a fool of myself.

The Ryans listened intently and nodded from time to time, as though I was explaining some abstruse philosophical concept which they were following but only by the skin of their teeth.

When I'd finished Ryan said, "Yes, we can take all that on board."

"And what about my script?" Tina said.

I still didn't have the balls to say I thought most of the script was garbage, but in any case I think I had come to the conclusion that the script was only confused and nonsensical because Ryan's conception of the film was confused and nonsensical. Or, more likely, despite his willingness now to take my criticisms "on board", he actually didn't have a conception at all.

"You want script approval?" Ryan suddenly asked.

I had a vague idea that script approval was something only demanded by the most difficult and temperamental Hollywood actors. I didn't want to start behaving like one of those.

"I don't think so," I said.

"Then how about this?" said Ryan. "What if you write the movie?"

"Oh come on," I said.

"Why not?"

"Because I'm not a writer."

"But Tina is. What if I stick to what I know best, directing, and you and Tina write the script?"

"I don't think so," I said.

"You won't be working blind. I'll be with you all the way. And hell, it'll still be my movie, my ideas, my vision, but you'll be helping to put it into words. You'll be able to write the kind of scenes you want to act, the kind of lines you want to deliver. It sounds like a good deal to me."

"I think we could work pretty well together," Tina Ryan said. "Don't you?"

"I just don't know," I said honestly.

Ryan put his briefcase on the coffee table in front of the sofa and snapped open the clasps. He raised the lid and took out two bundles of fifty pound notes.

"Don't make me beg, Jake," he said, and handed me one of the bundles.

I held it in my hand. It looked naked and vulgar resting there. I felt some need to distance myself from it, morally if not physically.

"I didn't do this in order to get more money out of you," I said.

"Of course not," said Ryan. "Call it a productivity bonus. More work means more pay, that's all."

I didn't see how I could say no to Ryan. So I said, "All right, I'll give it a go. But remember I'm not claiming to be a writer."

"I think you're going to do just fine, Jake," said Ryan. "Now put your money away somewhere safe. We're going out."

He picked up the other bundle of notes and pocketed it. He and Tina smiled at each other. I was past caring whether or not it was conspiratorial. By whatever dubious means I was back on the picture, which was what I wanted, being given more money, in what promised to be improved working conditions. What could I possibly find to complain about? We got into the Rolls and drove into the West End.

"Look at it like this," said Ryan. "Everybody gets up in the morning and they believe absolutely that they'll be going to bed that same night. They think they're going to survive another day. Well, here's the news: some of them are wrong. Some of them aren't going to make it. This is the last day that some people are ever going to see. And that 'some people' could include you and me."

He started to ramble on about having to make every second count, about living life to the full, about not going gentle into that good night. I couldn't find anything to disagree with, although it hardly sounded like the world's most original philosophy of life. Tina Ryan wasn't listening. She'd obviously heard all this before.

"Of course it helps to have money," said Ryan. "And it helps if you're good-looking and talented and charming and have a big cock. It helps if you're Errol Flynn."

We had arrived at a casino. I had never been to a casino before. Ryan was known there. The uniformed doorman took the car away to be parked and waved us inside. The place was plush yet businesslike, and it was not crowded. It was entirely without the louche and sophisticated types I would have expected. Ryan, still talking, changed his roll of notes into chips and headed for the blackjack tables. Tina and I followed in his wake.

"I know what you're probably thinking, Jake, that I have some kind of Errol Flynn fixation, that I'm trying to model myself on him, well that's just horseshit. Let me tell you about all the ways I don't resemble Errol Flynn. Like I'm not Australian. I don't hate my mother. I haven't been a slave trader. I'm not a morphine addict. I'm not a Nazi spy. I'm not a movie star. Hell, I haven't even raped anybody!"

That was meant to be a joke, but I couldn't laugh at it.

"But, if you're saying, do I wish I was Errol Flynn," Ryan continued, "well who the hell doesn't? He was rich, he was successful, he was admired by millions of people. He was loved. He got laid plenty. Isn't that what everybody wants?"

I might have argued that he was telling only half the story, that Flynn's life was indeed partly as he described but that it was also tragic, desperate and painful, but I still wasn't ready to contradict Ryan when he was in full flow.

"And Flynn's is one hell of a story," Ryan continued. "I love the guy. It's that simple. Since I was a kid. Always. I want to tell his story. Call me crazy, call me obsessive, but that's what I'm trying to do here in this movie, pay my respects to a great hero, *my* hero."

It was strange to think of Ryan as a hero-worshipper. He seemed too much his own man for that. I thought it was only the young, or at least the immature, who had heroes; the lonely, the inadequate, the incomplete. What did I know?

By now Ryan was at the green, kidney-shaped, blackjack table, receiving and rejecting cards from the dealer, placing large bets. The game moved fast and I couldn't tell whether Ryan was winning or losing. He said, "Look, Jake, I've had a chequered career. I've done some work that wasn't the best, that I didn't have my heart in, that I didn't do out of love, where I was just going through the motions, where I was only in it for the money. Well, enough of that, Jake. This time I'm doing it for real. This time I'm doing it for me."

He stopped talking and became completely engrossed in the game. Tina and I watched in silence for some time, growing increasingly bored. Ryan had assumed, rightly enough, that she and I had no desire to gamble, and yet he seemed to think we would be happy enough standing around watching him. He was wrong. Tina Ryan and I went for a drink.

The bar was empty and brightly lit. It was not welcoming or comfortable, the idea being, I suppose, that punters should knock back the booze and then hurry back to the gaming tables to lose some more money.

"So tell me about your girlfriend," Tina Ryan said.

"I don't have a girlfriend."

"I mean Sacha."

"She's definitely not my girlfriend," I said.

"No? Not your type?"

"Something like that."

"What is your type?"

"Someone who's not an actress."

"Sacha's not *much* of an actress," she said.

It was a bitchy thing to say but somehow it amused me.

"Ryan tells me she's interesting in the sack," Tina said, "but that's not everything, is it?"

I wondered what Ryan had told her, and whether I had any right to say that I knew quite a lot about Sacha and Ryan's sexual activities. I decided I didn't.

I said, "How come your husband tells you things like that?"

She said, "Because that's the kind of person he is."

"And do you tell him what you get up to?"

"I don't get up to anything, Jake. Monogamy may be boring but I find it very efficient."

"Even if the other partner isn't monogamous?"

"*Especially* if the other partner isn't monogamous. Monogamy lets you get on with what you really want to do."

"Like writing scripts."

"That kind of thing."

I tried to get her to talk about herself, about her past, what kind of choreography she'd done, where she originally came from, how long she'd been married to Ryan, things like that. I got nowhere. I wasn't sure whether it was reticence or secretiveness, but it came to the same thing. She was happy enough to admit that her husband was an adulterer and an alcoholic but she wouldn't tell me basic things like where they'd first met or how long they'd been married. After a while I gave up asking. Ryan showed no sign of leaving the blackjack table so Tina and I left the casino and went for an Italian meal.

Over veal escalope Tina Ryan asked me. "Do you think we can work well together on this script?"

"We can try," I said uncertainly.

"You haven't hated every word I've written so far."

"No," I said. "The Olivia de Havilland scene was great."

"I'm glad," she said, and she seemed radiantly happy. "It will be nice to have another collaborator. Ryan isn't all that easy to work closely with."

"I bet he's not easy to live with either," I said.

She nodded in gentle, somewhat pained agreement.

"He's an amazing man," she said. "Fascinating, exciting, very alive, but no, he's not easy."

I don't think she was asking for or expecting sympathy and it was as absurd to feel sorry for her as it was to feel sorry for Ryan, and yet I found myself feeling an unlikely compassion towards her. She was married to this wild man who drank too much, who got into fights, who was conspicuously unfaithful, and who had now also managed to rope her into writing this movie. She knew she wasn't the world's greatest scriptwriter and to her credit, that bothered her. She knew this film wasn't working, but she went ahead with it anyway. How come? Because she loved the guy, I supposed. For the first time it occurred me that being loved by Tina Ryan wasn't the worst thing that had ever happened to a man.

We ate our meal and returned to the bar of the casino. Ryan was still playing. We waited and had another drink, then another.

"How much longer are we going to be here?" I asked Tina.

"As long as it takes."

It was another hour or so before Ryan walked into the bar. He sat down at our table, saying nothing. He was empty-handed and I assumed he'd lost. I didn't know what you were supposed to say to people in these circumstances so I didn't say anything, neither did his wife.

Then he put his hand in his jacket pocket, took out a handful of chips and threw them on to the table in front of us. I could see some were for large denominations so I thought maybe he hadn't lost too badly after all. Then he dug again into a different pocket and pulled out more chips. And he carried on doing it. Trouser pockets, shirt pocket, inside pocket, breast pocket, all revealed little stashes of chips. He was like a conjurer pulling out silk handkerchiefs or producing playing cards. The chips clattered on to the table and looked rather wonderful, shaped in squares, discs and rectangles, all lurid acid colours, some flaked with silver, some with a pearl finish. They looked brash, cheerful and worthless. But they weren't worthless at all. The big rectangular ones were worth a thousand pounds each and Ryan had at least a couple of dozen of those. We were sitting and staring at what was surely tens of thousands of pounds. Ryan allowed himself to smile. I found myself laughing.

"The thing is, Jake," Ryan said, "it wouldn't have mattered

to me whether I'd won or lost. It's just the same thing. It's only money."

I thought he was being disingenuous. If he really didn't care, then why had he gone gambling in the first place? Equally, I couldn't believe in a film-maker who didn't care about money. Without money, a lot of money, films didn't get made at all. For all its problems, Ryan's film was at least getting made.

We had a celebratory drink and then left the casino. Ryan carried his winnings carelessly in his hands as a big, conspicuous, untidy bundle of notes. As we got to the car he handed them over to Tina. We got in and drove. I didn't know where we were going. I sat in the back, with Ryan driving and Tina beside him. After a while she said, "We're being followed, you know."

"I know," said Ryan.

They both talked so casually about it that I thought I might have misheard. I looked through the rear window and saw there was indeed a car quite close behind, a big, black estate car with four men in it, but that didn't seem to mean much. There were plenty of other cars on the road all heading in the same direction. I didn't feel any concern because Ryan didn't appear to feel any. Nevertheless it seemed to me that if you thought you were being followed the obvious thing to do would be to stick to the main roads where there were lots of lights and lots of other traffic. You would surely have more chance of losing someone there, that is, if you wanted to lose them. Ryan turned off the main road we were driving along and went into a network of increasingly quieter, darker streets. The other car stayed with us all the way. Soon there was no doubt at all that we were being pursued and I started to get scared.

Suddenly the other car accelerated and overtook us, but as soon as it was past the driver slammed on the brakes. Ryan stopped too, easily, instinctively, as though he had been expecting it.

"We may have to improvise our way out of this," he said, but he said it casually and as though he was looking forward to whatever was coming next. I wasn't.

Three men swaggered out of the black car, leaving the driver inside, and they positioned themselves around the Rolls. They were young, broad, wearing suits. They looked hard. It was possible they'd been in the casino watching us but I didn't recognise them. They looked as though they were putting on some kind of an act, behaving the way they imagined villains acted, but they were naturals in their parts. One of them beckoned for Ryan to get out of the car. Ryan looked unimpressed. He wound down his window.

"Yeah?" he asked dismissively.

"Step outside. We'd like to have a word with you," said the thug nearest him.

Ryan didn't say anything. I then saw that the thug was carrying an iron bar. He brought it down hard on the wing of the Rolls. Lumps of paint flew off it. Ryan still didn't react.

"Is this an attempted robbery?" he drawled.

"Get out of the car you fucking Yank. Get out."

Ryan casually got out of the car.

"My wife's carrying the money," he said.

"So tell her to hand it to you."

Tina leaned across the interior of the car and handed Ryan the money. He stooped and took it. Then he stood quite still beside the car, three villains around him, God knows how much money in his fist. And then I saw, and I have no idea how he'd done it, that he had a gun in the other hand. The three guys saw it too.

"It's not a real gun," one of them said.

Ryan lazily pointed the gun in the direction of their car and fired. The sound was like having someone punch you on both ears simultaneously. He'd shot out a rear tyre.

The thugs started to edge away. You could see they were considering making a run for it but they were scared in case that might make Ryan fire at them. Ryan placed the bundle of money on the bonnet of his car.

"Here it is," he said. "Come and get some of it. It's all yours if you can take it from me."

The one who had done the talking was still nearest to Ryan. He still had the iron bar. Ryan motioned for him to drop it. He did so meekly. He looked years younger now and not nearly so vicious.

"Hey, there's no need for the gun," he said.

Ryan took a couple of steps towards him and slashed the barrel of the gun across his face. It looked so easy, so natural when Ryan did it. The guy's face was suddenly covered in blood and he staggered backwards clutching his head, as though trying to keep it on his body.

The other two turned and ran, but there was still the driver of the car. He was smaller and even younger than the rest and he'd been too scared even to get out of the car when the tyre was shot. Ryan dragged him out. The poor kid put his hands up. Ryan slapped him round the head, not viciously, more to tell him he'd been stupid, then said to him in a stage whisper, "People get killed for less than you guys were trying."

Neither I nor the driver understood exactly what he meant by that, but the driver took his point. He stood rooted to the spot. I think he seriously believed Ryan was going to shoot him. I didn't, but I'm not sure on what I based my belief. Ryan gathered up his money and slid into the driver's seat of the Rolls.

"That's what I like about England," Ryan said as we accelerated away. "Fuck all."

He was still on a high from the danger and the violence. He was shaking a little and he was driving like a maniac. I was still in shock at discovering that Ryan was wandering around carrying a real gun and had actually fired it in a London street. Only Tina Ryan was calm. In fact she looked positively serene, and it seemed to me she was looking at her husband in total adoration.

"Hey, Jake," Ryan shouted, "the next time my lead actor gets all uppity and thinks about walking out on me, maybe he'll remember I carry a .38."

I said that I very definitely would.

8

Inevitably it got worse. Looking back on it I don't see how I could ever have expected anything else. I didn't have to walk through the streets of Lowestoft dressed as a swashbuckler but that was a very small mercy. When I got back to the house in Suffolk I stood in front of the rest of the crew and apologised as thoroughly as I knew how. I don't think anyone was very impressed by my apology but neither did they seem to hold my tantrum against me.

On my first day back we shot a scene where Errol Flynn is sitting at home and the Los Angeles police arrive to tell him he's been accused of statutory rape. At first Flynn thinks it's a practical joke but it gradually dawns on him that it's serious and that his whole life and career may be threatened. The two actors who were playing the LA cops had a pair of the least convincing American accents I'd ever heard, but I had resolved not to be too critical of my fellow performers, and at least we were now doing some "proper" acting.

Tina Ryan and I had a couple of "script conferences". Ryan was supposed to have been there too, but each time he failed to appear, later claiming that he'd had to make important calls to Los Angeles, again a claim I didn't believe. I did my best. I suggested some possibilities. How about a scene with Flynn and his mother? With his father? How about him in a drunken rage attacking Nora Eddington? How about a scene where he argues with Jack Warner? How about a court-room scene? How about a scene where Flynn is late for filming and is found being given a blow job by an actress, and he says, "Don't worry. I'll be coming in a minute."

I thought the last of these, supposedly a true story, would go down particularly well with Ryan, given that he'd enacted a fairly similar scene with the production designer. And I thought none of my ideas was any worse than some of the things we'd already shot.

Ryan would never give us much of a clue as to whether or not he liked the scenes. He always said, "This is great, give me more," which told us nothing. Tina Ryan found it as frustrating as I did. Now more than ever though, it struck me that this just wasn't the way to make a movie. Screenplays surely grew out of some kind of vision, or at the very least out of some urge to tell a story. The guy with the vision was pretending to be on the phone to LA. And if this movie was really going to be Ryan's act of hero-worship, why couldn't he at least turn up for script conferences?

Working with Tina Ryan was surprisingly easy. She was still nervous, she still chain-smoked, and did a lot of sitting down and standing up and pacing the room, but at least she seemed to trust me now. She knew we were both on the same side, even if, as it was starting to appear to me, that might not be exactly the same side as Ryan.

She constantly said how much she liked my ideas, and she had plenty of ideas of her own, most of which, it again seemed to me, were a big improvement on the dross that had appeared in the script to date, but perhaps that was what I wanted to believe. I was doing my best to help with the writing, but I was not pretending to be a writer; that was still Tina Ryan's job as far as I was concerned. I wanted her to keep that job and be seen to keep it. I didn't want anybody to think that I was trying to take over the film, that I was trying to be Orson Welles.

Incidentally, Tina told me at one of our meetings that it was Flynn who had introduced Orson Welles to the joys of cocaine. It was on board Flynn's yacht the *Zaca*, off Acapulco, and

Welles is reported to have enjoyed it so much he said that if he had a spare lifetime to waste he would devote it to taking cocaine. As it was he thought he'd better lay off.

She told me too that Welles appeared with Flynn in a movie called *The Roots Of Heaven*, shot in the Cameroons, in 125 degree heat. Flynn was in such a bad way by then that he needed regular shots of heroin to keep going, but the only source was the local missionary hospital run by nuns. The nuns quite reasonably refused to provide the heroin but Zanuck, the film's producer, is reputed to have offered to build them a new wing for their hospital. The nuns got their new wing and Flynn got his heroin. I couldn't see Ryan going to quite those lengths to get me what I wanted, but then my needs were much simpler.

We agreed there might be some mileage in having Orson Welles appear as a character in the film. A couple of good scenes might be written showing encounters between Welles and Flynn over the years. But somehow they never did get written. Tina and I kept coming up with ideas, but it was one thing to have ideas, and quite another to turn those ideas into a script. I was getting exhausted. We were still shooting every day, and we were shooting much quicker than Tina was writing. It was clear that unless somebody, preferably her, had a colossal bout of inspiration and productivity there would soon be nothing left to shoot. I tried to tell myself this was Ryan's problem far more than it was mine, yet I still felt its weight pressing ominously on my shoulders.

I didn't see much of Sacha immediately after my return. Ryan had given her a couple of days off following my walk out, she obviously wasn't in the scene with the two LA cops, and then I was busy struggling to help with the script. And when I did finally get to talk to her it was in fairly unusual circumstances. I was in my room in the Red Visitation. It was two in the morning and I should have been asleep since I had an early call, but my mind was buzzing too much. I was sitting on the floor trying to read. There was a knock on the door and it was

Sacha. My first thought was that there was some new trauma, that Ryan had abused her again. But she was not traumatised or abused. She was smiling. Her hair was long and loose. She was wearing a blue silk wrap and she was carrying a bottle of wine.

"I hope you don't mind if I come in," she said. "I can't get to sleep."

"Join the club," I said.

She sat on the room's one chair and I sat on the edge of the bed. I found a couple of glasses and she poured some wine. Then she started rolling a joint.

"Is it good to be back?" she asked.

"I wish I'd never gone away," I said. "I was scared of making a fool of myself in the film and yet I ended up making a fool of myself in real life."

"You did what you had to do."

"Would you have done the same?"

"Who knows? I'm not you. I can see there's a lot of pressure. This whole film hangs on you. For what it's worth I happen to think you're doing a very good job."

"Thank you."

"I think you're very brave and very clever, and very sexy. Very sexy indeed."

Now, there may be many men in the world who are more alive to sexual nuance than I am, but when there's a woman in my bedroom at two in the morning, plying me with drink and drugs and telling me how sexy I am, I think I can take a hint. All the same, I wanted to be careful. I didn't want her to think I was another rapist. So I went over to her and very gently stroked her hair, then kissed her very softly. I had not been mistaken. Sacha reacted enthusiastically.

After we'd been kissing for a while she got up. She stood in the middle of the room and very slowly let the silk wrap fall away from her. She was naked. I watched intently and tried to keep my breathing regular. She stroked her own body, probably a lot more expertly than I would have, keeping her eyes firmly on me the whole time. She was performing for me and I was delighted to be her invited audience. She came over and very slowly undressed me, pushed me on to the bed and then started to kiss me all over. I could barely believe my senses.

We started to make love. It was wonderful, of course. How could making love with Sacha have been anything else? This was one development I could never have expected. I was deeply surprised. I even thought I ought to be deeply grateful.

At one point she said, "Is this helping?"

"Do I need help?" I asked.

"Yes. You were so tense. You need to relax. You need to get the knots untied."

"I may be past helping," I said.

"No, it's never too late."

She massaged me. It felt very good but I wouldn't have said it was relaxing exactly. Then I did my best to return the favour. We kept the lights on. I liked that. Sacha's body was certainly one that you would want to look at, and certainly I loved looking at it, as well as kissing it, stroking it and all the rest. However, call me unromantic, I found myself looking for bruises. I didn't know what stage her relationship with Ryan was at, but I assumed that, despite everything, it was probably still continuing. I explored her body looking for marks, traces, evidence of the terrible things people do to each other. I found none.

But there is another terrible thing that people sometimes do to each other. They will be making love to one person but they will be imagining making love to somebody else. They have a real sexual partner in front of them but they try to make their sex lives more entertaining by fantasising about an unreal one, or at least about one who is unattainable, say an actress, a sex-goddess. This strikes me as unhealthy and dishonest and destructive, and to be avoided at all costs. However, I suspect that everybody in the world has done it at some time or other. No doubt a reasonable number of people have even fantasised about making love to Sacha.

So having sex with her now ought to have been a dream come true. Here I was with Sacha, doing in reality what most people wouldn't get to do in their wildest dreams. And certainly I wasn't complaining, but something very strange and probably rather terrible happened while I was making love with Sacha: I found myself fantasising about making love with Tina Ryan.

This was another great surprise. Finding Tina Ryan in my imagination was at least as strange as finding Sacha in my bed. I had grown to like Tina recently, but it hadn't crossed my mind that I actually wanted to make love to her. I still wasn't absolutely positive that I did, but I trusted my subconscious enough to believe it was probably telling me something I ought to take notice of. I could picture Tina's small, angular body, her nervous gestures, her lean face, and, ignoble though it certainly was of me, I came to the conclusion that making love to her would somehow be a lot more pleasurable than making love to the far more perfect and beautiful Sacha. I realised this was a conclusion not many others would have come to, and I wasn't sure quite how or why I'd come to that conclusion myself; but I suddenly had no idea why I was in bed with Sacha, and I realised I had no particular desire to be there.

I was no fool. I didn't say anything to her. I didn't complain, and I didn't kick her out of bed. In fact, by most standards, it was a good bout of lovemaking; sensual, athletic, extremely efficient. But there was no denying that Sacha was the wrong woman for me to be doing this with.

Afterwards I said to her, "Is this just a one night stand?" hoping desperately, I think, that she would say yes.

"I don't know," she replied. "Is it?"

"I don't know either," I said.

"I don't think we'll be getting married and living happily ever after if that's what you're worried about," Sacha said.

"I'm not worried about anything," I said.

"Good."

What a rotten liar I was. In truth I was worried about everything. Sacha had said that after she first slept with Ryan she'd thought it was a mistake. She would probably think that sleeping with me was a total disaster. And how would Ryan react if he found out? He had no right to demand faithfulness of Sacha, or of anyone else for that matter, yet my feeling was that he would demand precisely that. I thought he would not take kindly to somebody sleeping with his mistress. And what would Tina Ryan make of it, given that she didn't think Sacha was much of an actress, and given that I'd insisted Sacha wasn't my girlfriend and had said vehemently that I didn't want to get involved with actresses? And if I was really going to follow my subconscious and try to pursue Tina Ryan, then sleeping with Sacha was not the most obvious and sensitive first move.

I walked through the next day in a kind of weary trance. Partly it was because I hadn't had a full night's sleep, but it was more than that. I'd been seduced by Sacha; an event that had for me much the same status as winning the pools or being struck by lightning, that is, you assumed these things only happened to other people. But mostly I was stupefied by the realisation that I was, in some obscure but significant sense of the word, in love with Tina Ryan. I didn't know exactly why, but then I would be deeply suspicious of anyone who could give coherent and convincing reasons for being in love with anybody.

I hadn't the slightest idea, however, of what I was going to do about it. Once again I didn't want to make a fool of myself. Tina had said she didn't "get up to anything" and I took her at her word. I could have made a pass at her, told her I wanted to sleep with her, maybe even professed love, but why would that interest her? She had Ryan to contend with. She had her hands full. She didn't want some actor putting the make on her. It would only make life more difficult for both of us. I couldn't see that I had anything to gain from telling her how I felt and I thought I had quite a lot to lose. I certainly didn't have any reason to believe she had any reciprocal feelings for me.

I didn't abandon all hope but I told myself not to be clumsy, not to press too hard. I knew we'd be spending more time together working on the script. Things might develop. There was no need to rush. If it was meant to happen it would happen. If it didn't it would be all my own fault.

I was well aware that I was making unnecessarily heavy weather of all this. By "all this" I meant my life, my career, my relationships with other people. I knew that these things could be done more simply, more elegantly. You could take the money and run. You could "love 'em and leave 'em". You could just not give a shit. You could be "in like Flynn". But I couldn't do any of those things and frankly I still didn't want to. Unlike Dan Ryan, I still didn't wish I was Errol Flynn.

Something pretty odd happened to Ryan over the next couple of weeks. At the time I had no idea what the cause was but the effects were unmissable. It wasn't that he became more eccentric, but rather that his eccentricities took on a more intense, maybe even a desperate, character. Essentially he started to spend a lot of money.

Things and people began to arrive at the house with a profligate regularity. These things included several abstract metal sculptures each taller than a man. They were placed in locations around the grounds for use in some future, unspecified and certainly unwritten scene. Three classic cars, a Jaguar, a Cadillac and a Tucker, all of 1940s vintage, appeared in the drive one morning. A row of tents was erected on the front lawn; serious tents suitable for camping on some bleak rugged mountaintop. Pieces of art deco furniture – sideboards, chairs, cocktail cabinets – were delivered and disappeared into the house. There were fishtanks and animal cages, fortunately without fish or animals, although a collection of three stuffed polar bears duly arrived. There were several illuminated globes, each four or five feet in diameter. There were pin tables, juke boxes, a coracle, potted palms, freestanding vintage petrol pumps, even what looked like an orgone box, though I had never seen an orgone box before and couldn't be sure. As the items arrived they were accompanied by removal vans, delivery men and a flurry of interruption as production assistants signed delivery notes and gave instructions as to what should go where. Although these instructions were precise, they seemed completely arbitrary. If there was a plan, nobody bothered to tell me about it.

Then there were the people. Once I'd welcomed the presence of other performers as an indication that Ryan was serious and competent; but I didn't welcome this crowd. There were dancing girls, a troop of boy scouts, a string quartet, a Mexican mariachi band, jugglers and fire-eaters, male and female strippers, and a whole crowd of extras dressed as Roman gladiators, marines, nuns. There were three Clark Gable lookalikes, two Marilyn Monroes, one Mae West (probably a female impersonator). Then there were the freaks; some monstrously fat, some who were dwarfs, some who were missing legs or eyes or necks. It was as if Ryan had suddenly decided to become Fellini.

I had no idea how all or any of these people were going to fit into the film, and neither had they. They had been hired, presumably at some expense, and told to turn up, and they obviously expected that sooner or later somebody (a movie director, for instance) would say what was expected of them. It never happened. Ryan muttered something about deliberately trying to make a random and creative environment, an atmosphere in which anything could happen, but I didn't believe him. I thought he no longer had the faintest idea what he was doing.

Cameramen were instructed to film all the various comings and goings and duly did so but they clearly didn't know why they were doing it. And at one point I was filmed as Errol Flynn walking through the grounds of the house with all this chaos going on behind me. It must have made a lively backdrop for the shot but you couldn't have said that any of this paraphernalia of people and things was exactly crucial to what we were doing. But by then I no longer had any idea what was crucial and what wasn't. Everything was becoming increasingly peripheral.

By now Tina Ryan's role as scriptwriter had become so blurred it was almost invisible. Was she supposed to be writing scenes around all this activity? Was the sudden presence of stuffed polar bears or metal sculptures supposed to fire her imagination? If so it failed resoundingly. She continued to haunt the Gag Room but she seldom made any pretence of working on the script. Our script conferences became meaningless.

When I was there with her we'd talk as though we were still working on a sane and sensible movie, but that was a difficult pretence to sustain. Besides, I was no longer thinking of Tina simply as a colleague. Like a beast I was thinking of slowly undressing her and running my hands and tongue all over her lean white body. In my own way I even dropped broad hints that I was interested. I said I found older women very appealing. I said I thought monogamy was essentially a good thing but surely everyone needed a fling now and again. I discussed the difference between male and female sexual desire. All this under the guise of finding new themes and incidents from the life of Errol Flynn. Maybe I was being too subtle. Certainly I knew I was being a wimp, and that was part of the problem too. I suspected Tina Ryan didn't have much time for wimps, and therefore it seemed inevitable that she wouldn't have much time for me, so why even bother propositioning her?

Sacha, considerably to my relief, had told me we wouldn't be sleeping together again.

"I wouldn't say it was a mistake," she said. "Not at all. It was good. It was fine. But some things are good precisely because you only do them once."

I didn't feel that Sacha needed to give any apology or explanation for not wanting to sleep with me again. If anything needed explaining it was why she'd ever wanted to sleep with me in the first place. I could easily believe, in a general sort of way, in female lust, but I found it hard to believe in Sacha's specific lust for me. I was gallant enough to pretend I was disappointed that we wouldn't be sleeping together again, but it wasn't one of my better performances.

Sacha was enjoying every moment of Ryan's newfound weirdness. Each new arrival delighted her, opened up new possibilities and opportunities. I had always known that she and I approached acting in very different ways, but I didn't see how any actress could cope with the endless uncertainty and fluidity and lack of direction. By now I knew better than to discuss it with her. I didn't want to be reminded of my inability to submit, of my own suburban nature.

One of the better scenes we shot in this period, which isn't saying much, was one that Tina had completed before I started "helping" her. It involved Flynn and Earl Conrad, the man who was ghost writer for Flynn's autobiography. The two of them are driving along in a car, the 1940s Jag, and they need to pee. So they stop the car, both get out and stand at the roadside, peeing. When they've nearly finished Flynn looks down at his penis and says ruefully, "So this is what all the fuss is about; a perfectly ordinary-sized penis." Conrad takes a good look at Flynn's organ and says. "Yep, that's a perfectly ordinary-sized penis."

The incident is lifted more or less directly from Conrad's memoir of Flynn and it actually took place in Jamaica, but it might just as easily have happened anywhere else. The Suffolk countryside would do perfectly well as a backdrop.

We left the Red Visitation behind us, went out with a small crew and shot the scene at a secluded roadside with an absolute minimum of fuss. The actor playing Conrad was excellent and I thought we did a pretty good job. I had feared that Ryan might have wanted to show a lingering close-up of my ordinary-sized penis in this scene but in fact he, or rather Charlie Webb, his cameraman, shot it with considerable restraint. To my relief, penises and urine remained well out of shot.

Later Ryan told me it was completely unusable, but he

wouldn't say why. I was angry. So was Charlie Webb, who was positive the scene was fine. I didn't see how it could be unusable, but I just shrugged it off and said that was a shame. I asked if Ryan wanted to reshoot it but he said no. It was infuriating but I gritted my teeth and we carried on. I was determined that however bad things got I wouldn't walk out again, and that wasn't only because I knew Ryan carried a gun.

I thought the scene was a good one because it highlighted the problems that went with the myth of Flynn's supposedly colossal endowment. Flynn, according to all the stories, used to love showing off his penis to all and sundry. But if that was the case then all sorts of people would have known exactly how big it was. If, as Conrad says, it was of perfectly ordinary size, and if all sorts of people knew that, then how come the legend started that it was so big?

Also, if it really was of ordinary size, then Flynn must surely have disappointed an awful lot of people. All these people would go to bed with Flynn expecting him to have this mighty member and then find out they'd been deceived. Reputations are always hard to live up to, but that of phallic excess seems particularly doomed to failure.

One little theory I have is that Conrad could have been lying. Maybe Flynn's penis really was massive but Conrad preferred not to say so. Because he wanted to debunk Flynn, to cut him down to size. Or, more charitably, I think it's possible he thought he was doing Flynn a favour by playing down that side of his character, by asserting that he was more than just a stud, more than just walking cock.

I'm inclined to say we'll never know, although I suppose there must be plenty of people still alive who went to bed with Flynn, and they can't be in any doubt at all. They have first-hand experience. It's only people like me who'll never know, and it would be nice to say it's irrelevant, but who would I be fooling?

Once we had abandoned the Flynn-Conrad scene we ran out of script completely. My best efforts with Tina had produced nothing at all. My first guess was that Ryan would use this as a stick to beat me with. I thought the accusation would be that I hadn't liked his script so he'd let me write my own and I hadn't been able to come up with a damn thing. I was ready to take a lot of flak for that. But Ryan didn't give me any flak. He shrugged it off. "Okay," he said, "so there's no script. So we improvise."

And improvise we did. Sacha and I improvised a scene as Flynn and his mother. We improvised a scene with Sacha as Betty Hansen, one of Flynn's "rape" victims. I improvised a monologue direct to camera in which Flynn talked about his attitude to women. "Plain girls are swell, they don't tell, and they're grateful as hell," I said. I had always thought I was pretty good at improvisation, and I thought my Flynn improvisations were nothing to be ashamed of. Maybe the scenes were too long and slow, but they could be edited, and my improvised exchanges with Sacha were no worse than some of the scripted dialogue we'd already delivered.

"Hey," said Ryan after we'd finished the scene between mother and son, "that was good. Real chemistry. Real sexuality. I love it."

Ryan never said that he knew Sacha and I had slept together although remarks like that suggested to me that he did. But if he chose not to acknowledge the fact directly that suited me fine.

And on we went, improvising increasingly meaningless scenes: Flynn talks to a stripper. Flynn talks to a troop of boy scouts. Flynn sings with a Mexican mariachi band. Ryan suggested I should get drunk to play one or two scenes so I would know how Flynn felt. I knew it was barmy. I knew I couldn't act when I was drunk. Flynn presumably had no such trouble, that was why he did it. But I didn't argue. I got drunk and I tried to improvise a scene where Flynn is on a quiz show answering questions about sailing. Ryan had gone to a lot of trouble. The set of a 1950s American quiz show had been constructed in one of the barns, but it seemed like a ridiculous waste of time and effort to me. Sober I might just have got the scene to work, drunk it was hopeless. Ryan told me I was doing fine but I didn't believe him, and there was no longer any way of knowing whether I was really doing fine or not. Ryan had stopped screening rushes. He said they were too distracting. Then he suggested I take some morphine because Flynn had been addicted to morphine as well as alcohol. Despite my pledge of obedience I said no to that one and Ryan laughed as though he'd been joking. But if I'd said yes I'm sure he'd have come up with some morphine.

I had no idea what Ryan was taking these days. He no longer got so conspicuously drunk but he looked as though he was still using plenty of something or other. If I'd had to guess I would have said he was on a mixture of dope and cocaine as well as the drink. It probably wasn't doing him any good, but on balance it was probably better than the booze on its own.

Finally we were even running out of scenes to improvise so Ryan started shooting miles of documentary footage, because, he said, he wanted to show the process as well as the product. He filmed interviews with extras and designers and the handyman who came with the house. He interviewed me and asked me "how it was going".

I looked straight into the camera and said, "I don't know. I really don't know." I was prepared to leave it at that but Ryan kept pointing the camera and I felt compelled to say more.

"I guess it's okay," I continued. "I mean I don't know what sort of movie we're making any more, I mean maybe I never did. I always knew it was going to be strange but not how strange, and I knew it was going to be experimental but I didn't know what kind of experiment."

I was standing outside the rear of the house as I said all this. Behind me a bakery van was delivering a couple of hundred real custard pies, intended for some slapstick scene that never got filmed, and nearby two actors dressed as cowboys were passing a joint back and forth.

"Does it worry you?" Ryan's voice asked me off camera.

I couldn't be sure how generalised he intended that "it" to be, but I gave the camera what I thought was a suave, devil-may-care Errol Flynn style and said, "What the hell, sport, it's only a movie."

"What the hell," said Ryan off camera, "it's only my life."

"I have absolute confidence in my director," I said deadpan to the camera.

You would have thought that having all these extra people around would have given Ryan much more reason and scope for shouting. Curiously enough he became quieter. It wasn't that he was withdrawing or becoming sullen, he was just more accepting. He wasn't losing control exactly but he was behaving like a man who no longer needed to exert power. Anything that happened was fine by him. If the drum majorettes arrived in the morning he'd try to get someone to film them, but if they didn't arrive till the afternoon that was fine, and if there was nobody to film them that was okay too. And if the majorettes' bus happened to drive across some exterior shot that his cameramen were very carefully arranging, well that became the kind of "creative accident" that Ryan said he thrived on. Maybe it was his choice of drugs. Maybe it was a Zen thing, a going with the flow. In a way I almost admired it. There were certainly times when I wished I could have emulated it, but I still couldn't quite accept all of what was going on around me.

Despite the frantic activity, there were days when nothing at all got done. People arrived late or not at all, or took long breaks, or couldn't be found when needed. The worst of it was nobody, least of all Ryan, seemed at all concerned.

Then one day the whole crew was stinking drunk. Nobody could hold a microphone boom steady, nobody could focus a camera. A light got knocked over and smashed through a bay window. I was perfectly sober and it took a lot of effort to keep my mouth shut and not tell everybody they were behaving atrociously. The sense of waste and absurdity was really getting me down. I knew it was pointless talking to Ryan but I thought something had to be done, so I talked to Tina instead. I thought, in my naïve way, that perhaps even now if we could get a couple of scenes written, something concrete, with specific needs, a specific set, a specific group of actors, then that might help pull things back from the brink. I knew I was grasping at straws.

Tina Ryan was in the Gag Room as usual, sitting at the word processor, doodling at the keyboard. Words would appear on the screen and she would immediately erase them. Her eyes looked red and raw, as if she'd been crying or not sleeping, or as if she'd been staring at the monitor screen for too long. She looked delicate and vulnerable and miserable, and I felt the urge to put my arms around her. I had the urge to do other things too but they were the kind of urges I suppressed.

She saw me coming into the room and she turned away from the word processor. She didn't acknowledge me directly but she lit a cigarette and said, "There's been a phone call. It's all over."

"What is?" I said.

"So many things. The dream. Yes, I guess the dream is over."

"Which dream is that?"

"Oh, the belief that I could write a script. It wasn't even my own dream. It was his. He believed in me, which wasn't very smart of him, I guess. But I believed in him too."

She was somewhere else, somewhere distracted and floaty. I didn't want to have to deal with this. I didn't want to deal with somebody else's crisis. I had one of my own, thanks very much. I pressed on regardless.

"Script or no script," I said, "things are getting seriously out of hand. I'm not being temperamental. I'm not being a prima donna. I'm not threatening to walk out. But all these people, all these props, all this money that's being wasted, what's it all for? And today the crew are all pissed out of their brains. It's insane."

"You think that's no way to make a movie, right?"

"That's right."

"You should tell him," she said.

"I think he already knows how I feel, and that doesn't mean much to him. But if you told him."

"Because I'm his wife?" she said. "That's probably another thing that's over; my marriage."

"I'm sorry."

"I don't know if I am or not."

She looked like she was about to cry. I gave in to one of my urges and put my arm around her. It could have been construed as brotherly but I hoped she would construe it some other way. It was crass and boorish of me but I couldn't stop myself thinking that if her marriage to Ryan was over then maybe the way was open for me. She didn't react at all to my arm around her. She didn't flinch or shudder with disgust but neither did she say, "Oh Jake, I've been waiting so long." She just let my arm rest there and after a while it seemed redundant and I withdrew it.

"You've got to talk to him," I said.

"Sure," she said.

I had imagined that she would wait and pick her moment, presumably when they were alone together. I thought it might even be a subject for pillow talk. But no. She got up from her chair and walked out through the open french window and I followed her as she set off to find her husband. He was unloading two superb-looking palaminos from a horse box and didn't look round until she was at his shoulder.

"It's all over," she said again.

Ryan left one of his assistants to take care of the horses as Tina drew him aside.

"Do you mean what I think you mean?" he said.

She nodded, then said something to him that I couldn't hear. Ryan nodded too, whispered something back. I didn't know what the hell was going on. They were speaking to each other in some code that I didn't understand. I didn't know what she was telling him, but it meant a lot to him. Ryan looked calmer than I'd ever seen him. He turned to me and said, "That's it, Jake. It's a wrap. The show's over."

I still didn't understand at first, but very rapidly Ryan went round the crew, the cast, the extras, the hangers on, the delivery men, telling them all that it really was over. At first I thought he might be fooling around, but it looked perfectly serious. I didn't know why this moment had been chosen, but something vital had happened. The plug had very definitely been pulled.

Perhaps Ryan's mysterious backers had simply arrived independently at the same conclusions that I had, that things couldn't go on any longer. Maybe that was what the phone call had been. Somehow it didn't seem like the whole story, but whatever the whole story was, once again I felt sure that nobody was going to let me in on it.

There were a lot of baffled looks among the drunk and suddenly unemployed crew, but I thought there was also a palpable feeling of relief and release. It was as if they had always known this day was coming sooner or later and now that it was here they actually welcomed it. They were glad it was over. And for all that it came as a strange and dispiriting blow, nobody was more glad than I.

I must have been standing there looking shell-shocked when Charlie Webb, the cameraman, the one who'd told me that the best films always start out badly, said to me, "Don't worry, kid. It happens."

Ryan went around thanking people and assuring them that they'd get all the money they were owed. People appeared to believe him. He even started handing out fifty-pound notes as leaving presents, not that anyone showed any signs of leaving. Some of the girls were in tears and one or two said they'd be prepared to carry on working for no money, and several said it had been a privilege working on the film and they'd never been on a shoot like it. They got no argument from me on that one.

Finally Ryan came over to me again and gave me a bear hug. There were tears in his eyes.

"Hey, Jake," he said, "it ain't over till it's over. I'll sort this out. I'll get a package together. We'll shoot some more film. We'll work together again."

I disengaged from the bear hug and looked him straight between the eyes, and very slowly, very actorishly, I said, "Over my dead body."

I said it to annoy him more than anything, but I'd had enough. I wasn't going to let him off the hook. The whole project had been a fiasco and that had been entirely Ryan's fault as far as I could see. If the madness had finally stopped, that was a cause for rejoicing not for tears. He looked hurt by what I'd said, and that suited me fine.

Nevertheless, and for all the misery he'd put me through, I still thought of him as a remarkable and in some ways even an admirable guy. In some bizarre way I still had faith in him, and I still thought it was perfectly possible he might pull something out of the hat. And if eventually he came to me again asking me to do some more shooting, I knew I would probably have been fool enough to agree. He didn't know that, of course, and that suited me fine. But for this moment it didn't really matter either way. And in the end it didn't matter at all. Ultimately I was proved quite wrong. There was nothing to be pulled out of the hat. There wasn't even a hat. We never did shoot any more film. We never did work together again, although that wasn't entirely my fault.

9

There was a party in the house that night but I didn't stay for it. It would just be another excuse for everybody to get drunk again. I drove back to London experiencing a whole acting class of emotions on the way. I was sure there was a good film to be made about the life and times of Errol Flynn and I thought that the film shouldn't just be a quick jog through the "facts". It did need a director with the courage to be strange and off the wall, and in some ways Ryan probably was the right man for the job, but in all the important ways he was completely wrong.

The end of filming was going to leave a big hole in my life. What was I going to do all day? Go to auditions? Go back to working in a photocopying shop? What was I going to think about for every waking hour? But the real gap would be the absence of people. I had never been naturally gregarious and yet I had grown to enjoy being part of a team. Perhaps I especially enjoyed being one of the big wheels in that team. But it was Sacha, Ryan and Tina I was really going to miss. There would be no more Italian meals with Sacha and certainly no more nocturnal assignations. There would be none of Ryan's manic energy and none of Tina's bewitching neurosis. They hadn't always been easy to live with and yet it seemed I had become addicted to them.

I still felt bad that I'd never had the nerve to push my case with Tina. In some peculiar and adolescent way I was infatuated with the woman. Telling her how I felt might not have come to anything but at least I would have tried, and who knows, maybe I would have been pleasantly surprised. Maybe if I'd stayed for the party I'd have got up enough drunken courage to try seducing her. By then I'd certainly have had nothing to lose. But it seemed to me that even in the world the Ryans inhabited it would be considered bad form to try seducing a man's wife on the very day his production folds.

I got back to London, feeling that I needed to talk to someone. I had been out of touch with all my friends for so long, had been so involved with *The Errol Flynn Movie* that there was nobody I felt comfortable calling. I didn't want to ring up and say, "Hey, I know I've been out of touch for three months but now the film I was working on has collapsed so I'm in need of someone to talk to." They would have thought I was a wanker and I would have agreed with them.

So I phoned my parents. I thought they, if anybody, would show some sympathy. In fact they were depressingly philosophical about it. They'd heard that this kind of thing happened all the time in the world of film-making. They advised me not to brood.

They were right, of course. I knew I had no justification for brooding. Three months earlier I had all but given up acting. Then someone had offered me the lead in a movie and given me a lot of money. What was so terrible about that? It was all experience and it wouldn't look bad on a c.v. even if the film never did get completed. Yet I felt the whole business had chewed me up and spat me out. I felt, and I know I had no right to feel it, used. It was as if the Ryans had given me a life and then briskly snatched it away from me.

A couple of days later I went to see my agent and told him the story. He too was philosophical. He said it sounded like par for the course, at least I'd been paid a reasonable proportion of my money. He looked at his copy of my contract and said we had grounds for suing Ryan, but he could see no point. It would go on for years and even if we succeeded, by the time the lawyers had taken their cut I could still end up out of pocket. But it had never occurred to me that I would sue Ryan. It would have been kicking a man when he's down. I didn't believe in doing that.

My agent told me there were one or two interesting parts coming up, parts that he thought I'd be just perfect for, and he described a West End musical, a new TV police series and a touring production of *The Double Dealer*. I couldn't get excited by any of it, which was just as well since despite my agent's best efforts I didn't get called to audition for any of them.

I telephoned the Red Visitation but the line had been disconnected. I wasn't surprised, but I was disappointed since it was the only possible way I had of trying to get in touch with the Ryans. They had never given me a home phone number. I had no idea where their home was or even whether they had a permanent base in England. I don't know what I'd have said if I'd got through. Probably something like "No hard feelings, Dan. Let's have a drink one of these days." Or I might have got Tina in which case I'd have been completely tongue-tied and would probably have said nothing at all.

I did have Sacha's number by now and I rang that. I got her answering machine and left a message asking her to call me, but I suspected she was the kind of woman who didn't return calls so I kept trying the number. Over the days her message changed and the final one said, "This is Sacha. I'm out of the country right now. I got an unexpected call from Dino de Laurentiis's people and I'm filming in Tunisia. You can contact me via my agent." I knew Sacha was in demand as an actress but this was ridiculous. I wished I had somebody who would call *me* unexpectedly and require me to go to Tunisia. As things stood nobody required anything at all of me and that was the whole problem.

My flat was still cluttered with Errol Flynn memorabilia: the film stills, the books, the videos. I probably should have got rid of them all, but instead I found myself gazing at the stills, rereading the books, watching the videos over and over again.

I was also having trouble ditching the Errol Flynn image. I'm not saying it had taken me over or anything absurd like that, but I looked better as Errol Flynn than I did as myself. I had grown attached to my pencil moustache and couldn't bring myself to shave it off. By nature I had always been something of a slob but now I didn't want to go back to being slobbish. I wanted to stay suave and elegant. I wasn't intending to live my life as an Errol Flynn impersonator but a little of his swagger and self-confidence had rubbed off on me and I didn't want to lose it.

I found myself often thinking about the Ryans. Partly it was an unhealthy kind of instant and thoroughly bogus nostalgia, but more often I simply wondered where they were and what they were doing. Were they running around trying to set up new deals and get more money to complete the film? Was Tina still working on a script? Or, I thought it was just possible, had Ryan perhaps decided he'd shot enough film to be able to cobble together some avant-garde masterpiece? At the very least I thought he must have enough footage to make quite an interesting documentary, called something like, *The Errol Flynn Movie: the masterpiece that never was*. But for all I knew he might have abandoned the whole project, decided to cut his, or his backers', losses and move on to the next thing. Maybe Tina Ryan had gone back to choreography, maybe she was putting some chorus line through its paces even now. The one thing I felt sure of was that Dan and Tina Ryan weren't thinking about me nearly as much as I was thinking about them.

I started doing things I wouldn't normally do, nothing desperately wild or eccentric, but for example I would go to films and plays that normally I would have had no interest in seeing. I would go to expensive clothes shops and try on incredibly stylish suits that I had absolutely no intention of buying. I attended the Boat Show at Earls Court. I even found myself sitting in clubs and hotel bars looking for women to chat up. And that's all I would do. I would talk to them, convince myself that I'd made a good impression and then say I had to leave.

I had no desire to sleep with these women much less have any sort of "relationship" with them, but I wanted to know I had enough charm to be able to do so if I wanted to. I sometimes wondered if this meant I was still carrying a torch for Tina Ryan, and in some futile way I suppose I was, but I certainly didn't consider myself to be pining. I was eager to get on with the rest of my life, but the rest of my life was refusing to happen.

Then, a couple of weeks later, I got a call from Charlie Webb, the cameraman who had told me that all good films started badly, and when *The Errol Flynn Movie* had folded that "It happens". He was very engaging on the phone, and asked me if I wanted a drink. I hadn't spoken to anyone connected with the film since it had ended and while I didn't want to wallow in reminiscences about "the good old days", it seemed to me that talking to someone who had been around as much as Charlie had might help me get the events into perspective, might even help me to get them out of my system. I should probably have been surprised that he called me. I knew that technicians don't generally do much socialising with actors, certainly not after a project's finished, but I was still green, and I was eager to talk.

I went to his office in Soho. I had no idea he had an office. It was a small, scruffy, open plan affair with five desks and five telephones. He said it was just a temporary base and that he shared it with four others but he was the only one there that evening. I had assumed we'd be going out to a pub but Charlie produced a bottle of good whisky and two glasses and showed no sign of wanting to leave his office. We exchanged pleasantries and told each other what we were doing now and what we had lined up. It took him longer than it took me. Then we got round to Ryan and we both said we hadn't heard from him.

"Charlie," I said, "you know this was my first movie and so I don't have much to compare it with, but wasn't that a pretty weird experience we all went through on that movie?"

"They're all weird," said Charlie. "The thing is, they're all weird in different ways."

"But Ryan, wasn't he fairly unusual?"

"Well, like you say, what are you comparing him with? Compared to someone like Werner Herzog, Ryan is just plain folks."

"Was he any good? Did he know what he was doing?"

Charlie gave a small, non-committal shrug.

"He wasn't a complete tosser. He knew about cameras. He knew about lighting. Not that that means anything. Look, some of them know what they're doing and some of them don't. Some of them *think* they know what they're doing but they don't. Some of them are very good at convincing other people that they know what they're doing but they still don't. And some of them haven't a bloody clue what they're doing and everybody knows it. The only problem is, the ones who don't know what they're doing are every bit as likely to make a decent film as the ones who do."

"And Ryan?" I asked.

"Well . . ." Charlie took a long, meditative, somewhat over-acted pause. "I never knew what Ryan was up to, but I think *he* did. And I'm not sure it had anything much to do with making movies."

"What do you mean?"

"I don't know for sure but I reckon it all had to be a con, didn't it?"

"What do you mean?"

"I mean that Ryan was a con man, right? There's nothing wrong with that. All movie people are con men. They have to be. They have to talk people into doing things they don't want to do, talk people into giving them money, right? But I reckon your mate Ryan was much more of a con man than he was a movie-maker. I reckon this whole Errol Flynn thing was a front."

"For what?" I asked.

"I don't know, Jake, but I could offer you one or two suggestions."

"Go on then."

"Well, how about a tax fraud? Ryan sets up the production and spends, what, half a million dollars, but manages to come up with bills that say he's spent a couple of million. I don't know about you, Jake, but so far I haven't had every single penny I was promised."

"No," I admitted.

"And the way he started lashing out on props and extras towards the end – he looked to me like a man who was desperate to lose money quickly."

Some of this was making a lot of terrible sense. I had frequently had the feeling that this wasn't the right way to make a movie; but if movie-making wasn't the real purpose of the exercise that would explain a great deal. I didn't necessarily believe it and I certainly didn't want to believe it, but Charlie Webb was a man whose opinions I thought were worth listening to.

"Maybe he was just trying to spend his way out of trouble," I suggested.

"Look, Jake, I'm not saying I know for sure. I'm just saying I get the feeling."

"Okay," I said. "What else?"

"Another option would be some kind of laundering operation. I don't know exactly how these bloody things work but let's say you wanted to get drugs into this country and money out, then an American film production that kept splashing money about all over the place across two continents might offer all sorts of opportunities for a smart lad like Ryan. Or maybe it wasn't drugs. Maybe it was guns or porn or protection money. What do I know? But I'd be very interested to know who these bloody American backers were. And how come nobody ever saw them? I've worked on pictures where the money men are on the set twenty-four hours a day."

Charlie could see I was taking all this very badly.

"Look," he said, "I'm not saying Ryan was the devil incarnate, but my gut feeling is that he was up to no good."

There was no reason why I should argue with Charlie, nor any reason why I should defend Ryan. If anything I felt it was I who needed defending. I was the one who'd put all the work and all the effort and all the commitment into creating this character called Errol Flynn. It probably hadn't been one of the world's great performances but it had meant a lot to me. It had cost me something. To think that all that work had been irrelevant, that it had just been a diversion to disguise Ryan's other, more important, illicit activities made me feel sick with disappointment.

Ryan's enthusiasm for Flynn and for making this movie had appeared authentic enough to me, but that was surely how con men worked. They had to be good actors. Their performances had to be utterly convincing. Charlie's theory fitted a lot of the facts, and there was plenty of other evidence that could characterise Ryan as a villain; the violence, the rape, the gun. I didn't want to think of Ryan as a con man because it made me one of his dupes, perhaps the most thoroughly duped of all. It meant I should have taken his money and run.

"At least we had a good time on that picture," Charlie said.

"Did we?"

"Maybe you didn't, but the rest of us did. I've never had such a laugh on a picture."

No doubt he could see my disapproval. I was one of those boring old kill-joys who didn't do things just for a laugh.

"Look Charlie," I said, "I think I'd better be going."

"What are you talking about? We haven't even got round to why you're here yet."

"I thought I was here having a drink."

Charlie laughed, as if to say how could I be such a twerp as to believe he would want to have a drink with me.

"I've got something for you," he said. "I've got three things in fact. But they're not free."

"What's this all about, Charlie?" I said.

"You'll see."

"I don't want to buy anything," I said.

"It's okay. There's no obligation. But I think you'll change your mind when you see what I've got."

I realised then that I had completely misread Charlie Webb. I had thought he was that rare thing, "a nice bloke". I was now thinking of him very differently, and I had great qualms about what he might be trying to sell me. I thought maybe it was precisely those things he had accused Ryan of dealing in: drugs, porn or protection. But it was worse than any of those.

He unlocked a metal drawer in his desk and took out two videotapes. They were in unlabelled, though not identical, boxes. He dropped them down on top of the desk and pushed them towards me.

"I'm going to step outside for a little while. You watch these two videos. Start with this one. The whisky's here if you need it."

He picked up one of the tapes and slapped it into my hand. I wanted to protest but it seemed futile. Charlie Webb turned on a video cassette player and a television, then left the office. He locked the door from the outside. I was getting very nervous. I put the cassette in the machine, pressed "play" and sat down to watch.

The screen crackled into life and titles came up, simple white letters on a black background, that read "Pounds of Flesh – A Film by Daniel Ryan". Then the film started with a very tight close-up of a woman's face. It was undoubtedly Tina Ryan, although the film must have been made twenty or twenty-five years ago. She was younger and less thin, and she looked like a child of the sixties, eyes heavy with make-up and a mass of long, black tangled hair. I know that youth is supposed to be attractive in itself, yet the young Tina Ryan in the film wasn't nearly as attractive or as appealing as the Tina Ryan I knew. For some reason that made me feel very good.

After dwelling on the face for a long time the camera drew back to reveal that she was sitting on a simple wooden chair in a small, characterless room, possible a motel room, and that she was naked. She looked perfectly comfortable with her nakedness. She was sitting the way an artist's model might. The effect was neither prurient nor sexy, though I couldn't help noticing what a nice body she had. I wondered if the years had been kind to it. The film was grainy sixteen-millimetre that had been transferred to video. The lighting was harsh and contrasty. A soundtrack started: 1960s psychedelic electric guitar, sometimes quite tuneful and rippling, sometimes sinking into painful feedback. By now I had no doubt that I was watching a genuine "underground film", the kind of thing that was usually guaranteed to bore me to an early death. I mean I have seen Warhol's *Chelsea Girls* and I would rather have my eyeballs surgically removed than watch it again. But in this particular case the content of the film held a special fascination for me.

Tina Ryan got up and moved around the room. You couldn't have called it dancing exactly; it certainly wouldn't have needed to be choreographed, but it was a movement made for the benefit of the camera. It was more or less in time with the music on the soundtrack. Then she stopped dancing, smoked a cigarette, took a drink, sat on the chair again.

Then scratches began to appear on the film. At first I thought it might just have been a bad print, but after a while the scratches became regular and patterned. The image of Tina came and went under the onslaught of the scratches. Then there were flashes of colour, sudden blobs of brown and red that looked as though someone had daubed paint on the surface of the film itself. Then there were patches where holes had been gouged in the film, and stretches where the film had melted, been reduced to bubbles and blisters. It was a curious and disturbing effect. Some kind of assault was going on. The film was being attacked. But was the real object of the attack the celluloid of the film itself or the image *on* the film? Or, to push it one stage further, was it the image of Tina Ryan that was being assaulted or Tina Ryan herself? In the most literal sense of course she wasn't being assaulted at all, but these days we're sufficiently alive to these things to know that attacking images of naked women is a thoroughly unwholesome activity. And even in the days of underground film it must have been a bit dodgy.

There was something very nasty about the film, but the nastiness was clearly intentional, and if you wanted to defend the maker of the film you might have said that he was aware of the issues involved, and maybe we were intended to ask ourselves whether the assault wasn't coming from the viewer as much as from the film-maker.

The film went on for quite a long time, too long for my taste, although again endurance may have been part of the intention. Finally the scratches and blotches and burns stopped, and the naked image of Tina Ryan could be seen clearly again. Now she was talking to someone off camera and she was upset. The music on the soundtrack stopped. She was shouting and getting more angry the whole time, but there was no sound, no lip sync. She was mouthing, "You bastard," but it was a piece of silent film and the fact that she couldn't be heard only made her predicament worse. But her words were obviously being heard by whoever she was talking to, and he was obviously talking back, and he wasn't being placatory. Tina started to cry. She crouched on the floor, frail, naked and terribly vulnerable, and held her face in her hands. She wasn't acting. Her distress was real. At which point a man entered the frame. He had his back to the camera but I knew it had to be Ryan. He went over to Tina and knelt beside her and tried to comfort her, but it didn't do much good, and the fact that he was male and clothed while she was female and naked made her seem more vulnerable still. I had a feeling he was going to do something terrible to her, but fortunately I was wrong. Finally he turned round and the camera zoomed in on his face. He was laughing. The features were recognisably those of the Ryan I knew. They were younger and more delicate and he had longer hair and a moustache. He looked pretty much like Errol Flynn. But as the image on the film faded to black I realised with a strange sense of recognition, that he looked far more like me.

Of course, I should have recognised this much earlier. Even in the bar of the Savoy I had seen that Ryan resembled Flynn. Since I had spent a fair amount of time trying to remake myself in Flynn's image, it shouldn't have surprised me that I now also resembled Ryan. But it did. Maybe I was an idiot, but this was the first time this perfectly obvious fact crossed my mind.

I sat there after the film had ended trying to make some sense of it all. Had Ryan picked me as his actor because I looked like him? If he had, did that mean he was making a film about himself rather than about Errol Flynn? If so that wasn't particularly reprehensible in itself, but it would have been nice to have been told. It was bizarre, but no more bizarre than some other things Ryan had done. I was glad to have seen the movie but I couldn't think why Charlie Webb would think I wanted to buy it. I popped the cassette out of the machine and shoved in the other.

The second film had no titles, in fact, as I soon discovered, it was, in some sense of the word, a porn movie. It simply started with a shot of a bedroom. The lighting and the picture quality weren't great but you could make out a bed, one chair and a man sitting on the floor reading. It took me longer than it should have to realise that the room was the one I had occupied in the Red Visitation in Suffolk, and even longer to realise that the man on the floor was me. I suppose it took me that long because I knew nobody had ever filmed me in that room, and I didn't see how anyone could have filmed me without my knowing. Then I recalled the layout of the room. There was a mirror on the wall that more or less corresponded to the position from which the camera was filming. It seemed preposterous but I realised I must have been filmed by a hidden camera shooting through a two-way mirror. That felt very strange indeed.

I watched with a growing dread, and even before the door of the bedroom opened and someone entered I knew what was coming. It was a film of the night I'd spent with Sacha. She came in and before long she was standing in the centre of the room undressing, and then she was undressing me. Then we were making love on the bed and the camera moved in, panning up and down our bodies like a dirty, wandering hand.

I suppose it wasn't as explicit as most porn films. There were no lurid close-ups of blow jobs and penetrations and cum shots. Perhaps it was even rather tame. It was just a film of two people making love and that in itself certainly wasn't obscene. We did nothing that most people haven't done at some time or another. What made it pornographic was the obtrusive presence of the camera. I couldn't bear to watch.

I turned off the video. I was so angry my hands were shaking. I couldn't think. I was torn between the desire to smash up the office and break down in tears. Then I heard the key unlocking the office door. Charlie Webb came in, looking far too cheerful and pleased with himself for my liking.

"What the fuck's going on?" I demanded. "Where did you get this film?"

"Never you mind."

"I bloody do mind."

"Tough."

"Who filmed it?"

"Not me," he said hastily.

"Ryan?"

"Presumably."

"And Sacha must have been in on it too."

"Looks like it, doesn't it? By the way, the thing you've got there is only a copy."

"Are you trying to blackmail me?" I demanded.

"Not me. Maybe Ryan is. Maybe he thinks you're going to be a big star one day and he can make some money out of you trying to keep this out of sight."

"Come on," I said, "that's not Ryan's style, is it?"

"I don't know what his style is. But you're probably right. Maybe he's just a pervert."

"But why would Sacha do it?"

"Same answer maybe. I dunno."

He could see I was all confused and furious and floundering, and in other circumstances he might have been the kind of guy you'd expect to be helpful.

He said, "Sit down. I told you I had three things for you."

I sat down, but the idea that he might have something even worse up his sleeve didn't do much to calm me down.

"I also said I had something to sell. I'm not stupid. I don't expect you to pay very much for the videos. In fact you can have them for nothing. But I do have something that I think you're going to want to pay for."

"What's that?" I said.

"The Ryans' current address."

Charlie Webb was even smarter and more manipulative than I'd thought. He knew exactly what I wanted, which was to confront Ryan face to face, to ask him what the hell he was doing. I wanted to tell him exactly what I thought of him for filming me with Sacha. I also wanted to get the original of that video. And if there was some wonderful, "innocent" explanation, and I didn't see how there possibly could be, I desperately wanted to hear it.

"How did you get their address?" I asked.

He shook his head. He wasn't going to tell me.

"How do I know it's for real?"

"You're going to have to trust me," he said.

I could think of no reason whatsoever for trusting Charlie Webb any more but I paid up. It was my only hope. I had to go out to a cash machine to get the money. It was a lot to pay for an address but I'd have been prepared to pay more. Charlie Webb wasn't greedy. He gave me an envelope inside which was a slip of paper. There was a handwritten address on it, but no phone number. I looked at it with dismay.

"But this is in America," I said.

"They're Americans," Charlie replied.

"It's in Las Vegas, for Christ's sake," I said.

"That's not my fault, is it? I hear they have these things called aeroplanes these days. I'd get on one if I were you."

The next day, like a fool, I did.

10

The person who got on that flight to Las Vegas (via Minneapolis) was a complete mess. And I became even more of a mess as the flight went on and I ate the awful meals and drank too much. But that was on the inside. Outside I was nattily dressed, as nattily dressed as, say, Errol Flynn. I looked good. I looked smooth and suave and capable. It was quite an act.

This whole thing was not my style. It was not my style to get on aeroplanes at the drop of a hat and fly to America. It was not my style to seek out confrontation. It was certainly not my style to travel five thousand miles to have an argument with an ex-director. Yet that was precisely what I was doing. Maybe I was developing a new style, becoming a new person. That suited me fine.

In my head I rehearsed all the questions I was going to ask Ryan, all the smart things I was going to say to him. Was he really making a film or was it just a con? Why had he filmed me having sex with Sacha? What was Sacha's part in it? What in God's name gave him the right to treat people like that? I worked as hard preparing for this performance as I'd ever worked on any. Despite the inner turmoil and the possibility of stage fright I was determined to appear tough, confident, like a difficult son of a bitch. Ryan was going to give me some answers, and he was definitely going to give me each and every last copy of that film of Sacha and me. I was going to have the power. I was going to be in control. I wasn't going to be scared or intimidated by the force of his personality, or by his shouting or by his gun.

Then, and it did occur to me that this was actually a much better reason for making this trip, I was going to see Tina, and I was going to say, "Damn it all, woman, I'm in love with you. How about it? How about ditching that crazy husband of yours and coming away with me and being mine for ever and a day?" I told myself some stuff about a faint heart never winning a fair lady, and some other stuff about when you ain't got nothing you got nothing to lose. And if she thought I was a complete idiot and hadn't the slightest urge to be with me, that was okay too. It was better to have tried, confessed and been thought foolish than to have said nothing at all.

I knew these scenes were all slightly corny and I knew it wouldn't take much to ruin my plot. But I still thought I was a pretty accomplished improviser, and I thought I could handle anything they threw at me. And whether the ending was a happy one, a tragic one, or just a bunch of old clichés thrown together haphazardly, at least it was better to be out there doing something than sitting at home kicking my heels and licking my wounds.

In Minneapolis I had to kill three hours and when I got on the internal flight to Las Vegas I was surrounded by people in violently good spirits. They were on the way to Vegas to spend a wild few days, to party, to hit the casinos, maybe to break the bank. I didn't share their exuberance and I felt like Banquo's ghost. I was the only person on the flight who wasn't going to Las Vegas to have a good time.

Before leaving England I had bought a guide book to Vegas, looked down the list of hotels, selected one that appeared to be near the airport, and had phoned through to make a reservation. All this was unusually efficient of me. Once we'd landed and got through the terminal building, I looked for a taxi to take me to my hotel. It was easier to hire a limousine than it was to hail a cab. White, chauffeur-driven Cadillacs were lined up, waiting to take you to your hotel in conspicuous luxury, but I still didn't have quite as much style as that. I knew I was going to need a car in order to track down Ryan, and I could have hired one at the airport, but I was too tired, drunk and disorientated to want to risk American traffic yet. That would have to wait until tomorrow.

I eventually found a cab and gave the driver the name of my hotel. It was night and I saw very little of the town, although even on that short trip you couldn't avoid seeing the glow and hustle of the Strip. My driver wasn't the chatty type, but I mentioned the address of the apartment block where the Ryans were living, and asked if he knew it. He said sure, but it was some mouse warren miles out of town on the edge of the desert, who the hell did I know out there? I said it was just an acquaintance. He laughed when I used the word "acquaintance", said it wasn't a word you heard much these days. He dropped me off at the hotel. I felt he'd overcharged me but I tried to behave like a high-roller who didn't care about these things.

I didn't have much luggage but a female porter insisted on taking my bag from me and portering it to my room on a little trolley. The whole ground floor of the hotel was a casino, and she led me between tables, past bars and restaurants, into a network of carpeted corridors that brought me finally to my room. I tipped what I considered to be generously.

When the porter had gone I looked around this needlessly vast and luxurious hotel room, with its pair of twin beds and its marble bathroom, and I felt not so much like an actor, but like a complete impostor. What on earth was I doing here? How did I get cast in this part? Did I really know my lines? And the fact that I knew precisely what I was doing here, the fact that I had done my own casting, and was writing my own lines as I went along, didn't help to make me feel any more authentic.

I turned on the TV. There was an in-house channel that endlessly showed a short movie extolling the delights of the hotel and casino. I watched it through twice, like a zombie. There were big mirrors all round the room and I no longer felt very secure in front of mirrors. You never knew quite what was going on behind them, not that I was doing anything that anyone would have wanted to watch.

Next day I hired a car and bought a good map of Las Vegas and the surrounding area. I tried hard to be smart, smooth and efficient, but it took me hours to accomplish it all. It was late afternoon before I set off to look for the Ryans.

I drove north, up the Strip, getting used to the car and to the other traffic. The big casinos and hotels crowded in on either side, sparkling and vulgar, and for all their vast impressiveness, somehow temporary-looking. Eventually I left them behind and I passed the wedding chapels and the cheap motels and the pawn shops, and came to the edge of town, to the start of the desert. Everything was strange and unsettling: the billboards, the giant scrapyards, the trailer parks. It was like being in a movie, though not one starring Errol Flynn. I felt I should be playing a tough guy rather than a stylish charmer, although Flynn was both, of course. But I wanted to be someone more indestructible; Bogart or John Wayne or Arnold Schwarzenegger.

It was surprisingly easy to find the apartment block. It was brand new and sprawling, all white stucco and red Spanish tile roofs, and there was a courtyard with palm trees and fountains. It stood surrounded by scrubby, beige-coloured desert that ran flat and featureless all the way to some distant blue mountains. It looked as though the building had been snipped out of a glossy magazine and pasted in position. It looked classy enough to me, but there was a big sign outside giving the rates for renting and it wasn't so very expensive. I'd expected better from the Ryans. I pulled the rented car into the driveway, and was confronted by a locked gate and a big security guard in a Ruritanian uniform.

"Can I help you, sir?" the guard asked, though he didn't sound as though he enjoyed calling people sir.

I gave my best charming actor's smile and said, "I'm here to see Mr and Mrs Ryan."

"What apartment would that be, sir?"

I consulted the piece of paper Charlie Webb had given me and told him the apartment number. He in turn consulted a clipboard and said, "Are you expected, sir?"

"Oh yes," I lied.

"I wonder if you'd mind stepping into the office for a moment, sir."

I continued to smile and I graciously consented to follow him into the office.

"Do you have any ID, sir?"

"Yes, but I don't see why . . ."

"Are you English, sir?"

"Yes," I said.

"Here on vacation?"

"No, on business."

"And what kind of business would that be exactly?"

"The same business as Mr Ryan. The movies."

That didn't impress him one bit.

"Okay, now you see my problem is that we don't have anyone living here by the name of Ryan."

I felt my heart sinking. Was it possible that Charlie Webb had sold me a dud address? Or, equally possible and rather more hopeful from my point of view, was Ryan perhaps using a different name? I hoped it was that simple.

"The people I'm looking for," I said, "are a man about fifty, big build, bearded, loud, and his wife's a little younger, black hair, very thin, nervous. It is just possible they may be using an assumed name."

But the guard wasn't listening. He'd decided I wasn't worth listening to.

"You understand," he said, "Las Vegas is the kind of town attracts a lot of crazies. You understand if we're careful. I'm going to have to ask you to leave."

"But you do have two people living here who fit that description, yes?"

"You know I can't tell you that."

"Why not?"

"Security, sir."

"Well, look," I said, "can you at the very least tell me who does live in that apartment?"

"What do you think?" he sneered.

We stood there in hostile silence until I said, "I've come a long way to see these people."

"I'll bet you have."

"And look, sport, they're friends of mine. I'm not going to rob them or anything. Can't we come to an arrangement about this? A financial arrangement? I mean, how much is it going to cost me for you to tell me a couple of simple things that any decent person wouldn't even want paying for?"

He remained impassive as though waiting for me to make him an offer. I got out my wallet and slipped him a hundred dollars. He took it willingly enough, then said, "A hundred dollars doesn't buy you anything in Vegas."

"You are a cheap son of a bitch," I said, doing my best to rise to the occasion.

"Out," he said.

"Look, all I'm asking . . ."

"Out!"

With a certain amount of physical encouragement from the security guard I left the office, well aware that I hadn't played this very well. He bundled me into my car and made sure I drove away. I thought of going back after his shift had ended and seeing if I could get any more information out of a different guard. Somehow I doubted it, and I didn't have all that many hundreds of dollars to spare. But I wasn't going to give up quite that easily. I drove aimlessly for a while, then turned the car around and drove back to the apartment block. There were no other buildings around, nowhere to park inconspicuously, nowhere to hide. I pulled off the tarmac and brought the car to a halt behind a couple of scraggy creosote bushes at the side of the road. The car was still visible enough, but I hoped I was far enough away from the office not to draw attention to myself, and that the security guard wasn't so conscientious as to be looking out for me.

I sat for several hours watching the apartment block. Nothing happened except it got dark. I was hoping to see Ryan or Tina leaving or arriving. If they left I would follow. If they arrived, at least I would know I'd got more or less the right address. By midnight I'd seen nothing and was about ready to go back to my hotel. But then I saw the security guards changing shift. A new one arrived and a little while later my man left. He was out of uniform now and he was in a pick-up truck. I could have tried my luck with the new guard, but instead I decided to follow the one leaving. It wasn't a very considered plan. It just seemed like the right thing to do, like something I'd seen in a movie.

He drove a couple of miles into town and pulled into the car park of a rough-looking bar. He went inside. I gave him a couple of minutes then followed him in. He was sitting at the bar drinking beer with chasers. Very casually I sat down on the stool next to him. He raised his eyes and looked me over dismissively and without surprise.

"You come to give me more money for nothing?"

"Money's not a problem," I said, aware that I was quoting Ryan. "But I do need to know about these friends of mine. Now that you're out of uniform I thought maybe you'd have more to say to me."

At first he didn't. He kept looking at me and didn't say a word. He twirled his beer glass around in his hands. It was of far more interest to him than I was.

"What the fuck are you supposed to be?" he said at last. "Are you a pimp or a faggot or a gigolo, or what? Whatever it is, you're not much good at it. And then you try to come on like some sort of tough guy, and you've got this phoney English accent. I don't know what you are, pal, but you're definitely a fake."

It was one of the worst reviews I'd ever had. Actors like to say they don't care about bad reviews but they're usually lying. I did my best to appear unconcerned.

"I really do need to find these people," I said, still in my phoney English accent.

"Well you're going the wrong way about it."

"So tell me the right way if you're so smart?" I demanded.

"There you go again," he said, "with this stupid, snappy dialogue, straight out of a lousy B picture. Be straight. Stop play acting. Be a real person."

Now I was the one who had nothing to say. I sat there feeling gawky and childish and useless. He kept looking at me and slowly his contempt turned into something like sympathy.

"Look, kid," he said, "there's nobody called Ryan lives in that building. That apartment you're asking about belongs to an old guy who used to be a shill for one of the big casinos. He just retired."

"A shill?" I asked.

"It doesn't matter. And yeah, there are some couples living there but nobody fits your description. The place is new. It's only been open six months. It's still mostly empty."

I nodded to say thanks. He turned away and got back to his beer. I felt I'd probably had my hundred dollars' worth, though I could no doubt have had the information cheaper. I left the bar and went back to my hotel. Everything was still in full swing there: the gaming tables, the bars, the buffets. I stayed up till three in the morning, drinking and losing money on the one-armed bandits. It was good for me. At least it stopped me thinking. It stopped me worrying about what to do next, and just as important, it stopped me wondering who the hell I was and what the hell I thought I was playing at in Las Vegas.

Next morning I got up late, went into the hotel buffet and pigged myself on bacon and fried potatoes. I didn't bother to shave and I couldn't be bothered trying to look smart any more. I wanted to put some distance between myself and the ludicrous character I had been playing. I sat there a long time and looked around at the other people having breakfast. They all looked buoyant, in high spirits. They made me feel even more like a loser, and Las Vegas was no town in which to believe you were a loser.

I tried to organise the few facts I knew and came to the conclusion that I knew nothing. I didn't know whether or not the security guard was lying, though my intuition told me he wasn't. So then I had to decide whether Charlie Webb had deliberately sold me a false address, or whether he'd genuinely believed that was where the Ryans lived. Again I tended to think Charlie hadn't deliberately deceived me, but I wasn't sure, and of course I had no idea at all how he'd come by the address. It came down to the fact that I didn't know whether I was looking in the right place for the Ryans. I didn't know for sure whether I was in the right town or even the right country. For all I knew they might never have left England and could be living in a flat round the corner from my own place in London.

I had flown to America feeling strong, capable and larger than life, ready for drama and confrontation, ready for some big scenes. All that had gone. Now I felt much more like my old self and it depressed the hell out of me. Maybe it was time to go home.

But I still wasn't quite ready to do that yet. I didn't know what good I was conceivably going to do myself by sitting in Las Vegas for a few more days, but that was what I decided to do. Maybe something would happen. Maybe I would have some brilliant idea. Maybe, entirely by accident, by some incredible stroke of luck, I might even come across the Ryans.

Of course it didn't happen like that. I spent the next three days doing what for most people would count as doing nothing. I visited lots of casinos, though I never gambled on anything except the slot machines. I lost a little money, of course, but nothing worth worrying about. I looked at the rubbish for sale in the souvenir shops. I bought a lot of cups of coffee, had a lot of cheap meals, drank a few beers. I fell into conversation with one or two waitresses and with the occasional fellow-gambler, but they weren't the most entertaining conversations

I'd ever had. I began by telling myself I was looking for something or waiting for something to happen, but increasingly it didn't feel like that. Eventually I no longer felt as though I was looking for the Ryans at all, no longer waiting for the brilliant idea or the incredible stroke of luck. I was just a bum hanging out in Las Vegas, wasting my time, letting my beard grow.

Las Vegas is a twenty-four-hour-a-day town. Nothing ever closes. There are no clocks in the casinos, and no windows. I stopped caring about the time. I stopped caring about much of anything. I couldn't have said I was bored exactly, but I was becoming increasingly inert and without desires. It felt okay to me. In some ways it felt a lot better than being my old self.

Then finally I was in the Desert Inn Hotel and Casino. I hadn't chosen it for any particular reason, in fact all the casinos looked and felt pretty much the same to me by now. But I was well aware that this was the hotel that Howard Hughes had once owned, where he'd lived, and where, according to Tina Ryan's wretched script, he'd had his encounter with Errol Flynn. I walked around the tables, watched the play at a roulette wheel and at a craps table. I didn't even know the rules of craps but I stood there and watched it just as a spectacle. I went to one of the bars, had a draught beer, had another and was just picking up my change when a female hand came down gently on mine. It was a hand I knew quite well, long elegant fingers and short square nails painted a deep red.

"Tina," I said, and I turned, and the person I saw standing next to me didn't look at all like Tina Ryan. She was blonde for a start, though I could tell it was only a wig, and the lips and the eyes were done differently, and the clothes looked far too frumpy and middle-American for her. It was a shock, but underneath all that clutter it was undoubtedly Tina Ryan.

"Why the disguise?" I said automatically.

"It's necessary," she said in a way that permitted no argument. "What took you so long to get here? Where have you been?"

This wasn't the joyous greeting I'd been hoping for from Tina.

"I've been looking for you and your bloody husband mostly," I said, but even as I said it I didn't understand what was going on. She was the one who was supposed to be surprised to see me, not vice versa.

"You knew I was coming?" I asked.

"Of course."

"How?"

"Once Charlie Webb showed you the videos and gave you the address I knew it would only be a matter of time."

"How do you know about Charlie Webb?"

"Because I sent him the tapes and the address and told him to give them to you."

"He didn't give me anything. I paid through the nose for that address."

"That stubble really doesn't suit you, Jake," she said. "You don't look at all like Errol Flynn."

"That's right," I said. "This is the real me. Boring isn't it?"

"Not necessarily."

That was far more the kind of thing I wanted to hear from Tina Ryan. If I tried really hard I could almost believe she was flirting with me. But I didn't want to get sidetracked.

"Why did you involve Charlie Webb at all?" I asked. "Why didn't you send the address straight to me?"

"Buy me a drink, Jake," she said.

I ordered her a vodka martini. The barman made it sloppily but quickly. Tina watched him in silence and lit a cigarette. When he'd set down the drink and gone away she said, "Think about it. I could have sent you the films and the address anonymously and maybe you'd have caught the next plane out here, but then again maybe you wouldn't. So I could have phoned you or written to you and asked you to come, but you said 'over your dead body' and I thought you probably meant it. So how else was I to get you here? I knew you trusted Charlie. I knew he could be relied upon to get you all stirred up.

And he had instructions to get you so stirred up that you caught the next plane to the States. Looks like he did a good job."

"Good old Charlie," I said bitterly. "But why did he give me the wrong address?"

"He gave you the address I gave him. Obviously I couldn't give you the actual address in case you were being followed. In fact I still can't."

"Who'd want to follow me?"

"I can't tell you that yet, either."

"Am I going mad here?" I asked. "What is all this nonsense with wigs and disguises and being followed? Why can't you people ever do anything in a simple straightforward way?"

"I had to have you here," she said. "I couldn't take any chances."

"Why do you have to have me here?"

She looked troubled and just for a second I thought she might be about to declare undying love for me, but I didn't get that lucky.

"Because of the movie," she said.

"What movie?" I said.

It was a stupid thing to say, and of course I knew what movie, but I was feeling pretty stupid and I couldn't believe that even Ryan was planning to continue making *The Errol Flynn Movie* in Las Vegas. She didn't answer.

"Did he get some more money?" I asked.

"Not exactly, but circumstances have changed."

"I'll bet you can't tell me what those circumstances are."

"I'm sorry. Not yet."

"What if I've had enough of this whole thing?"

"Then we're in trouble. But I don't think you've had enough. Not yet. You're here, aren't you? You also haven't got the original of your little porno extravaganza with Sacha."

"Is that Ryan's deal, then? I work on the movie in exchange for the video tape? You're married to a really nice bastard."

"That's not exactly the deal," she said.

"Is that the only reason he filmed me? So he'd have some power over me?"

"That's not the whole story either," she said. "Once you know the whole story you'll feel differently."

"When do I get to hear the whole story?"

"Not yet, but soon. Ryan's working on it."

My head was swirling from all this stuff. I felt trapped, exasperated, like I was losing my reason, and there was Tina behaving as though everything was sane and logical and normal. For her maybe it was. She ordered two more drinks and she leaned over and kissed me very gently on the mouth.

"It'll be okay," she said. "Trust me."

I looked at her. Even with the absurd blonde wig she still looked beautiful to me. Despite all the continuing madness, I felt overwhelmingly glad to be sitting next to her in a casino bar in Las Vegas.

"I do trust you," I said. "It's your husband I worry about. I used to believe in him a lot more than I do now. And I don't think I believe in his film at all any more."

"Well, at least you're here."

"I'm not here for the sake of any Errol Flynn movie," I said. "And maybe I'm not even here to get that porno film."

She looked at me suspiciously.

"Just before the filming stopped you told me your marriage was over," I said. "Is that still true?"

"Yes. I think it was probably over before we ever started filming. But the professional relationship goes on, of course."

"You still live together?"

"We don't sleep together if that's what you're asking. Is this important?"

"Yes," I said. "I saw you in that film he made."

"Well of course you did. I thought you might enjoy seeing me with nothing on."

Now my head was swirling for quite a different reason.

"In other circumstances I'd have been fascinated," I said.

"You didn't get even slightly horny watching me?"

"Is that what you wanted?"

"I guess so."

"Are you saying what I think you're saying?"

"That we'd be very good in bed together? Yes."

It was precisely what I wanted to hear. I couldn't believe my ears or my luck. I should probably have just scooped up my winnings like any other Las Vegas gambler, but I wanted more.

"Look," I said, "I don't know how things are with you and Ryan, what kind of relationship you've had in the past and what kind you're going to have in the future, and yes, of course it would be nice to go to bed with you on any terms whatsoever, but you know, I guess I'm in love with you or something and that somehow makes things different, and I know you're probably not in love with me, and why should you be, but the thing is, I want to sleep with you but I don't *only* want to sleep with you, if you see what I mean. I don't want to go to bed with you just for fun."

"You want more than fun?"

"Yes."

"You ask a lot."

"Yes," I said.

"If you don't ask you don't get," she said.

"Sometimes not even then."

"You've come a long way," she said.

"Yes."

"And you *have* asked me very nicely," she said, smiling at me slyly. "So how can I refuse?"

Very easily, it seemed to me, but to my astonishment, I saw I was not being refused. We went back to my hotel room and we discovered just how good we could be in bed together. Tina took off her strange, unsuitable clothes and her wig, and we made love in pitch blackness. Our lovemaking had an abstract, almost an impersonal quality to it. Yes, it was me and Tina, these two imperfect, messed up people, but there was also something elemental and fundamental about it. There was no sense of giving a performance. Neither of us was showing off for the sake of the other person. Everything we did was as natural and as normal as breathing, but every movement and every touch set off depth charges of dizzying sensuality. I know comparisons are odious, and it wasn't as though I had a great deal to compare, but I had never experienced anything better. More than that, I couldn't even imagine anything better.

"If I'd made a pass at you while we were in England would you have accepted?" I asked later.

"Perhaps, but it wouldn't have been like this."

"You told me you believed in monogamy."

"I do. Sort of."

"Are we going to be monogamous?" I asked, but she didn't answer.

I started to doze, and then I felt her getting out of bed, and I could hear her putting her clothes back on.

"I have to go now," she said. "And you have to trust me."

"If I have to then I suppose I will."

"It's all right. Things will be all right."

"But what happens next?"

"Well," she said, "if we're lucky we get rich, live happily ever after and keep on having great sex for the rest of our lives. You know, like in the movies."

"And when do I get to see Ryan?"

"Later. Soon, I hope. It'll be okay, Jake, really. It'll be difficult but it'll be okay. Be careful. I'll be in touch. And I'll definitely be back for more."

She finished dressing, kissed me and went. I fell asleep wondering if this hadn't perhaps been the happiest day of my life.

11

I woke up feeling terrible. There were plenty of reasons why I shouldn't have felt terrible. After all, a good part of my "mission" had been accomplished; especially the fun part. I had found Tina Ryan, and despite the great unlikeliness of it all, she was happy to be found. She was even happy to sleep with me. I should have been deliriously happy. Who could have asked for anything more?

Well, I could, of course. I still wanted to get to Ryan. Tina had told me that would happen "soon", more than that she had implied that when I knew everything I would forgive everything. I still found that hard to believe. I didn't see how he could possibly justify filming me having sex, although I didn't have the slightest doubt that he would try.

And was I really going to get inveigled into shooting some more scenes as Errol Flynn? I certainly didn't want to, but that didn't necessarily mean anything. I suspected that as soon as I met Ryan again things would get infinitely more complicated. I would no doubt get manipulated, might well be talked into something. I would resist, but I knew myself well enough to doubt my resolve. And if the price of destroying the footage of me and Sacha was that I had to do a little more work for Ryan, that might, however much I resented it, be a price worth paying. And at least I would still have Tina.

But then I started doing some serious thinking about Tina, and that didn't make me very happy either. I started turning things around in my head and I didn't like all the angles. It all came down to symmetry. Suddenly it occurred to me that my night with Tina was all too reminiscent of my night with Sacha. Was it possible that Ryan was behind both? Having Sacha seduce me had given him a hold over me. Perhaps my feelings for Tina now gave him another, and potentially far more sturdy kind of hold.

I knew Ryan was a control freak. He liked to have power, and perhaps he especially liked to have power over women. Perhaps that meant he got to sleep with lots of women, maybe even got to tie them up and play SM games. But perhaps his power was such that he could even force his women to sleep with other men. "Hey, Sacha," he must have said, "I need some incriminating film of Jake. Go and fuck him, will you?" And maybe he'd said to Tina, "Jake could cause trouble. Go to bed with him and keep him quiet." It made me feel sick with anger and disgust.

Of course none of this was what I wanted to believe. I wanted to be wrong. I wanted to believe that Tina Ryan was in love with me, and a part of me almost dared to believe that. But whenever Ryan entered the equation I knew nothing could be taken for granted, nobody could be trusted, everything and anything might be a lie. And as I tried to think my way around the convoluted deceptions and double bluffs that Ryan might, or might not, be employing, I realised I had started to think in terms as devious and twisted as he did. That didn't make me like myself very much.

I spent the day in a mounting fury of uncertainty. There were so many things I wanted to know, questions I wanted answering, things I wanted to get off my chest. Ryan was at the centre of most of them, but for all I knew Tina could have been weaving little mysteries entirely of her own. She had told me to trust her, but why should I?

The fact that I had no way either of venting my irritation or of relieving the uncertainty made for a rough day. My head kept speeding around and the time passed very, very slowly. Then at seven in the evening, as I was slouched in my hotel room watching MTV, Tina knocked on the door, swept in and suddenly I was happy again. She certainly gave every indication of being in love with me. For the moment I had not the slightest doubt it was genuine, and I thought I'd been an unworthy fool ever to have doubted her. We went to bed and there was no need to waste time asking questions. Actions spoke infinitely louder than words. She left after a couple of hours, and I continued to glow with pleasure for a long time after she'd gone. But gradually the glow faded and by the next morning I was lost again, and full of the same old questions.

The next day I had a new theory to worry about. I had been trying to make sense of things but maybe there was no sense to be found. I thought maybe Ryan was just committed to power for its own sake. Maybe there was no plan, no governing principle, that he was using me and messing around with my head just because that was the kind of thing he enjoyed doing. It was power for its own sake, destructive and corrupt and not to be explained by reason. Certainly I was being paranoid, but paranoia was as good a weapon as any when dealing with Ryan. And my paranoia only departed when once again Tina arrived at my hotel room later that day and made the world seem simple and bearable again. It was another kind of plate-spinning.

I tried, rather ineptly, to get some kind of promise or guarantee from Tina. I wanted her to say that she loved me, and she did say it, though not quite with enough conviction for my tastes. And I wanted her to describe, or at least imagine, a future in which we would be together, but that was a game she refused to play. I was disappointed but hardly surprised. I had tried to imagine a future for myself, and hadn't been able to come up with much. Would we live together in some sort of cosy domestic bliss in my flat in London? I couldn't see it. Would we live in Las Vegas? I thought not, given that I had no idea what we were doing in Las Vegas in the first place. Or would we be globe-trotting "film people" like she had been with Ryan? Surely not. Nothing seemed to fit. When Tina was with me this didn't matter too much, but in her absence this lack of a future only added to my doubts. A large part of me knew it was absurd even to think about this stuff, but I couldn't help it.

This was the pattern for three consecutive days, days spent alone, becoming increasingly wound up and frantic, and then a brief, blissfully therapeutic visit from Tina, who would arrive in her wig and strange clothes and mercifully shed them the moment she entered the room. As a domestic routine it didn't have much to recommend it, but I went with it because, in some nebulous and halting way I was still trusting Tina.

It was seven o'clock on the evening of the fourth day. There was a knock on my door. I didn't bother to say come in, since I knew it would be Tina and she would walk right in. But the knock was repeated and I went to open the door. It wasn't Tina. A uniformed porter was standing there smiling at me, and he had a trolley with him as though he was delivering something from room service. But he pushed the trolley into the room and I saw it was bearing a video cassette player.

"I think you must have the wrong room," I said.

"No sir. Mrs Ryan made a special arrangement."

He took over and began connecting up the room's television with the video player, and looked pleased with himself when it was done. Fearing the worst from any special arrangements I said nothing.

"Mrs Ryan sends her apologies. She regrets she cannot be with you at this time, but she hopes this will more than make up for her absence."

He said all this as though reading from a manual, then added, obviously in his own words, "I guess it's pretty hot stuff."

He handed me a video cassette and left. I felt two equal and opposite sensations of weariness and dread. Again I found myself sitting in a strange room about to watch a video of unknown content and uncertain provenance. I thought "here we go again" but I also suspected we were going into brand new areas of intrigue and confusion. For once I was right, but I'd have much preferred not to be.

I slipped the cassette into the mouth of the player and waited for the worst. There were no titles and when the image came it was a simple one: Dan Ryan sitting on an old chair by an open window. He was in some kind of broken-down shack. The room was bright with sunlight and it was just possible to see the view outside, which was of a harsh, empty stretch of desert. Ryan looked different. He had lost a little weight and had shaved off his beard, adopting instead an Errol Flynn pencil moustache. He looked a lot like Flynn, more than I ever had. It was the ageing Flynn, the careworn, slightly fading actor. It was a very convincing impersonation, and it was helped, if that's an appropriate word, by the fact that Ryan was wearing a sort of all-purpose British military uniform, the kind of costume Flynn might have worn for *The Charge of the Light Brigade*. The effect could have been absurd, yet Ryan wore the uniform very convincingly. He looked good. He looked better than I thought he had any right to.

He seemed powerful. The camera liked him and he was at home with it. The scene was shot on video, not film, but it was of professional standard, and it was all one continuous take. My guess was that Ryan was alone with the camera. He had simply turned it on and then talked directly to it. He spoke slowly and effectively. It was a highly controlled and extremely accomplished performance.

Maybe he was putting on an act for the camera, but there was something in his manner that I had never quite seen before. I was used to him being loud or extrovert but that had now gone, to be replaced by a strange concentration and intensity. I wouldn't have said he was manic, but there was a compelling edginess about him. You felt you were watching a dangerous act.

"So the movie starts like this," he said. "We have an aerial establishing shot. The camera's in a helicopter moving across a huge expanse of Nevada desert. There's nothing to see, no roads, no houses, nothing. Suddenly, up ahead, very small, very far away, there's something glistening in the sun, and as we get nearer we see it's one of those beautiful 1950s silver Airstream trailers, and eventually we see there are five cars parked around it. They're unlikely cars to see there in the desert: there's a Cadillac, a Lincoln, a couple of Porsches, a Ferrari.

"Then we're inside the trailer. The place is like a kitsch palace. It could be a mobile brothel maybe, all velour padding and gold light fittings and oak panelling. But it's not a brothel, and we see that five guys, obviously the owners of the five cars, are using it as a gambling den. They're in there playing poker.

"The camera moves round the table. One of the guys is dressed like a dude cowboy, one is a big fat Italian with a huge cigar and lots of gold jewellery. The third guy looks like a college professor, except he has a scar all the way along one cheek. The fourth guy is foreign, a Hawaiian maybe or a Samoan. The fifth guy, and the camera stays on him just a fraction longer than the others, is a good-looking guy about fifty, big but not fat, with trim grey hair and a beard. Maybe he looks a little like a movie director.

"You can tell these guys have been gambling a long time. They look like they've been up all night. The air's thick with smoke, the ashtrays are all full. And this is serious gambling going on here. There's a lot of money on that table, a hell of a lot, upwards of a million dollars. But as the camera shows us each player's pile of money it's clear that nobody's made a killing yet. Things are still pretty even, nobody's cracked yet, and that's making them even more tense.

"Then we go outside again. Two trail bikes are coming in from across the desert, two masked riders dressed in dirty leathers. When they get within earshot of the trailer they kill their engines and start to wheel their machines. They get pretty close to the trailer, then prop up the bikes, take guns out of their panniers and advance on foot.

"Then we're inside again with the gamblers. They're totally engrossed in the game and don't know a thing about what's going on outside. Then there's a warning shot, the door of the trailer bursts open and the bikers explode into the room. The gambler with the beard has his back to the door and the bigger of the two bikers grabs him by the neck and puts the gun to his head. If anyone tries anything he gets his brains blown out. But all this is silent. There's not been one line of dialogue yet.

"The other biker goes round the table, gathers up the money, puts it in a sack. It's very quick, very efficient. Then they start to leave but they drag the bearded guy out with them as a shield.

"One of them goes over to the five parked cars and systematically blasts out all their tyres so they can't be followed. They get to their bikes, club the bearded guy over the head so he falls unconscious. Then they get on their machines and head out across the desert.

"The four other gamblers step out of the trailer, see what's been done to their cars. They're foaming mad, but what the hell can they do? Then the camera starts to ascend and move again. We see the trailer and the cars, and the two trail bikes getting further and further away, and before long the camera is so high that they're all just specks in the desert and soon after that they disappear completely.

"That's the pre-title sequence. First scene after the titles, an abandoned desert motel, some time later. Camera zooms in on one of the windows. Interior shot: we see a man sitting in a wrecked room on the frame of an old bed. It's the gambler with the beard, the one who was used as the shield. He looks a little jumpy, though he's trying hard to hide it. He looks out of the window. The two masked riders reappear. They pull up outside the motel, dismount and head for his room. They're carrying the sack with the money in it. The bearded guy gets up off the bed, opens the door, lets them in. They take off their masks and we see that one of them, the shorter, slimmer one who collected up the money, is in fact a woman; lean, pretty, black-haired. She goes over to the bearded guy and gives him a big, passionate kiss. Then she puts the bag on top of an old packing case and starts counting out the loot. Obviously all three of them are in this thing together, but the guy with the beard is clearly the brains. As the woman divides up the money we see that the other biker only gets a very small cut. He protests just for a moment but he knows there's no point arguing. He takes his money, gets on his bike and goes.

"The couple are alone in this trashed motel room. They start kissing again and before long they're naked and making love on the ground in amongst the dust and sand and wreckage. The camera moves out again, draws way, way back until the motel itself is just another speck in the desert.

"So that's the opening. Personally I like it a lot. I'm not saying it's the greatest opening sequence anybody ever shot, and I'd probably agree that it's definitely not the most original, but I like to think it has a certain amount of style, and a certain compelling quality. And the thing is: this is a true story. I *am* that bearded man."

Ryan laughed as he said that and he reached out of shot for a beer. He took a swig from the can. He drank slowly, giving his story time to sink in, giving the audience, me, time to wonder just exactly what he was confessing to here. After a while his face and his attention moved back to the camera.

"So there you have it," he started again, "a couple of scenes from the life of Daniel Ryan. And like any good cinema audience you're saying to yourself, hey, what's the motivation here? Okay, flashback time.

"1950, black and white movie; a ten-year-old kid sneaks into a cinema in LA without paying. We see that the cinema is showing an Errol Flynn double bill: *Captain Blood* and *The Sea Hawk*. The kid goes up to the balcony and gets a front row seat. The movie starts and he's instantly and completely entranced. We see one or two shots from *The Sea Hawk* interspersed with the boy's face. It's obvious that Flynn is an absolute and utter hero to him.

"Then we see someone sit down next to the boy. It's a man, tall, shadowy, maybe a little sinister. He's behaving a little furtively. The boy takes no notice of him at first, but the man leans over and sits real close. Obviously it's a dirty old man, although in fact he's not that old. We see his hand reach out and touch the boy's knee. Close up on the boy's face. He's still trying to watch the movie but it's not so easy now. He's distracted. He turns to look at the man (and here the audience isn't sure if we're into a fantasy sequence or not) and the man is the spitting image of Errol Flynn.

"Now we have a series of rapid cuts between the man's face, the boy's face, and the face of Flynn on the cinema screen. Finally there's a long lingering close-up of the boy's face. We realise something untoward is going on down below, just out of shot, but we don't know exactly what, although let's face it most of us could make a damn good guess. And the boy's face undergoes a transformation, unsure at first, then submitting, and finally looking as though he's really enjoying himself, but his eyes are fixed firmly on the movie screen image of Errol Flynn the whole time.

"Yeah? Well, put that in a movie script and try selling it to Hollywood, and see how far you get. Polymorphous perversity isn't very saleable in Hollywood this year, or any other year. Again, it really happened. I *am* that ten-year-old boy in the cinema but I know that's no reason for putting it in the movie. And I don't know if the scene really tells you anything. I don't know if it really explains why our hero grew up wanting to be a movie director with an Errol Flynn obsession, and with a fairly wide range of sexual tastes. But grow up he certainly did.

"Time for the autobiography. I spent a lot of my childhood in movie theatres. My parents lived in LA and both of them worked in and around the movie business. They both had talent. My mother worked for one of the big agencies. My father was a musician. Sometimes he did really well and got to write a little incidental music. Other times he was reduced to giving singing lessons to aspiring starlets. They never made it big, but they survived, and they loved the movies.

"It was assumed, especially by me, that I'd grow up and work in the movies too, maybe as an editor, maybe as an actor. It didn't seem to matter much. The important thing was just to be involved. But by the time I was old enough to think for myself I decided the only job worth having was that of movie director. He was the big guy, the one with the power. That's what I wanted to be. It was a big ambition, but there was no point in thinking small.

"Now this was the time when the first film schools were opening. If you wanted to be a movie director that was the place to go. I enrolled at UCLA. I lasted two months. I hated it, hated every damn minute of it. I left. My ambition looked more unlikely than ever. I spent the next few years drifting around the movie industry, getting a few menial jobs from people who knew my parents. I told myself I was paying my dues, that the big break would come one day. But I got tired of waiting for it. And you know, my plan had always been to start at the top not the bottom.

"I never did drugs, didn't even drink much in those days, but I did like to gamble. I always had. I was a fair poker player. I knew how to bet and I knew when to quit. There were years when I made more out of playing poker than I did out of working in the movie industry. And that only made me want to be a movie director even more.

"By now I'd figured out that in order to make a movie you didn't need talent or ability, all you needed was money. I'd also realised that nobody was going to come running up to me and put a few million dollars in my hand and tell me to go away and make a movie. I was going to have to hustle the money for myself. I had precisely one thousand dollars to my name. I was pissed off with my life and my career, and I decided to go to Las Vegas for the weekend. I knew that a movie director had to be something of a gambler. I knew he needed luck. I had some crazy idea that I was going to take my thousand dollars to Vegas, hit a winning streak, and return with enough money to bankroll my first low-budget independent feature film. I was insane.

"Within three hours of getting to Vegas I'd lost my thousand dollars and signed markers for three thousand dollars more. I was completely broke, more than broke. I only had what I stood up in. There was no way I was ever going to be able to pay back the casino. I realise now that if I'd just run out of town I'd most likely have been okay. They wouldn't have chased me to the ends of the earth for the sake of a few thousand dollars. But back then I knew nothing. I felt sure I was going to get my legs broken.

"So I went and told my sad story to the pit boss. He could see I was a nobody and a nothing, but obviously he wasn't going to pat me on the head and tell me to forget about it, so he must have decided he'd get some work out of me. He offered me a job as a blackjack dealer, so he could stop what I owed out of my wages. I took the job. I didn't think I had a choice. It wasn't as if Hollywood was calling me home, and in any case I thought I had no choice. In my family you didn't go crawling home to your father and ask him to pay off your gambling debts.

"But working for a Las Vegas casino turned out not to be so bad. Even after I'd paid back the debt I carried on with the job. I wouldn't have believed it, but it was more satisfying than any of the shit work I'd done in the movies. And after a while I met a girl. She was a dancer in one of the casino shows. She was good. She was called Tina. Twenty-five years later we're still together, more or less.

"I had a little money by now. I bought a used Arriflex, shot an avant-garde movie called *Pounds of Flesh*. I thought this would be the big one. Once somebody saw my work I knew I was going to get 'discovered'. I thought I was bound to be acclaimed as the genius I'd always known I was. I was going to be the next Warhol, the next Orson Welles, the next Jesus Christ. I entered the movie for one or two competitions and festivals. I got zero response. Nothing. Not the slightest tremor of interest. I told myself that the world's indifference meant nothing, and I was right of course, but that didn't stop it hurting. The master plan was going seriously wrong. I needed some time to lick my wounds, and I still needed to make a living so I stayed working at the casino. I stayed a long time.

"I started to live with the idea that I'd be an undiscovered genius, making movies my own way, by myself, for myself. And for a long time that's what I did. I worked in a Las Vegas casino and I financed a few very cheap, very obscure movies, written and directed and produced and shot and edited by Daniel Ryan, American auteur. Only a handful of people ever saw them. Even fewer people ever wanted to. Maybe the movies had an integrity that comes from independence, though frankly I'm not certain about that, but they sure never had an audience. They were just a great way of losing money.

"Tina and I got married. She kept dancing. I kept dealing blackjack. But gradually I worked my way up to casino manager. It was a big job and I was pretty good at it, and we carried on like that for a few years but in the end I was getting bored and so was Tina. We both needed something new. Then someone suggested Tina should start doing choreography. It seemed like a good idea. You can't keep dancing for ever. And then we thought, why not do this as a team? I was supposed to be this visually-oriented guy, I was good at organisation, what if Tina did the choreography and I did the stage direction? We went for it.

"We had to start pretty small, in some real low-budget dives, and let's face it, we never made it all the way to the very top. Caesar's Palace didn't come begging us to do their floor show for Liza Minnelli, but, you know, we moved up, we did okay.

"We did some good shows: all singing, all-dancing, topless showgirls and a good band and some very slick lighting effects, a lot of glitter, a lot of feathers. In fact I even based one or two of the shows on Errol Flynn movies. There was a Robin Hood sequence, a *Captain Blood, Elizabeth and Essex, Don Juan,* even a version of Custer's last stand from *They Died With Their Boots On.* Of course I'm not saying that the audience grasped all the filmic references. They were just there for the dancing girls. But I was pretty happy with it all for a while.

"And that's what happened to Daniel Ryan the famous movie director. He spent about twenty years telling topless dancers how to smile, where to stand, when to make an exit, how to take a curtain call. It wasn't art but it was a living. They were full years and they weren't bad years but they went by way too quickly.

"And then somehow I got to be fifty years old. I didn't feel fifty. I still felt twenty-one, and all those youthful ideas and ambitions were still there. I still wanted to be a movie director. So I discussed it long and hard with my wife and finally she agreed we had to go for it again. I had to try to make a big movie. We had to do whatever it would take to make the dream a reality.

"But, of course, nothing much had really changed. I had more than a thousand dollars to my name but I sure as hell didn't have the kind of money needed to finance a movie. Yet I was surrounded by money all the time. I saw fortunes change hands at the gambling tables every day of the week and I thought there had to be a way of getting my hands on some of it. The sons of bitches would gladly lose half a million dollars at a roulette wheel and shrug it off but they wouldn't put up one thin dime to fund a Dan Ryan movie, and who could blame them?

"But I'd learned my lesson a long time ago. I knew that gambling wasn't the way to get rich, but fortunately a lot of people hadn't realised that yet. So I organised a poker game. It took place in an Airstream trailer in the middle of the Nevada desert, and I think you more or less know the rest.

"It was set up by word of mouth and it was done in such a way that I didn't appear to be the prime mover. The buy-in was high, a quarter of a million dollars. I had to do some real hustling to raise that, had to borrow from all over the damn place, but I managed it. The great thing was, when the five of us were in that trailer I knew that even excluding my own money, there was at least a million dollars sitting there on that table, just about enough to make a movie. These guys didn't know it but they were going to be my backers.

"I found the biker who did the actual robbery, made sure he hit me a couple of times to avoid suspicion, and of course Tina was with him to make sure he didn't get any ideas about taking the money for himself. I always feared he was going to be trouble, but there was no way Tina and I could pull off the job without outside help.

"When word got around about what had happened out there in the desert, there were plenty of theories about who was behind the robbery, but nobody ever mentioned me. Why would they? I had very conspicuously lost everything. In order to pay back what I'd borrowed to get into the game I even had to sell my apartment. I took it badly. I took time off work. I said I'd had enough of Las Vegas. I told anybody who'd listen that I wanted out of that world. And after a respectable wait, Tina and I got out. We left for England saying we were looking for a new start, a new life. It wasn't so far from the truth.

"I thought it was quite possible that sooner or later someone might join up the dots and work out what had really been going on in that trailer, at which point I would be in serious, probably lethal, shit. But that didn't really bother me at the time. So long as I could make my movie I didn't much care. If they caught me and killed me, well, that seemed like a reasonable price to pay for having the chance to make my movie.

"So I got to England and I had my money and there was nothing standing in the way of me making a film; nothing except my own lack of ability and experience, that is. It'll sound crazy but I really hadn't decided what my film was going to be about. I knew it was going to be about my life, about power and risk, and life and death and sex: you know, the Big Themes; but I hadn't worked out how to talk about them. It took a while to realise that I had to make a film about Errol Flynn. I had to make *The Errol Flynn Movie*.

"Flynn genuinely was, and is, my hero. When I was a boy he was a swashbuckler who fought hard and nobly, and defeated the villains. When I was an adolescent he still seemed like a hell of a guy. He fucked everything that moved. He drank hard. He played hard. He said 'Fuck you' to the whole world. He never let himself be bored. I admired that. And now when I think about Flynn I think what a great and brave and tragic character he was. He had just about everything: talent, charm, money, success, love, and the poor bastard hadn't the slightest idea what to do with it. And I find that kind of heroic too.

"When my wife gets really mad at me she says I should grow up and stop playing at being Errol Flynn. But she's wrong. I don't try to be Errol Flynn. I know I couldn't do it. I haven't modelled myself on him. I haven't tried to emulate him. I like sex and drugs and drink the way he did, but that's not all Errol Flynn was about. He was a much better man than I could ever be. He had control over his own life in a way I've never managed to have. I know movie directors are supposed to be powerful and in control. And I wasn't. And maybe that's why I was such a fuck up as a film director.

"Okay, let's talk about sex. Sex is about power, dominance, control, violence. And anyone who tells you any different is an asshole. Now, you liberals out there don't want to believe that. You say sex is only about that stuff when it's bad. Well, you're wrong. The crazed feminists know better than that. They say all men are wicked, violent, dangerous monsters; and that's why they hate them. But see, not all women are like that. Some women like monsters. All you have to do is find one.

"'Why I like tying up women', an essay in self-justification by Daniel Ryan the little-known pervert. Sure I like tying up women. Why not? Look, half the women in the world lie there and do nothing while you're fucking 'em anyway, so what difference does it make if they have a few ropes and chains around them? But yeah, sure, it feels good to have someone in your power, someone who's powerless and who you want sexually. You know you can do anything you want to them. You can kiss them and touch them and stroke them and tease them. That's standard. But, because they're bound, and probably gagged and maybe blindfolded, you could do all sorts of other things too. You could hurt them, or cut them with razors, or burn them with cigarettes, or strangle them or maim them, or even kill them. You could do all that. They couldn't stop you. But the important thing is you DON'T. That's the point. That's the punchline. That's what this is really all about. You have absolute power over somebody but you choose to use that power benevolently.

"And let's get this straight. This has nothing to do with rape fantasies. This has nothing to do with coercion. The dominant partner is not forcing the victim to do anything he or she doesn't want to do. The submissive partner has agreed to all this. The dominant one only has power because the submissive partner has given in to him.

"And maybe, just maybe, there's some half-assed comparison to be drawn between this and making movies. A movie director supposedly has a bunch of actors and technicians in his power. At the very least he has to try to get them to do what he wants. And sometimes he only has to ask, but usually it's more complicated than that. Usually he has to persuade and charm and flatter and convince and cajole and beg and plead, and most of the time the director still doesn't get what he wants. He finds himself surrounded by a bunch of assholes who want to improve on what he's doing. They want to be creative. They want to give of themselves. And the director's left asking himself why the fuck can't they just do what they're told.

"Or else they *don't* want to give of themselves. They don't want to take risks because they're scared of looking stupid. They don't want to do anything different from what they've always done before because what they've done before has always worked out fine for them. They want to keep their egos and vanities nicely intact. At least that's how it was when I tried to make a movie.

"I got to England, me and my wife and my money; and I put the word around that I was making a film about Errol Flynn, and of course a lot of people wanted to be involved. I looked like a fool with a lot of money and plenty of folks wanted to part me from it.

"I didn't know how I was going to make this movie, but I was sure I wasn't going to make it the way anyone had ever made a movie before. Like I never really wanted a script but my wife said I needed one. And maybe she was right. I was surrounded by a lot of people who thought a script made a very good security blanket. But no way did I want to get stuck with storyboards and budgets and all that bullshit. Hell, I was a radical film-maker.

"I thought I could wing it, make it up as I went along. The film would be the story of itself. I would tell the story of Errol Flynn and also the story of the story of Errol Flynn. A lot was riding on this movie, but I wasn't afraid to take risks, and I wasn't afraid to fuck up. Just as well.

"I did find an Errol Flynn of sorts. His name was Jake. Never mind his other name. It doesn't matter. You won't have heard of him. I know this is going to sound weird and faggoty but he looked perfect. He looked just enough like Errol Flynn but he had something else, a quality, an appeal. He had a look that I thought was attractive to both men and women. He was too young to be Errol Flynn really, too innocent and too soft. But I thought a) I could work with him, and b) even if he never got to be a convincing Errol Flynn there might be some mileage in the ironic distance between the actor and his part. Some hope.

"But the real reason I wanted him, and this will sound like the faggoty part, he reminded me of myself, a younger, better version. Even my wife agreed about that, And I don't know if I buy this idea about homosexuality being a form of narcissism, but it could be. Maybe I found him attractive because he was like me. He was a good-looking kid. I mean he was no Errol Flynn. I'm not saying my tongue was hanging out for the guy, but you know, give me a few beers and I wouldn't have kicked the lad out of bed. Christ, give me enough beers and I wouldn't kick my own mother out of bed. Or maybe I'm just kidding myself. Maybe what I really wanted was to shack up with him in some chichi lavender-coloured apartment and go into the interior decorating business, but I don't think so.

"I still didn't know how I was going to pull it off but somehow this young English actor was going to portray *me* as well as Errol Flynn. He was going to tell my story as well as Flynn's. I was nothing if not ambitious.

"Probably I was asking too much of the poor guy: maybe it was too much to ask of anyone, but Jake didn't come up with the goods. He tried. He wasn't a complete jerk. He was even pretty good in a couple of scenes. He was especially good in one of the sex scenes, but that was probably because he didn't know he was being filmed. On balance he was okay, but okay was never going to be enough.

"But hey, I'm not blaming Jake. He wasn't the reason the production was a disaster. *I* was. Simple as that. All my life I'd wanted to be this big shot movie director, and here I was being a big shot movie director. It was everything I'd ever wanted. I was the kid who'd broken into the candy store. And for maybe the first week of shooting it was fine, although even then I had one or two problems. It dawned on me, not all that gradually, that I was just no fucking good as a director. I was a good blackjack dealer, a good poker player, a good casino manager, a good director of Las Vegas floor shows. The one thing I was no good at was directing movies. I just happened to be no good at the one thing I'd spent my whole life wanting to do. I was fucked up by it. I was more or less suicidal.

"But I carried on. I put on a brave face. I didn't know what else to do. I thought I'd keep going until the money ran out and then see what I'd got. I knew I hadn't got much, but maybe I could find an editor to make something out of it. So I started spending, wasting a lot of money on props, sets and extras. Running out of money seemed like a good reason for abandoning a movie. Realising you were an asshole didn't. But in fact the money never did quite run out. In the end that wasn't the reason I pulled the plug on Errol Flynn. Something much more important happened.

"Tina got a phone call from a man in Las Vegas. He was a poker player. He called himself the Cowboy and he wore all the western gear. He was one of the guys in the Airstream trailer, one of the guys I robbed. I don't know how the hell he found us.

"He told Tina that a friend of mine was dead. He said he'd killed him. The guy in question turned out to be no friend of mine at all, but it was the guy who'd helped us do the robbery, the biker, the guy who'd used me as a shield. I wasn't inclined to shed any tears over him, but the Cowboy said he'd worked out the whole scam and next he was coming to get me.

"And, believe it or not, that changed everything. Suddenly death didn't seem such a reasonable price to pay for making my crappy movie. Maybe it would have been different if I'd thought the thing was any damn good, but suddenly I wanted to save my skin.

"I ditched the movie. I left England fast. I wasn't going to sit there and wait for some son of a bitch in a stetson to come and blow me away. I flew back to America with one thing in mind. I was going to find the Cowboy before he found me. I was going to find him on my own terms, and when I found him I was going to kill him. I thought that was the right thing to do, the brave thing, the tough thing. I thought that's the way Errol Flynn would have played it.

"This is an interim report. I haven't found him yet, but I'm still looking. I'm getting closer. Once I find him I can finish him off. And what's more, I think I've thought of a way of finishing my movie.

"Okay, maybe this is crazy, but it's occurred to me that maybe this is my real story, me sitting here talking direct to camera, telling the story of my life, telling the truth, talking about sex and death and Errol Flynn. And, hey, I'm not an idiot, I know nobody wants to watch a whole film of somebody just talking, so I'm going to intercut this monologue with the stuff I shot in England, the scripted scenes, the improvised scenes, the scenes where actors fluffed their lines, the documentary footage, the porno, maybe even some footage from Flynn's own movies. It'll be wild, weird, magnificent. Okay, so it's a long shot, and even if it works I don't know who the hell is going to pay to see it, but, you know, I still have hopes, just so long as I live to tell the tale.

"Does any of this make sense to you out there? Does any of it sound plausible? Do you think an audience would buy any of it? I don't know. I sure as hell don't know any more."

Ryan smiled weakly, partly to himself and partly to his imagined audience. He looked composed and in control but he also looked very sad, as if he'd been wounded. He reached down to the floor beside his chair and picked up an enormous black gun. From having watched a few Clint Eastwood movies I knew it was a Magnum and that it could blow mighty big holes in people. He lifted it and pointed it straight into the camera lens and pulled the trigger. There was a dry impotent snap. This time at least, the gun was empty. Ryan laughed and said, "That's all, folks," and the film abruptly ended.

12

I had watched a pretty good piece of cinema. Ryan was a compelling performer, and let's face it, I had every reason to be compelled. Although Ryan was telling his own story, in lots of areas he was also telling mine. Not that I found it at all reassuring. Once again I was lost and unsure of myself. The plot had been given another twist. A new set of motives and meanings had fallen into place. The script had been given another rewrite.

There was, however, one small crumb of comfort I could derive from all this: Ryan's production had not been set up as a front for other, more profitable and less artistic, activities. Ryan may have been a liar, a thief, a crook and a pervert but the bottom line was, he genuinely wanted to make a movie about Errol Flynn. I felt strangely relieved. Ryan had undoubtedly been using me, but at least I now knew he'd been using me as an actor, not as some irrelevant stooge.

By his own admission Ryan was an exploiter, but at least it could be said he was doing his exploiting in the name of art. I wasn't sure exactly how I felt about that. Is a man who exploits you for the sake of art better than a man who exploits you merely for the sake of money? I thought he probably was, although I couldn't have argued the case with much conviction. Normally I would have said that the same rules apply to artists that apply to anyone else, that artists can't get away with being selfish, callous or wicked simply because they're artists. For Ryan, however, I was somehow prepared to make an exception.

Any way you looked at it, Ryan was a brave man. He had taken some gigantic risks in order to be able to make his film. I wasn't sure, however, if those kind of risks can ever really be justified. Maybe it all depends on the quality of the finished product. To gamble everything and come up with a masterpiece seems worthwhile, maybe even noble. But to gamble everything and come up with a piece of trash, seems just plain stupid. Ryan had certainly not made a masterpiece but somehow I still didn't think of him as stupid. Not that my opinion mattered. Ryan hardly needed glowing reviews from me in order to feel good about himself.

For me, however, it was different. In the video Ryan had given me another bad review, my second of recent days. Okay, he was probably right. I probably hadn't delivered a great performance, but if he wanted to argue about it I had some pretty good excuses, the best one being the lousy director I'd had to work with. But what the hell, I wasn't going to argue and I certainly had nothing to apologise for. Even Ryan seemed to be admitting that. But bad reviews went with the territory. Far more difficult to deal with was Ryan's "weird faggoty stuff".

For some reason a lot of straight men like to go around believing that gays are just dying to have sex with them. I've never worked out why they believe that, but it seems to make them feel good. In my very limited experience they're completely wrong. Obviously there are exceptions, but it seems to me that if you don't give off the right kind of signal then gay men aren't going to be interested in you at all. And heterosexual men don't give off that signal. The main reason I'm not attractive to gay men is because I don't want to be. So I don't really see what Ryan was telling me. That he fancied me? Well, that didn't really fit with my experience of Ryan. I wasn't giving him any signals, but neither was he giving me any. Was he telling me then that I was a stand in for himself when young and that he wanted to screw his younger self? I couldn't believe that. It was taking narcissism way too far.

For my part, call me an old square, I certainly had no desire for sex with Ryan, however many beers I'd had. I didn't see him as an older version of myself, and even if I had, that struck me as just about the world's most unlikely reason for wanting to have sex with somebody. Then I asked myself why I was even bothering to think about this stuff. What did it matter? Ryan's psyche was a mystery, and as far as I was concerned it was probably better if it stayed that way.

But I began to worry again about Tina's role in all this. By now I was more or less convinced that she wasn't sleeping with me just to please Ryan. For one thing I could see that her pleasure in sleeping with me was extremely personal, not taken on behalf of any third party. What concerned me now, however, was that she might only be interested in me because I resembled her husband. Ryan was getting old. He was, by his own standards, a failure. All vestiges of youthful promise were finally gone. Their marriage was over, so what was more natural than trading in Ryan for a younger, but (in her own eyes at least) similar model? This did not make me at all happy.

I was coming rapidly to the conclusion that I'd had enough of Ryan messing around in my life, especially in my sex life. I thought I was still in love with Tina, but I didn't see any hope for us while we both continued to flap around Ryan. His influence was all-pervasive and seldom positive. Above all, I came to the conclusion that I simply wanted to get out.

Retrieving the video of Sacha and me seemed very small potatoes now. Ryan was out there in the desert somewhere fighting for his life, trying to find and kill this Cowboy character. He surely wasn't going to try blackmailing me. If he did I simply wouldn't play ball. And what if he used some of the pornographic footage in this new film he was talking about? Would it really matter? I couldn't believe it was a film anybody would ever see. I thought that I was probably also an actor nobody would ever want to see, but if, by some miracle, I did become successful and well known, and if the film then came back to haunt me, well, I'd just brazen it out and say, So what? Who cares? Fuck you! Very Errol Flynn.

This wasn't indifference exactly, because in one way I would have been very happy for Ryan to finish his movie, and I even wanted it to be good. I had no reason for wanting Ryan to fail. I just didn't want to be involved. It was Ryan's own problem now. And, of course if the Cowboy found Ryan before Ryan found the Cowboy, then little matters of film-making would all be irrelevant anyway.

A part of me wanted to believe that Ryan's story was all a fantasy, just part of his self-dramatisation. That would have made it much easier to wash my hands of the whole business. Yet it seemed likely to be absolutely true. Ryan was a liar, but I didn't think he was lying about this. Common sense told me otherwise. It was obvious even to me that if you stole a million dollars from some heavy Las Vegas gamblers then you were likely to be in some serious trouble. It was entirely Ryan's own fault, but I still felt sorry for him. I wished there was something I could do, but I thought Ryan was beyond any help that people like me could give him. He needed a few hired guns, not some English idiot with an Equity card. This was not my territory. The rules, the stakes, the players were all unfamiliar. I was scared. The idea of even knowing about people who wanted to kill each other terrified me. Did that make me a yellow coward? If so, I was perfectly at ease with my cowardice. Running away seemed more than ever the best game plan.

Ultimately I couldn't for the life of me see why Ryan had wanted me in Las Vegas. In the video he'd said nothing about wanting to shoot any more footage. So what was I doing there? Cynically, I thought perhaps my real function was to serve as an audience for Ryan's lurid and self-created dramas. But this audience was about to get to its feet and walk out.

There was a knock on the door of my hotel room and I let in Tina. She was still in disguise, and that now struck me as totally ludicrous. The woman I thought I was in love with was completely concealed under the wig and the strange clothes. This time she didn't attempt to take any of it off.

"You've seen the video," she said.

"Yes."

"And?"

"I think it's going to be a big hit," I sneered.

"Didn't it tell you some of the things you wanted to know?"

I said wearily, "It told me *more* than I wanted to know."

This was obviously not the reaction she'd been expecting. I got the impression she thought the video would have left me stunned but enlightened, and ready to turn to putty in her hands. Seeing that this hadn't happened she moved rapidly to the next big revelation.

"Ryan's ready to see you," she said. "He's ready for me to take you to him."

"Oh, is he really? His Holiness is ready to give me an audience, is that right?"

"Don't talk like that, Jake."

"Like what? So Ryan's ready to see me. Well, so what? I mean, big fucking deal. Am I supposed to be honoured? Well, here's some news, I'm not ready to see *him*. I'm never going to be ready to see him. If I never see him again that's fine."

Tina looked hurt and yet determined. "I have to insist," she said.

"Oh, do you?" I replied.

"He needs to see you."

"What does he need to see me for?"

She fell silent. She looked helpless. She said, "I can't tell you that. Not yet."

I said, "Oh, bullshit. I've had enough of this."

She looked even more hurt.

"Have you had enough of me too?" she asked.

"No, not of you. But enough of this situation. I just want to go home."

"Not yet, Jake. Please."

"And I want you to come with me," I said.

"You know I can't."

"No, I don't know that. Why can't you?"

"Because Ryan needs me," she said. "He needs us both."

"Bullshit," I said again. "Come with me to England. Walk away from this mess. Leave him to it."

"Leave him to get killed, you mean."

"Ryan getting himself killed doesn't have anything to do with me," I said. "And I don't see why it has to have anything to do with you either."

She shook her head like she was seriously disappointed in me. She was close to tears but I wasn't going to fall for that one, and she said, "Maybe you're not the person I hoped you were."

I said, "Well, thank God for that. Look, I only have one offer to make. Please come back with me to England."

"I can't," she said.

"You'd rather be with Ryan."

"At this moment, yes."

I hadn't been trying to provoke such a simplistic conflict. I hadn't intended to demand that she choose between him and me. Why would I? When it came down to it I suppose I always knew that she wouldn't choose me. Yet that was the conflict that it had been reduced to, and now that it had happened there was no point avoiding it. At the same time there wasn't much to be said about it. She was saying, "Please don't go," and I was saying, "Please come with me," and it was useless. There was no room for negotiation, and nothing to debate. Neither of us had the slightest chance of persuading the other. She came over to me and started to kiss me, but I wasn't going to let that get to me either. I pushed her away, not violently, not petulantly, but I hoped decisively.

"Then I'm going alone," I said. "Let me know if you ever get sick of Ryan and his games."

I swept out of the hotel room, my own hotel room. I ran away along the hotel corridors. I heard her calling after me, shouting, "It's not a game!" Her voice was tearful but I suspected the tears were because I'd failed to fall in with her plans, not because I was leaving her.

I got out of the hotel. It was a hot, arid night. I left my car behind and caught a bus going up the Strip. I got off when we came to a record store and went in and browsed for a while. But this was Las Vegas and browsing in record stores is not the thing to do in Las Vegas. Before long I was back in another casino. I played the slots but before long they seemed deadly dull. It wasn't real gambling. I had my credit card with me. I went to the cashier's window and got a thousand dollars' worth of chips, the amount with which Ryan had supposedly first come to Las Vegas.

Normally I was no gambler, and it wasn't that I was feeling lucky tonight, if anything the opposite. It was more that I wanted to have nothing left to lose. This had been an unlucky town for me. If it now took an extra thousand dollars from me, well, that would finally confirm how truly terrible life was. And then I could return to England feeling totally and utterly washed up. That was precisely how I wanted to feel, but in the event it wasn't quite that easy.

I'm told by serious gamblers that the real joy of a winning streak is the feeling of omnipotence it gives you. You know exactly which hole the roulette ball is going to drop into. You know exactly what the next card is going to be. When it starts you feel that you're performing a simple act of prediction. But after a while you don't feel that you're just guessing, not even playing a hunch, you feel that you're actually *willing* the cards or the ball or the dice or the horses to do precisely your bidding. Things happen because you will them to happen. The world obeys your whims. You are in complete, God-like control.

I didn't get all the way with this feeling, but I got far enough to see how it might be possible. I saw how a run of luck might make you think that you were somehow above the laws of chance and probability, might even fool you into thinking you were actually in control.

I started small, and let's face it, by the standards of Las Vegas I stayed pretty small, but by my own standards it soon got big. I played one of the roulette tables, making little ten- and twenty-dollar bets on the evens and two to one chances. I employed no system, kept no records of the plays. I just placed my chips here and there, more or less at random, and after a while I increased my bets to fifty and a hundred dollars, and in no time at all I'd doubled my money. It felt good. It was a new sensation, and not one I'd been expecting.

I moved to the blackjack table. I'd only ever played pontoon before, and that was with the family at Christmas, playing for pennies, but it was enough to be able to participate in blackjack. There was a guy sitting next to me at the table who knew far less than I did, and the dealer had to keep explaining the rules to him. It wasn't at all the cut-throat, high-powered sort of gambling you might have expected from a Las Vegas casino, but the winning and losing of money was perfectly authentic. The game moved very fast. Each hand seemed to be over in a matter of seconds. And again I won.

A waitress brought me a drink on the house. I started to feel like a real high-roller and I carried on playing and winning, betting freely and without any inhibition or pattern. I wasn't being reckless exactly, but then again I didn't really care whether I won or lost. When I left the blackjack table I had about four thousand dollars. I walked round the casino feeling rather fond of myself. I looked at the craps tables and thought about giving them a whirl. If my luck was in maybe it wouldn't matter that I didn't know how to play. But lucky or not, I decided that was just plain stupid.

I put money in the slots again for a while, the ones where you could win a shiny red sports car, but I didn't win anything there so I returned to the roulette table where I'd been lucky before.

I sat down, received another free drink, and continued to win. All round me the other gamblers were taking things very seriously. Their faces showed they were involved in a sombre and stressful ritual. For me it was just a game, and that was surely the only way to gamble. Across from me was a young, wholesome-looking woman who had the same attitude as me. She was alone. She had a big pile of chips in front of her and she was methodically and cheerfully losing them. From time to time she would look over at me, then smile and shrug. I guessed she was losing somebody else's money: her husband's or her boyfriend's.

I kept gambling. It was exhilarating in some ways, although I can't say I got wildly excited about it. However, gambling did concentrate and clear my mind. I no longer had to worry about Ryan or Tina or Errol Flynn. Of course it was solving nothing, but I wasn't sure there was much solving to be done. Sitting at the roulette table, watching the wheel and the chips, the rakings in and the payings out, I felt better than I'd felt in a long time. And my winnings wouldn't stop coming. After about an hour and a half I had a little over ten thousand dollars in front of me. Okay, it didn't break the bank. It wasn't enough to change my life, but for an out of work English actor it was very good money.

It was time for a break. I gathered up my chips and went over to the bar area. I was planning to have one drink then return to the tables. I had barely sat down when the woman who'd been cheerfully losing money joined me.

"Mind if I sit here?" she said.

"Of course not."

"What's your system?" she asked.

"I don't have one."

"It's okay, I wouldn't expect you to tell me."

"It's just luck," I said.

"Ah well, lucky at cards, unlucky at love. Hi. My name's Betty."

I told her my name and asked if she wanted me to buy her a drink. She did, of course. She smiled at me a lot. I knew this was an attempt at a pick up, maybe an attempt at something more. I knew she was smiling at my winnings rather than at me, but I thought I could handle the situation. I wasn't averse to the idea of having someone to drink with.

"I'll bet you're in the movie business," she said.

"How did you know that?"

"Just a lucky guess. Can you help me break into the movies?"

She was joking. "Sure," I joked in return.

"Would I have to go on the casting couch?" she asked.

I was getting the hang of these sexual come-ons by now. It wasn't subtle, but that was okay. I was pleased to be with someone who was simple and direct in their dealings. I assumed she was a prostitute. I assumed she would demand quite a big slice of my winnings in exchange for her services. I wasn't very tempted. I had never been with a prostitute, had never liked the idea. I didn't take any moral high ground on the subject. I just thought, in my suburban way, that sex with someone you didn't know very well or like very much was unlikely to be all that enjoyable. I thought I had proved this with Sacha. I decided to be simple and direct in return.

"Look," I said, "I'm very happy to buy you a drink, very happy to talk, but if you're only after my money, you'd better try some other mug."

"You're not gay are you?" she asked.

"Maybe that's it," I replied. "If I don't want to pay to have sex with you I have to be gay, is that right?"

She looked confused. I looked away. I felt no need to defend or define my sexual preferences for the benefit of this complete stranger.

"I'm sorry," she said. "I didn't mean to insult you."

"It's not an insult to be gay," I said. "I just happen not to be."

That confused her even more. She studied me closely, as if she was looking at something very weird. Finally she said, "Oh, okay, I guess you're just English."

I wasn't sure whether or not that was meant to be a joke, but I laughed anyway. It seemed to please her that I was laughing.

"You know who you look like?" she said. "Errol Flynn."

That was the moment I should have guessed it was a set up, because at that moment I didn't look at all like Errol Flynn. But even if I *had* guessed, I still wouldn't have known what was coming next, and I still wouldn't have been any better prepared for it. She said she was a fan of Errol Flynn and I fell for it. I was extremely surprised but I was also interested. Apart from Ryan I'd never met anyone who claimed to be a fan of Errol Flynn before. Betty told me her favourite Flynn films; *Gentleman Jim* and *The Santa Fe Trail*: the latter, incidentally, also starring Ronald Reagan.

"You know," she said, "Flynn and Reagan were just about contemporaries. Just imagine if Flynn had lived to become President of the United States. The whole country would be a different place."

That was one angle on Flynn I'd never considered. Of course I should have worked out it was too much of a bizarre coincidence that I ran into an Errol Flynn fan on the very day I was running away from the Ryans; but my life had been rather full of bizarre coincidences lately. I found myself telling Betty the whole story of *The Errol Flynn Movie* and the Ryans. She was a good listener, and as I talked I realised how much I needed someone to talk to. It took several rounds of drinks before I'd finished.

"God," she said sympathetically, "you've really been through it."

"Yes," I said, feeling that her sympathy was entirely justified.

"And where's this Dan Ryan guy now?"

"Somewhere in the desert," I said.

"Where exactly? There's a lot of desert round these parts."

"I've no idea," I said. "And it's probably better that I don't know."

She gave me a peculiar look that I couldn't read at the time, but later it took on a lot of significance. We got up from the bar and went back to the roulette table. I dumped the whole of my winnings on to red. The people round the table thought I was a real big shot. Either that or a lunatic. Somebody said I should place at least a small bet on black as a kind of insurance, but I wasn't interested in that. Perhaps a part of me wanted to lose it all. I watched the croupier spin the wheel, flip the ball, and I knew. I absolutely knew that I was going to win. And as it happens, I did. I'd doubled my money again, but I felt no thrill whatsoever. Winning had become tedious. I cashed in my chips and agreed to go home with my new friend Betty. I still didn't feel I was committed to a sexual transaction with her, though I was resigned to the fact that this part of the evening was going to cost me some, if not all, of my winnings.

She had a car, and we drove to a bungalow on the outskirts of Las Vegas, a very long way from the lights and glamour of the Strip. We went in. It was homely and comfortable, a little threadbare. It certainly didn't look at all like the home of a Las Vegas hooker, but I was too tired and drunk to realise just how wrong all this looked.

I sat down on the lumpy grey couch and waited while Betty went into the kitchen to make us a drink. I thought back to a time before I'd met Dan Ryan, a time when it would have been utterly inconceivable that I would find myself sitting in a Las Vegas bungalow, with twenty thousand dollars hibernating in my pockets, waiting for a woman I'd picked up in a casino to make me a drink. I continued to think that life after Ryan was a lot more interesting than life before had been.

Then I heard men's voices, someone talking to Betty, and I stood up in time to see three men emerge from the kitchen. At first I assumed this was going to be a straightforward robbery, that Betty had some friends who were going to relieve me of my winnings. But then I got a better look at the men and realised it might be a lot more complicated than that. Two of them were heavies. The third was a lean, tanned man dressed in fancy cowboy gear and carrying a silver gun that was pointed in my direction. I knew this had to be Ryan's Cowboy. His outfit was meticulously neat and clean. He was an urban cowboy rather than a rider of the purple sage, though God knows there was nothing effete about him. His age was hard to guess. He could have been anywhere between twenty-five and forty, but he certainly looked as though he'd been around. He also looked hard, tough and extremely dangerous.

"Betty thinks you don't know where Ryan is," he said to me quietly in a soft western drawl.

"That's . . . that's right," I stammered.

"But I think differently," he added.

He said it without sounding angry or aggressive. He wasn't about to start playing the stage villain. He was far too cool for that.

"I wish I did know where he was, actually," I blustered. "I've got some unfinished business with him myself."

"Have you really?" said the Cowboy.

He obviously wasn't interested in me or my conversation. He only wanted to hear one thing from me. He took off his fringed jacket and placed it carefully over the back of a chair.

"There's an easy way of doing this," he said. "Tell me where Ryan is, and then Betty will drive you back to your hotel and that'll be an end of it."

"I really don't know where he is," I said, doing my absolute best to portray total trustworthiness and sincerity.

"Then there's the hard way," said the Cowboy.

I have been in very, very few fights in my life. I haven't taken many punches in my face, stomach or kidneys; but I can't imagine anyone ever hitting me harder than the Cowboy then proceeded to do. He was almost gentlemanly about it. It was a means to an end for him, and he took no great pleasure in beating me up. And he did the job himself, refusing to let his two henchmen join in. All he wanted was for me to tell him Ryan's whereabouts. It seemed a simple enough request. But the fact that I hadn't the slightest idea where Ryan was made it a long, strenuous and bloody session for both of us, though the blood, of course, was exclusively mine.

At first I tried to defend myself but it immediately became clear I had no defence against the strength and controlled violence of the man. He kept encouraging me to tell him where Ryan was, and my silence only spurred him on to hit me again.

"What do you think I am?" I said. "A masochist? You think I wouldn't tell you if I knew?"

Then he really started hurting me. After less than a couple of minutes or so of this treatment I was lucky enough to pass out. When I came to we were no longer in the bungalow. We were out of town, in the desert. There was no sign of Betty. I was tied up, and a long rope ran from my wrists to the rear bumper of a Jeep. One of the Cowboy's men poured water over my head to revive me, then got into the Jeep and started to drive, with me dragging along some way behind. My face, knees and elbows were cut open by the desert ground. I really thought there was every chance they would kill me but it seemed they wanted me alive, and before very long the Jeep stopped, the Cowboy got out of the cab and he continued to hit me and demand from me information that I hadn't got.

I wish I could say I acquitted myself with even the slightest degree of bravery or dignity while this was going on, but I did not. I cried and screamed and sobbed like a pathetic child. I humiliated myself. I behaved like a wimp and a coward. I begged and pleaded for mercy and it was not forthcoming.

Even while it was going on I couldn't understand how the Cowboy could possibly continue to believe I knew where Ryan was. Surely he could see that I would have told him if I'd known. I would have told him anything. Then he suddenly stopped hitting me. I couldn't work out why but I was very grateful. I lay on my back on the desert ground. I was covered in dust and pain. The Cowboy nudged me with his foot. I rolled over and was then face down in the dirt. Then he ripped my trousers apart so that my backside was naked, and he took his gun and shoved the barrel viciously into my rectum.

"Last chance," he said. "Tell me where Ryan is or kiss your ass goodbye."

I could barely speak by now, but it didn't matter. I had nothing to say, or at least nothing that my tormentor wanted to hear. I made a few grunts that indicated I still didn't know where Ryan was. The Cowboy waited a long time before doing or saying anything, and then he squeezed the gun's trigger.

I thought I was done for. I yelped and writhed, thrashed

around, and it was a while before I realised there had been no bang, that no bullet had been fired into my bowels, that the gun had been empty and that I was still alive. For a while I almost didn't believe it. Then I started to sob with pain and relief.

I heard footsteps walking away, and I heard the Cowboy saying extremely casually to his men, "You know, I don't think he knows where Ryan is."

A little later the Jeep's engine started. I expected to be dragged along again, but they had disconnected the rope, and I remained where I was, not quite daring to hope that the nightmare might be finally over.

I continued to lie there, listening to the silence, my whole body glowing with pain. I wasn't even sure I could stand up. I didn't know where I was. I was presumably some way out of town, possibly miles from the nearest road, but I thought I had to make a move. I managed to get to my feet, pulled up my torn trousers and, somewhat to my surprise, found I was just about able to walk. It was a tricky business, but I progressed very slowly, and in some agony, for what seemed like a very long time. However, I was not thinking straight, my sense of direction was blurred, and for all I knew I could have been walking round in circles. And then I saw some lights up ahead. They looked like car headlights though there was still no sign of a road. I walked towards them.

I wasn't seeing too well at the time. The series of punches I'd taken to the head had left rings and flashes of light pulsing in my eyes. I couldn't see if there was anyone in the car or not, and I feared it might be the Cowboy returning to have another go at me. But as I got closer I could see it wasn't the Cowboy's Jeep. In fact it looked like some shiny, finned, 1960s limo. But what on earth would that be doing out here in the desert? It seemed too unlikely to fathom, and when I saw the figure standing beside it, I thought I must be hallucinating.

Standing right beside the car, I kid you not, I saw Errol Flynn; or rather Errol Flynn playing the part of Robin Hood. The figure in front of me was dressed in Lincoln green, with a bow and arrow and a cape. He was wearing tights and a jaunty little hat complete with feather. He was standing in a quite ridiculously heroic pose, and he looked as though he'd just walked off the set of *The Adventures of Robin Hood*.

"Jake, old sport," he said. "How the hell are you?"

It was a ridiculous question even for a hallucination to be asking. But hearing the voice cleared my head slightly. The voice was Ryan's, of course, and I immediately realised that I was looking at Ryan, not at Errol Flynn. But he had perfected his Flynn impersonation to an awesome degree. He was now an absolute dead ringer. I was too weary and in too much pain to ask myself why he should have bothered to do so. I staggered a few feet towards him. His appearance was simultaneously comic and creepy. I was finding this all too strange and difficult to deal with. A second later I fainted at the feet of this apparition. It was the greatest act of submission I'd ever made to a director.

13

Dan Ryan said to me, "The movie starts anywhere, any time, on any set, whenever two or three are gathered. There's a sunset or a seashore or a Wild West saloon. And Venus rises from the waves, and a ship appears on the horizon, and Errol Flynn steps down from the carriage. There's a chase. There's a love scene. There's a sword fight. It's a genre movie, a romantic comedy, an art house film, it's drive-in fodder, the late show, for adults only. You want in, Jake? You want a bit part? A cameo? Or is it starring roles only from now on? You want your name above the title? You want points?"

I said, "Look, Dan, I really think I ought to get to a doctor." But I was talking to myself.

I was lying on a bed in a cabin somewhere in the desert outside Las Vegas. This was Ryan's base, his hiding place. It might well have been here that the video was shot, but I couldn't have guaranteed it. It was pretty much your standard issue desert cabin. There were two camp beds, one on either side of the room, a table and a couple of rickety chairs. There were windows, but they were broken, and there was a door but it kept flapping open. The only other room was the kitchen. There was no running water but there was a tiny generator outside the back door that provided enough power to run a fridge and the electric light. There was also a filthy old stove that ran on bottled gas.

"The art of story-telling," Ryan suddenly announced, "is the art of telling lies. Okay, so in scene one a guy says he likes dogs; then in scene two you see him stroking a dog. Well, so what? The audience has fallen asleep by now. But try this: in scene one he says he likes dogs, but in scene two you see him *kicking* a dog. Well, yeah. You've got a movie. Or like Errol Flynn. In scene one he says he's going to love some dame for ever, then in scene two he's in bed with another one. Or he says what a red-blooded male he is, and then we see him in bed with some Mexican boy prostitute. That's good stuff. We should have shot that and got it in the movie. You and Tina should have written that, Jake."

Ryan was standing in the centre of the room leaning on a big packing case. It was full of film cans, most of which had burst open so that their contents were spilling out and tangling round each other. As far as I could tell this was the negative for *The Errol Flynn Movie*. Such negatives, I knew, were normally treated like the crown jewels in order to keep them perfect and unscratched. Ryan wasn't worried about that. Sand and dust blew around the cabin, settled on the negative, penetrated its loops and coils.

Not that the state of Ryan's negative was the main thing on my mind. I was in pain. Thanks to the Cowboy, every bit of me hurt, and I thought I possibly needed some medical attention. Ryan had made some perfunctory attempts to clean me up and bandage me, but his heart had not been in it. He had other things on his mind too.

Quite apart from the packing case of negative, the other remarkable presence in the room was half a dozen swashbuckler costumes, in acidic primary colours, complete with boots, swords, plumed caps and outrageous codpieces. Ryan was finding it necessary to change in and out of these costumes at regular intervals, and as he put on each outfit he would erupt in a flurry of manic ham acting, which included mimed sword fights with imaginary and invisible brigands, and a lot of improvised dialogue about the gallows, buried treasure and her liege the Queen. Errol Flynn had done it all rather better. Ryan looked definitely, and I suspected dangerously, mad, but it came and went in waves. There were occasional, if rare, moments of what sounded like lucidity.

"How did you find me?" I asked. "How did you know where I was?"

"The desert's a big place but nothing ever really gets lost there," said Ryan studiedly.

I suspected that was as much of an explanation as I was going to get.

"But what are we doing here, Dan?"

"We're waiting. We're waiting for the Cowboy."

"I don't understand."

"You will," he said. "I've finished running. I'm ready for the finale, the climax, the big gundown. The Cowboy's on his way and we've got to be ready for him. Are you feeling lucky, Jake?"

I felt in the pockets of my torn trousers and they were still full of money. I couldn't believe it. A little must surely have fallen out while I was being dragged behind the jeep but most of it was still there. I pulled out a handful of notes and showed it to Ryan. He wasn't interested, but I couldn't help finding it pretty funny.

"You see," Ryan said, "you're feeling better already."

"No, really I'm not," I said. "I think my nose is broken."

"No it isn't," he said with finality.

"And possibly my ribs," I added.

"Well, there's not much doctors can do for broken ribs anyway. Have a beer."

I took a beer from him. I couldn't have thought of anything I wanted less, but at least it was cold and thirst-quenching, and I hoped the alcohol in it might act as something of an anaesthetic for my pains.

"You're not going to see any doctor, Jake, so forget it. You can beg and plead. You can even offer to suck my dick, but you're not going anywhere, understand?"

"No, I *don't* understand."

It was the wrong thing to say. A full-blown fury immediately seized Ryan, which in turn led him to seize me. He lifted me off the bed and threw me across the room. I landed in a corner amid the loose sand and dust balls. The experience of being thrown around was all too familiar, though Ryan's violence wasn't nearly as purposeful as the Cowboy's.

"We're here because we're waiting for the Cowboy," Ryan said. "And because I say so. Because I have the power. Because I'm the movie director and you're just a piece of garbage. Are you following me?"

I nodded cautiously.

"Christ," said Ryan. "Everybody wants power these days. Women want power and blacks want power and gays want power. Well, I say tough titty. It's real simple to understand. By definition not everybody can have power. If everybody had power there'd be nobody to have power *over*. So you see why you're here, Jake. You see how necessary you are to the scheme of things."

He was calm for a while. He sat at the table. Then he put on a yellow swashbuckler's outfit. It had elaborate red braiding and waves of ruff burst out at the neck and cuffs. He looked pathetic, like an off-duty clown. It was almost possible to feel sorry for him.

"How was my wife?" he asked.

"She was okay when I last saw her."

"Don't fuck around with me, Jake. I mean how was she sexually? How was she in bed? Was she good? Was she hot stuff?"

I didn't answer. Ryan picked up a cutlass and waved it at me. I thought it was only a prop but I couldn't be sure, and he could probably poke my eye out with a blunt cutlass as easily as with a sharp one. But I didn't know what to say to him. He tried to prompt me.

"Well, was she compliant?" he asked. "Was she up to scratch? Would you recommend her to your pals? Did she do the things you like to have done? Did she satisfy any of your more interesting fantasies?"

I continued to say nothing. I hoped he was just raving and that sooner or later he'd rave on about something else. But he was decidedly stuck on the question of me and Tina.

"How did you like her breasts?" he demanded. "I've always thought they were a little too small. I offered to pay for enlargement but she wouldn't go for it. And how about her ass? And how about her cunt? Did she suck you? Did she lick your balls? Did she put her tongue up your ass? Did she let you come on her breasts? On her face? In her mouth? Tell me. I'm interested."

"I'm in love with Tina," I said.

In the current circumstances and surroundings it sounded stupid and wholly irrelevant, but I thought it was worth saying. For Ryan, however, it was just a great joke. He let out some operatic laughter and patted me on the shoulder.

"You know," he said, "there are plenty of husbands who would happily kill their wife's lover if they found themselves alone with him in the desert. They probably wouldn't be able to help themselves. It would be a crime of passion. I'm a very passionate guy, Jake, as you well know. I might lose my cool. You might push me into doing something I'd later regret. But hey, I'm a civilised guy too. I'm not a beast. I'm not a murderer. I'm not going to blow away my star actor just because he's been fucking my wife? Am I?"

"No you're not," I said encouragingly.

"And what's more I need you to help me blow away the Cowboy. He's coming, you know, real soon. I know it. I can feel it."

"How does he even know where we are?"

"Maybe he doesn't know yet, but he will. He'll find out. He'll ask Tina. She knows where I am. Maybe she won't tell him at first. Maybe he'll have to slap her around a little, inflict a little bit of pain, but sooner or later she'll tell, and then he'll be here. And we'll be ready."

He then walked out of the cabin and I was left behind, wondering exactly what my predicament was here. If Tina knew where we were then there was every chance that she might come along and rescue me from this situation. But if Ryan was right and the Cowboy was going to extract the information from her, then he would get to us first and we might have to play out the drama exactly as Ryan envisaged. All we had to do was wait. But waiting was a long, painful business. I hoped that none of my cuts turned septic, and that the Cowboy hadn't caused me any permanent internal injuries.

Time passed on that first day, but only very slowly. Occasionally Ryan would produce some food; beans and frankfurters out of a tin. I ate as eagerly as my loose, aching teeth would allow. Sometimes Ryan would deliver long monologues about the art of film, or about sex or about gambling, but other times he would sit completely still and silent.

He spent a lot of time perfecting his look, making sure he remained the spitting image of Errol Flynn. By now, of course, I didn't look even remotely like Flynn. My beard had grown and my features had been thoroughly knocked out of shape by the Cowboy. When I saw my face in a mirror I was shocked. It didn't look as though I was going to be playing any pretty boy roles for a while.

Night fell and I managed to get some sleep. It was a long night and I had some bad dreams. They were vague but full of dread, about strange presences and hidden threats. The night had a strange, hallucinatory quality to it, although as far as that went, my days with Ryan were hallucinatory too.

On the second day I staggered out of the cabin and looked at the surrounding desert. It was bleak, forbidding terrain. There was no way I was going to walk out of there. The horizon was low and a long way off. No road led to or from the cabin, although there were sets of tyre tracks showing which routes Ryan had taken in the past.

Not far away from the cabin, Ryan had set up a kind of shooting range. There were bottles and tin cans and lumps of wood arranged at different heights and different distances. He had given it a lot of use, and his success at destroying the targets had been considerable. There was also one of those free-standing wooden targets, the shape and size of a man, with a series of circles around the heart. Ryan had taken a colour photograph of Flynn's face and stuck it on the face of the target. This seemed horribly significant but I wasn't sure how. Flynn's features beamed out, smooth, smiling and unconcerned, oblivious to the fact that his heart had been peppered with bullet holes.

I hadn't actually seen Ryan brandishing any firearms this time, but a man who carried a gun while driving through the tame streets of London would surely be armed to the teeth out here.

Ryan's car was parked beside the cabin and it looked tempting as a means of escape. But Ryan had the keys, and my boringly well-spent youth hadn't taught me how to hot-wire a car. Besides, I suspected that if I tried to escape and failed, Ryan's anger might get completely out of control.

Ryan must have noticed me looking longingly at the car. "Hey," he said, "I've had a great idea. Let's get in the car, drive into town, pick up a couple of girls, get 'em good and drunk, bring 'em back here, drug 'em, fuck 'em, chain 'em up, dismember 'em and strew their remains all over the desert? What do you say?"

"No," I said calmly.

"You don't ever let me have any fun," he said.

Ryan, I guessed, was not quite as crazy as he sounded. I don't think he really wanted to cut up girls in the desert. I think it was his idea of a joke. On the other hand, even to joke about such things suggested to me that he was in a pretty bad way.

Later that day he started teaching me how to shoot. I had never even seen a real gun until I saw Ryan's that night in England. I had certainly never held or fired one, and I'd never had any desire to. But if Ryan was right about the Cowboy's imminent arrival, and the more I thought about it the more I thought he was, then there was suddenly every reason to learn.

He produced a small suitcase full of guns, and suggested I try the Smith and Wesson .38. It was all much the same to me. I was not a natural with a gun. My hand wasn't steady. I couldn't stand the noise and the smell, and the recoil made my arm ache. I spent a lot of time failing to hit the target that had Errol Flynn's face on it. But after a whole day of spraying bullets around the desert I had just about learned enough to be able to hit a man-sized target so long as it stayed fairly still and didn't shoot back.

The Cowboy could certainly have killed me in the desert or even in the bungalow, but he had chosen not to. It seemed that Ryan wanted him to have another chance. That was if Ryan didn't kill me first himself. But Ryan was now treating me as an ally. I was now supposed to be his gunslinger, his deputy, and together we were going to defeat the Cowboy. I didn't doubt that the Cowboy wanted to kill him but I wasn't quite sure that I could see myself being much use in this imagined shoot out, much as I wanted to be. Perhaps we were acting out our own version of Custer's last stand, like Flynn in *They Died With Their Boots On*. At least it partly convinced me that Ryan didn't mean me any serious harm. It seemed unlikely that he would teach me to use a gun if he intended to kill me. Surely he wouldn't want me to have the means of fighting back. Or maybe he just wasn't operating rationally at all.

"And how did you find Sacha?" he asked. "Actually, you don't have to tell me how good she was in bed. I know. I'm sure she did everything you wanted. Well, maybe not everything. Not for you. Maybe you're just not masterly enough. Maybe you just don't have that kind of authority that women go for."

Again I didn't reply.

"Sacha would do anything for me, you know. Anything. She slept with you because I told her to, no other reason. And she didn't *ask* for a reason. I told her to do it so she did it. You don't think she liked you, do you? And I'm very glad to have got it all on film. I don't mind telling you, sport, when I sat in the adjoining room filming you through the two-way mirror, watching you and Sacha go to it, I got hot. I got very hot. I just couldn't keep my hand off my pecker. It's all in here somewhere." He kicked the packing case containing the negatives. "One of these nights we'll watch it, eh Jake?"

He was drinking beer as he said this, and as he kicked the packing case a rush of beer flew out of the can and splashed over the negatives. He saw it happen but it didn't bother him. My mission to get back the footage of me and Sacha had become totally irrelevant by now. Ryan was destroying his film as effectively as I ever could. But I still needed to talk to him about it.

"Why did you shoot that film of me and Sacha?" I said.

"You can't ask a question like that of an artist," Ryan said.

"Did you intend to use it in the finished film?" I persisted.

"Sure. Why not? Let's tell the truth about sex once in a while, show it how it really is, though I'd have had to use a bigger actor for the inserts and the come shots. Would have had to use myself as a stand in."

"I don't think you should have filmed it without asking me first."

"But you'd have said no, you repressed, hung up, English asshole. You know the real reason I shot it? Because I'm a sick pervert. Okay? That what you want to hear?"

"In the video where you talked to the camera . . ."

"A masterpiece, huh?" he interrupted.

"You said something about having power over people but using it wisely."

"Yeah. I probably said that."

"Well do you really think you used your power wisely with Sacha? Getting her to sleep with some guy she didn't want to sleep with? Getting her to appear in a piece of pornography? Was that benevolent?"

Ryan didn't say anything. I wasn't sure if I was doing good here or not. He was calm but it could have been the calm before the storm.

"And Tina," I said. "I don't know much about your relationship with her; but I now know that you got her to take part in a robbery. She could have gone to jail. She could have got killed. Maybe she still could."

"She did it because she wanted to do it," Ryan said, but he didn't sound at all confident. "She did it because she loved me."

I didn't feel able to argue about that.

"And what about me?" I said. "You've got me here, and God knows I'm in your power. You can keep me here as long as you like. You can kill me. You can do anything. How about a bit of benevolence?"

I don't know if I really got through to him, but it had some effect. He didn't say another word for the rest of the night, and the next day he ordered me to do extra shooting practice.

At night Ryan drank beer and whisky, and took various combinations of drugs. He got the mix as he wanted it. The various substances made him ragged and paranoid, but they kept him awake and alert. He didn't sleep more than a couple of hours a night as far as I could tell.

I, however, was glad to take as much sleep as possible. I liked to think it helped me get my strength back, and it certainly made the time pass. But if I ever woke up in the middle of the night I would look around the room and Ryan would be there, awake and watchful. It could have felt threatening but somehow it didn't. In some curious way I came to think of Ryan's watchfulness as reassuring. Rather than my captor, he began to feel like a bodyguard, not that he was ever consistent.

Next day, for instance, I saw a small plane overhead. It seemed to be circling above us. I just stood outside the cabin and looked up at it. I certainly wasn't trying to wave at it. I had no thoughts of being rescued. But Ryan thought I was signalling and he hit me and knocked me to the ground. I knew it was pointless to protest and I said nothing. A couple of hours later Ryan sort of apologised.

"I'm sorry," he said. "I don't know. I guess it's a question of too many movies, too many clichés. The guy turns on the car radio the very moment the news comes on giving details of the crime he's just committed. The guy returns to his apartment and there's a naked girl in his bed. The phone rings unanswered. The creak on the stair, the jump cut, the lipstick on the collar. Too much mood music, too many special effects. You've got a good face, Jake. Would you say you have a love affair with the camera, Jake? Has success changed you? Are you still the same simple guy you always were? The lights go on in the apartment. Someone's cut the brake cable. The blood groups match. The objection is sustained. They have to get to the border before sundown. The hooker has to find her heart of gold. Everybody has to find themselves. There has to be a showdown, a shoot out, the arrival of the US cavalry. The monsters must be destroyed. The fucking show must go on. And we have to wait for the Cowboy."

Waiting for the Cowboy was becoming a full-time occupation. This was my third day in the desert with Ryan and I was both incredibly tense and incredibly bored. I didn't want to be involved in an all-action finale but if it had to come I wanted it to come soon. The anticipation was killing me.

"You know," Ryan said, "Errol Flynn was old enough to be my father."

I'd never given it any thought. It was obviously true, but this seemed like the ultimately wrong time to discuss it. That didn't bother Ryan.

"My parents were working in Hollywood at the same time as Flynn," he said. "I used to ask them if they'd ever met him. My father said he'd once been at a party where Flynn turned up. He said Flynn was a pretty nice guy. Of course that wasn't what I really wanted to hear. I wanted to hear stories about him getting drunk and punching some guy's lights out, and making it with scores of chorus girls. Of course my father was a very straight guy. Even if he'd witnessed Flynn doing any of that stuff he wouldn't have recounted it to his young son.

"So then I asked my mother if she'd ever met Flynn. And she said, 'Just once. And once was enough.' Of course I didn't know what the hell she meant by that, but I was a dirty-minded little son of a bitch, and the more I thought about it, the more it sounded like something sexual. I mean, Flynn met a lot of women just once, and that was enough because once he'd fucked them he was through with them. Right?

"Well obviously you can't say to your mother, 'Hey, did you ever fuck Errol Flynn?' so I kept quiet but I kept thinking maybe my Mom did it once with Flynn. I found that pretty exciting. And then I thought well, maybe I was the result of that one time. I kept looking at myself in the mirror and I didn't look at all like my Dad, whereas in the right light, from the right angle, I could look a lot like Errol Flynn.

"I felt pretty pleased with myself, thought I'd done a smart bit of detective work, found out Mom's dirty little secret. But, you know, you think a lot of dumb things when you're young. And a little time went by and I forgot about it, and I grew up and I thought it was just one of those dumb ideas that kids get into their heads.

"Then my father died. And not much later my mother died too, and I had to go back and clear out the family house. It was a tough job. I had to go through all their drawers and cupboards and all their papers. And I know it sounds corny, but one of the first things I found was a signed photograph of Flynn. Maybe it wasn't all that strange in itself, but how come I'd never seen it before? How come nobody had ever mentioned it? How come it was hidden away in a drawer?

"And then I found a purse of my mother's. It wasn't one I'd ever see her use. It had some old photographs in it, and some letters. Most of the letters were from my father. I read them. They weren't the most romantic things you'd ever read in your life, but they were from my Dad to my Mom and they had me crying like a baby. And then I found one particular letter that wasn't from my father. And you couldn't really call it a love letter. It was too raunchy for that. The writer described in great detail what he was going to do when he next saw my mother. It was all the usual stuff, you know, cocks and cunts and mouths and so on, kind of predictable. But it was also a bit of a shock to know that your mother read this stuff and liked it enough to keep in her purse."

"Who was it from?" I asked.

"Now wouldn't it be convenient if it were from Flynn? If this were a movie it would be signed 'Your loving Errol' and he'd be asking how his illegitimate son was doing these days. But in the event it was signed with a question mark, a squared off question mark."

"But that was Flynn's symbol."

"I know, I know," he said, as though I was boring him with my interest. "But it was also the symbol of a guy called Scotty Knight. Who? That's right, a nobody. He was a drummer. He was a friend of my father's. They did some session work together. Scotty had a big square question mark painted on his bass drum. I never knew why. I don't know if he got the idea from hearing about Errol Flynn or whether he thought it out for himself. I never asked him. There were a lot of things I never got to ask.

"So *you* figure it out. Either my mother was fucking Errol Flynn or she was fucking some no-hope drummer who was a pal of my Dad's. Well, which sounds more likely to you? Which would you rather believe? Which makes the better story?"

"They're different kinds of story," I said. "I'm not sure which is better."

"No, me neither."

Ryan left the cabin and walked off into the desert. I didn't see him for the rest of the day. I sat alone in the cabin feeling like one of those caged birds that refuses to fly away even after the cage door is open. When Ryan eventually returned he was worse than ever. He was obviously on some sort of drugs and he was looking mean and threatening.

"So let's talk about us," he said, slurring his words. "You know, Jake, we could be a team like De Niro and Scorsese. What do you say to that?"

"We'd have to complete a film first."

Ryan kicked the packing case containing the negative.

"This is complete," he said. "It's finished anyway. And, you know, maybe what I have to say about Errol Flynn isn't right for this medium. Maybe it's not a movie at all. Maybe it's a picture book, or a poem, or a computer game. You understand?"

I pretended I did.

"You know why Tina slept with you?" he asked.

"Tell me," I said wearily.

"I will. Tina worries about me, you see. She doesn't worry about me sleeping with girls, that's not serious. That's nothing to her. But she does worry about me sleeping with boys. That threatens her. Does that make sense? So the silly bitch thought I had the hots for you. And she was scared. Maybe she thought I was going to run off with you. Maybe she thought that was going to destroy her whole little world. And so she thought she'd better get to you before I did, head me off at the pass. What do you think of that? Bullshit or not?"

I didn't say anything. I didn't know. It made an appalling kind of sense.

"So, Jake, all you have to decide is, was she right or was she wrong? Here you are in the middle of the desert, with this homicidal sex maniac. Is he going to have his dirty way with you or not?"

He started to fiddle with his belt, to loosen his trousers. He gave me a dirty leer, but at first I wasn't sure if he meant it or not, whether it wasn't some sort of put on just to scare me, but I soon realised he was being perfectly serious. He really was after me. Maybe he was even going to try raping me. And when I saw there was a gun in his hand, the big black Magnum as seen in the video, there no longer seemed to be much cause for doubt.

"Well, you're the boss, Ryan," I said. "You've got the power. You've got the gun. You can force me to do just about anything you want. You win. I submit. Isn't that what you want to hear?"

"Yes. I like to hear that. Say it again."

Now his trousers were down and his penis was up. There is surely a theory which says that men who go on about how big their penis is, in reality have really very small ones. This wasn't the case with Ryan. It really was as billed. It was a huge, angry-looking thing and it was coming right at me.

I was still in some pain and I certainly wasn't feeling very strong, but I took an almighty kick at Ryan's genitals, and, more by luck than anything else, it landed in exactly the right spot. Ryan buckled, dropped to his knees, and the gun fell out of his hand. I swooped on it and picked it up. I didn't brandish it, didn't point it at Ryan, or anything stupid and melodramatic like that. I just held it down, out of harm's way.

"Look, Dan," I said, "we're in a crazy situation here. I think you need some help. God knows when or how you're going to get it, but in the meantime keep your hands off me, okay?"

Ryan sat on the floor and laughed at me. I took a mattress off the bed and dragged it after me into the kitchen. I was determined I would be sleeping alone tonight.

14

Somehow I got through the night. Ryan didn't try to molest me, and just as it was starting to get light I eventually fell asleep. It didn't last long. An hour or so later I was jolted awake. I knew something had woken me but I wasn't sure what. The likelihood, of course, was that it was Ryan shouting about something or other, or maybe firing one of his guns; but at the same time I somehow knew it was more than that.

I got up and went over to the kitchen window. I looked out cautiously and it was like seeing a clip from a movie. You didn't know exactly how the characters had got themselves into that particular situation, but the drama in the scene was sufficiently gripping that you kept watching and didn't ask questions.

There was a tense and highly elaborate confrontation taking place outside the kitchen window. Tina had duly arrived, as I had always hoped she might, but it was in circumstances I wouldn't have chosen. She was sitting in the passenger seat of a jeep. She looked as though she'd been beaten up a little and it didn't take much to work out who'd done the beating or why. The Cowboy was sitting beside her, alone, without either of his henchmen, and he was holding a gun to her head.

He was using the gun primarily for the benefit of Dan Ryan, but it was hardly having the effect he wanted. Ryan was standing beside the cabin and he was certainly aware of the Cowboy's presence, but he wasn't paying full attention. In fact he was making thrusts and parries with a sword, but he was only duelling with the air. The Cowboy wore what a lot of people might consider to be fancy dress, but he really couldn't compete with Ryan. Ryan's outfit for today was a Cavalier costume in electric-blue satin. It came complete with thigh boots and a plumed hat. I don't think Errol Flynn ever wore anything quite that foppish. The Cowboy must have thought this was very strange but he did his best to stick to the script.

"There's an easy way of doing this, Ryan," he said, "and there's a hard way. You give me back my money and you can carry right on living. Otherwise . . ."

He was still acting cool, but he wasn't finding it so easy. He still wanted to play it light and not too corny, but it was hard to play any sort of scene with Ryan at the moment. The Cowboy fired his gun in the air. It was a warning shot, perhaps meant to intimidate, but chiefly I think he fired it to attract Ryan's wandering attention, to let him know this was serious.

I saw Tina flinch as the gun was fired, and I thought of the various forms of pain the Cowboy might have inflicted on her, and I started to get very angry. I'd felt no such anger on my own behalf. I didn't want revenge on the Cowboy for anything he'd done to me, but what he might have done to Tina was a different matter. Was that terribly old fashioned of me?

The shot succeeded in bringing Ryan back to earth. He looked at the Cowboy as though through new eyes.

"You'd better come inside, sport," said Ryan, and he gestured expansively towards the cabin as though he was welcoming some visiting grandees to his vast country estate. "You'll find everything you want in there."

"I only want one damned thing," the Cowboy said, but Ryan swept towards the cabin, and the Cowboy didn't have much choice but to follow. He pushed Tina ahead of him.

Ryan began one of his monologues. "You know alchemy is just about the best way of describing it, the nearest analogy for what an artist does . . ."

They had to cross the front of the cabin in order to get to the door, and for a moment I couldn't see them. I moved away from the kitchen window, crossed the room, stayed hidden, tried to stay motionless, and watched the next scene through a crack in the kitchen door. I automatically picked up Ryan's gun.

Ryan was still talking as they entered the main room of the cabin. "The artist takes base metal and turns it into gold," he said. "He turns clay into art. He's a bit like God. He turns money into light."

"Yes indeed," said the Cowboy. "Money's what we're here to discuss. Now, where's my quarter of a million dollars?"

"It's right here," said Ryan, and he pointed to the packing case containing the scratched, dusty, beer-splashed negatives.

"You know you're about as funny as leprosy," the Cowboy said. "Don't get me angry, Ryan. Just give me my money."

Ryan looked at him with utter, pitying contempt.

"I told you, your money's right here, you dumb fuck," he yelled. "Christ, how much do you think it costs to make great art? You think you can turn it out on the cheap? Maybe get some low-price immigrant labour to do it for you? How much money do you think you have to spend on cast and crew and sets and costumes and the hire of location and editing facilities . . ."

"Shut up," said the Cowboy. But you couldn't shut Ryan up that easily.

"Let's face it," he continued, "what would you have done with your money if I hadn't taken it? Lost it gambling? Bought a new car? A new set of spurs? Spent it on some Mustang Ranch hookers? You have no imagination. No finesse."

The Cowboy looked at the mess of negative and I saw it slowly dawning on him that Ryan just might be telling the truth. He could see that Ryan was acting crazy, but he was gradually concluding that maybe it wasn't an act, that Ryan really might have spent all that money making a film. But the Cowboy still didn't want to believe it.

"Okay, so what if you did spend all the money on a movie?" said the Cowboy.

"Not just a movie," Ryan blustered. "THE movie; a film about life and death and Errol Flynn."

"Yeah, yeah, I've heard this story. It's a riot. But I don't care. I just want my money back. You've got assets. Sell the damn movie. Sell your car, your house, your ass. Just give me my money."

"I've no assets," said Ryan. "You're standing in my house. My car's a heap of junk. My ass isn't worth two bits. There's nothing. It's all gone. It all went into the movie, and the movie's a piece of crap."

He reached down into the packing case and dredged up a handful of tangled negative which he proffered to the Cowboy.

"If this is true," said the Cowboy, "if I really start to believe this is true, you realise I'm going to have to kill you?"

"I know that," said Ryan.

"You understand why I can't let you get away with this?" the Cowboy continued. "If you take what's mine, I have to take it back. I have to make you pay. If you can't pay in money, you have to pay some other way."

"Well, of course I understand," said Ryan. "It sounds like a very sporting arrangement."

"You can see he's sick," said Tina. "What pleasure would you get out of killing him?"

"I wouldn't get any pleasure," the Cowboy replied. "It would just be business. Letting someone carry on living after they've stolen a quarter of a million dollars from me would be very bad for my business. And then I'd have to kill you for much the same reason. I can't have any witnesses. You can appreciate that. That's why it'd be so much simpler if you just came up with the money."

I was watching with a growing sense of panic. I could see that sooner or later I was going to be called upon to do something here, and it wasn't going to be telling everyone to shake hands and go home quietly. I had a gun. I had some idea of how to use it. This was the closing scene Ryan had always envisaged. If the Cowboy was about to try to kill Tina and Ryan, I would have to make a move.

My heart was jumping and my breath was erratic, and I was

wet with sweat, and suddenly like a complete idiot, I dropped the gun. The noise it made seemed to shake the whole cabin. The Cowboy shouted something, then ran over to the kitchen door.

He kicked it open, but that wasn't as easy as it might have been. The mattress was still on the floor behind it, and the door hit the mattress and bounced shut again. That delayed the Cowboy for just a couple of seconds and in that time I was able to grab the gun I'd dropped. It rested uneasily in my hot, wet hand. I felt its weight and power, and thought nothing about the implications of what I was about to do.

The Cowboy pushed the door open again, using his weight to move the mattress away this time. I had only the barest glimpse of him entering the kitchen before I fired. The shot made a loud, hideous noise and blew a vast, jagged hole in the wall behind the Cowboy's head. I had missed him by miles. I tried to fire again but I was shaking too much.

He had a gun too, of course, and he pointed it at me. I had not the slightest doubt that he was going to use it to kill me, when suddenly half a dozen bullets were fired into him from the main room of the cabin. They pock-marked his body and face, made ugly raw tears in his fancy Cowboy outfit. He was dead before he even got a chance to fire at me. Maybe that wasn't at all a sporting arrangement but it suited me fine.

Tough guy that I am, my first reaction was to throw up. I turned away from the Cowboy's body and vomited into a corner of the kitchen. Tina and Ryan ran into the room. They could barely get in for the corpse and the mattress. Ryan waved his gun around. I guess he had kept it hidden in the many folds of his costume. No doubt in more ordinary circumstances the Cowboy would have frisked Ryan for weapons, but frisking a man in full-blown Cavalier costume would cause problems for the most careful gunman.

Then Ryan shouted, "Cut! Cut! That was the worst fucking death scene in the history of the cinema. Let's do it again, and let's do it right this time. Let's have some pace, some passion, some excitement. Let's do it like we mean it."

I don't know who Ryan thought he was talking to, whether he saw himself as performing in front of a hallucinated movie crew, or whether it was just his crazy way of telling me he wished all this had never happened. Either way, the Cowboy was not available for retakes.

And yet he was right. As a climax, what we had just been through seemed remarkably unfulfilling and unsatisfactory. A man was dead, a man who certainly would have killed me, would possibly have killed all of us. And for what? For money. For a pile of scratched and unusable movie negative, for the sake of a movie that its maker wasn't skilful enough to finish. At the end of Errol Flynn movies there was always a greater sense of triumph, of honour. It ought to have been a big, dramatic finish. This was the finale, the big gundown, but in the event it felt inevitable, meagre, sad.

I was very glad the Cowboy was dead, but I was even more glad that I hadn't killed him. I'd tried to, and the only reason I hadn't succeeded was my sheer incompetence with a gun. If I'd had a steadier hand and a sharper eye, I would have been standing there with a murder on my conscience. As it was I could leave Ryan to worry about all that stuff, and I had the distinct feeling that it wouldn't worry him nearly as much as it would have worried me.

I suppose I was in some sort of shock. I looked across at Tina and I started to laugh. It was a wild, uneasy laughter and I was well aware how inappropriate laughter was in those circumstances, but I couldn't stop. It was caused by relief, at finding myself still alive, but it was also the joy at finding Tina again.

We put our arms around each other, and she said, "You're a complete fool, Jake." I continued laughing and I suspected I was getting close to hysteria. She kissed me long and hard and for quite a long time. That helped push away the laughter. It also hurt my teeth but it felt fantastic. It didn't even bother me that Ryan was watching us. He could have put a bullet through us both, and in other frames of mind perhaps he would have, but maybe he'd rationed himself to one killing per day.

I stood there with my arms round Tina, with a corpse on the floor, with Ryan preening himself in the corner, adopting classic Errol Flynn postures. And I felt, not exactly for the first time, that I was in completely the wrong movie.

We buried the Cowboy's body in what the newspapers call a shallow grave. Then we burned the negative of *The Errol Flynn Movie*. Then we got in the Jeep, drove into Las Vegas, went to the office of Ryan's lawyer, and then we went to the police and told them most of the truth.

I guess it could end there in a little ripple of montage; the grave, the black oily smoke rising from the negatives, Ryan's lawyer saying, "Either he's insane or it's self-defence, and either way there's no court in America is going to convict him. He's an artist. He blew away a piece of Las Vegas trash in self-defence. What's the problem?" And perhaps finally a shot of Tina and me, arms round each other, steadfast but tearful as we look into a long, shared future. Except it never happened.

Certainly we buried the Cowboy. That was to preserve the body as much as anything, to protect it from the heat and the coyotes, the birds of prey, or whatever other critters lived out there in the desert. And certainly we burned the negative. That was Ryan's idea, but I didn't take much persuading. We imagined the police would search the place and seize anything that looked like a clue. The movie was the biggest clue of all, and none of us wanted to have a bunch of tight-lipped Las Vegas cops watching our various ineptitudes; my bad acting, Ryan's non-existent direction, Tina's lame script.

As it burned Ryan said, "I'm such a liar, Jake. I've told such lies. There was no Airstream trailer; it was just a house. The cars weren't Ferraris and Porsches; they were just rented Buicks. And Tina and the other guy didn't arrive on trail bikes;

they had a pick-up truck. But it was in a good cause, wasn't it? It was for the sake of art. That's okay, isn't it, Jake?"

I told him it was just fine.

And yes, the scene with Ryan's lawyer certainly took place, and when Ryan handed himself in to the police (always a good move if you believe the TV cop shows) they seemed to think the lawyer had got it about right. Ryan would not be going to the chair for this. Some of them even knew Ryan. They were very polite, regretful that they had to put him in a cell, but they assured him he'd only be there until they'd sorted out bail: not very long, although there was a chance he might have to spend a night behind bars.

I had feared that I too might end up in jail, as accomplice, or even as attempted murderer of the Cowboy, but once they'd established I was English they seemed to think I was more trouble than I was worth. I thought that at the very least they'd want me as a witness and there'd be some of that familiar "Don't leave town" dialogue, but as far as the police were concerned I could have disappeared from the face of the planet and it wouldn't have bothered them one bit.

But the scene that didn't take place was the one with me and Tina looking to the future. I wanted it to happen. I almost expected it. A part of me even thought I was entitled to it, as compensation maybe, but it never happened. I didn't get the girl after all.

With Ryan out of the way, at least for one night, I played at being a hero and said I didn't need to see a doctor. I thought that if I'd survived this long without medical treatment I could probably survive a few hours more. If the Cowboy's beating had done me irreparable damage I'd have been dead already. So it was only cuts and bruises, and all they needed was time to heal. But more importantly I didn't want to be away from Tina.

For a while it looked very good. We went to my hotel room and we sat on the bed. I showed Tina my winnings from the casino but she wasn't impressed. So I ordered some room service and I thought we were going to have a major love scene. But all Tina said was, "It wasn't meant to be like this."

"Well, of course not," I said.

"I mean it wasn't meant to be like this at all. It wasn't what I wanted at all."

I still couldn't see anything to disagree with. How could anyone have "wanted" all the madness that had gone on? But I had the distinct impression that wasn't quite what she meant.

"Because a part of it went very well for quite a long time," she said.

I couldn't for the life of me think what part that was, but she soon told me.

"Ryan isn't the only one who can devise plots," she said. "Okay, so I'm not much of a scriptwriter but I can still make things happen."

From then on I suspect that my mouth began very slowly to drop open with disbelief.

"Ryan wanted you here, that's for sure," she said. "Maybe he wanted to film you, maybe he wanted to fuck you, I don't know. But mostly he wanted you to lead the Cowboy to him. That was what I wanted too. You arrived. I went along with it. Ryan wanted to confront the Cowboy. He wanted a fight to the death. I wanted that as well. The difference between us was that I wanted the Cowboy to win. I wanted the Cowboy to kill Ryan."

I may have gasped at that point.

"Such as it was," she continued, "that was my plan. I know the Cowboy said he'd have had to kill me too, but I don't think he would have. I wanted Ryan dead. I couldn't see any other way out. You weren't going to kill him for me. I couldn't do it myself. If I'd gone away with you he'd have chased after me, brought me back. You know what he's like, how powerful he is, how hard it is to say no to him."

"I didn't find it so hard," I said.

"Well, good for you. But for me it was impossible. It was the only way out. And for Christ's sake the Cowboy should have wiped the floor with him. Ryan was raving. He was drugged up to the eyeballs. Who'd have given him a prayer against the Cowboy?

"And that's where you came in, Jake. That's where you put your big foot in it. You are such a loser, Jake. Suddenly you're a gunslinger. The only problem is you can't hold a gun without dropping it. You can't even shoot a man dead from six feet with a Magnum. You can't even shoot the right man. And if you had to shoot the Cowboy why the hell couldn't you have waited until after he'd killed Ryan?"

I might have explained that I dropped the gun by accident. I might have said that by trying to shoot the Cowboy I was hoping to save three other lives, but I said nothing.

"The Cowboy would have got the job done if it hadn't been for you," she said. "Ryan would be dead. I'd be free, and you and I could have been together."

"Meaning we're not together now?"

"Come on, Jake, my husband's in jail. His movie's gone up in flames. He's got nothing except me. How can I leave him now?"

"But you wanted him dead."

"Yes. If he was dead maybe I could be with you. Alive there's just no way."

It wasn't an entirely new story. I'd had enough of both begging and reasoning with her.

I said, "Why did you ever sleep with me?"

She thought for a while then said, "Because you asked me nicely, Jake."

I said, "You say I'm a loser. Well I'm not the one stuck in some stupid freak show of a marriage. I'm not the one in jail. I'm not the one who wasted a fortune on a movie nobody's ever going to see. I'm not the one who can't write a script, can't direct a movie, can't even get his sex life to make sense."

"That must be why you're so happy, Jake."

Those were the last words she ever said to me. After that we both knew there was no point talking. We did make love.

It was for old times' sake, I suppose. I wish I could say that I didn't enjoy it, that perhaps I'd fantasised about someone else while it was going on. But I didn't. It was intense and special and powerful, and I felt all the worse for that. When we'd finished, Tina got out of bed and slipped away without a word, and I made no attempt to stop her.

I flew back to England next day. I phoned my parents and my agent. They all asked if I'd had a nice holiday. I said sure. I went along to my GP and showed him my cuts and bruises. He said he'd never seen such an efficient bit of beating up. I assured him that the culprit wouldn't be doing it again.

A lot of time has passed, though perhaps not enough. I'm still in London. I am still an actor, though I'm still waiting for that legendary big break. I'm not holding my breath. I get enough work to survive, and I turn in perfectly competent performances, but I've decided that maybe the secret of good acting, as Errol Flynn constantly demonstrated, is not to care too much and not to try too hard. That's my excuse anyhow. Also I suspect, and fear, that I may have already played my greatest role, and all evidence of it went up in smoke over the Nevada desert. Or maybe the real performance took place off screen.

I have a few friends, no girlfriend at the moment, but that suits me fine. When I'm not working I spend a lot of time alone. I've started to drink too much. I haven't spoken to anyone who was involved with the *The Errol Flynn Movie*, although I still read the occasional newspaper or magazine interview with Sacha. She never mentions Dan Ryan or the film. I don't blame her. Her career is still on course. She is still enigmatic. I hear that Charlie Webb is doing all right for himself too. He's started directing episodes of up-market TV whodunits. I imagine he's rather good at it.

Needless to say I've heard nothing from or about the Ryans. A part of me knows it's better that way, but I still feel the loss. I am no longer sure about the need for beginnings, middles and ends. I know that one phase of my life is over, the phase where I was involved with the Ryans, but I don't feel that anything has been concluded. I have experienced no satisfying sense of an ending. I did not come out of it feeling purged or cleansed. I may have experienced pity and terror, but there has been little in the way of catharsis. Ryan, of course, is the tragic hero, the one who suffered so grandly and picturesquely. I was only the attendant lord, the spear carrier.

Typecasting is always depressing, but if you're an actor you have to live with it. It's probably worse in the movies than in the theatre, and in life it's worst of all. I never wanted to be cast as the hero. I didn't want to play the great lover. I never thought I was an obvious choice for Errol Flynn, but like most actors I took what was offered and did my best with it. Sometimes I think of that whole period as a kind of dream sequence, a flashback; but it's never my dream, the flashback is to a past that I don't recall. I'm like the amnesia victim who doesn't even recognise his own life.

If I look at it one way it seems that the moment I met the Ryans my life became painful and confused, but somehow that was okay. It was better than the life I'd had before. I didn't relish the pain or confusion, but I welcomed the sense of involvement, of being alive. It seems to me now that I rather enjoyed the dangers and the difficulties. It took me out of myself. It made me someone else. Now I'm my old self again. And what dangers and difficulties do I face now? I go on stage and perhaps I'll dry, or corpse, or experience first night nerves. Maybe there'll be a troublesome audience to win round. Maybe I'll have an argument with some useless director. Big deal. Jesus.

I ask myself this: is "real life" about sex and death, guns and gambling, all that flashy fictional stuff, or is it really about getting on quietly with your life, doing your work, doing your best, keeping your head down? Once I would certainly have said it was the latter, but having lived through a certain amount of the former, and despite never wanting to have to go through it again, I'm not so sure.

Maybe that was Ryan's problem. For better or worse he was "larger than life", but he wasn't able to get that largeness down on film. The business of making a movie must have seemed a little tame and pedestrian after all that sex and guns and gambling.

And maybe that was Errol Flynn's problem too. He'd lived a whole life before he ever became an actor; a life of smuggling and sailing and slave-trading. Learning cues and lines must have seemed pretty inane after that, and that's how they now seem to me too.

I don't want to sound like one of those terrible, patronising movie-star biographies but I think that in the case of both Ryan and Flynn their lives were their true art forms. They were bigger and greater than the movies they were involved with. Good for them. But I'm not like that. My life is small-scale, undramatic. You wouldn't pay to see a movie about it.

I'm not about to turn into some cut-price version of Errol Flynn, but I think I understand him better now than I ever did when I was trying to portray him. Ryan said that Flynn suffered from a terrible sense of boredom, and at the time I didn't know what he meant. Now I do. And despite the fact that I've grown my hair and shaved off the moustache, I perhaps "resemble" Flynn more now than I used to. I don't have his taste for sex or drugs or drink or adventure, and the fact that we're both actors doesn't mean much either. But it's precisely that sense of boredom with the self that links me and Errol Flynn.

But boredom can get you two ways. Flynn lived and died running, fighting hard to keep that boredom at bay. My technique seems to be to sit here with it, letting it slowly suffocate me.

I was a boring, unsuccessful actor before I met the Ryans and today I'm a boring, unsuccessful actor again. When I'm lucky enough to get work I go on stage and act out the great dramas of love and death, and then I go home and I'm boring again. This is not news. Of course the actor who plays King Lear isn't as interesting as King Lear, otherwise he wouldn't be an actor. Most actors are fairly dull and shallow, that's why they're actors.

Maybe I'm not much of an actor. So what? I can take that. That's not the worst insult I've ever received. A lot of people would say precisely the same thing about Errol Flynn.

Author's Note

In writing this novel I have referred to many books which describe the life and work of Errol Flynn. I would like to acknowledge a particular debt to the following:

My Wicked, Wicked Ways, Errol Flynn
Errol Flynn: The Untold Story, Charles Higham
Hollywood Babylon, Kenneth Anger
Errol Flynn, A Memoir, Earl Conrad
An Open Book, John Huston
Orson Welles, Barbara Leaming
A Biographical Dictionary of the Cinema, David Thomson

GEOFF NICHOLSON
STREET SLEEPER

'Call me Ishmael' announces Barry Osgathorpe as he abandons his dull job and unadventurous girlfriend to hit the road in a decrepit VW Beetle he names Enlightenment. But he soon finds that the M62 is a poor substitute for Route 66 as Fat Les the Beetle mechanic, a gorgeous hitchhiker who turns out to be a con-artist and a band of hippies who have sold out join him in a climactic battle with the forces of darkness.

'Witty, zany and brilliantly comic, STREET SLEEPER is a genuine original . . . Part madcap car chase, part hymn of praise to the Volkswagen Beetle . . . going the wrong way round the Spaghetti Junctions of life on two wheels and a Zen prayer. Tremendously enjoyable'
J. G. Ballard

'Geoff Nicholson has resurrected the genre of the road novel in an updated and anglicised form . . . pokes merciless fun at the entire Beatnik ethos . . . Light, fast and highly entertaining'
James Fergusson in the Literary Review

'It makes ON THE ROAD and ZEN AND THE ART OF MOTORCYCLE MAINTENANCE look like they're wheel clamped on double yellow lines . . . hugely entertaining, very Rabelaisian and a great debut in pumping good gas. Could become a cult book, particularly among Beetle fans'
Val Hennessy in the Daily Mail

'Silly, mad and clever . . . also a lot of energy and invention'
Hilary Bailey in The Guardian

'A rollicking farce . . . skilfully co-ordinated'
The Sunday Times

sceptre

GEOFF NICHOLSON
THE FOOD CHAIN

London's Everlasting Club is dedicated to sustaining gluttony. For three hundred and fifty years the fire in its hearth has burned as the members eat, drink, make merry, collapse, are carried home or revive and carry on. But when Virgil Marcel, the Golden Boy of Los Angeles cuisine, is invited to join the club he is puzzled. Is this Old World decadence, simple excess or a dark paean to Dionysus? Taken on a sensualist's Grand Tour of Britain, he soon detects more sinister items on the menu than the pleasures of gastronomy.

'An enjoyable black study of avarice and revenge . . . compelling'
The Observer

'A very funny, subversive writer'
The Times

'Hilarious . . . outrageous comedy . . . tremendous verve and wonderfully comic detail'
Literary Review

'An excitingly inventive novelist'
GQ

sceptre

GEOFF NICHOLSON

HUNTERS AND GATHERERS

Steve Geddes' research for a book on collectors leads him to some very eccentric people: from obsessive amassers of beer cans, bizarre sounds and lovers to the filer of 527,345 jokes. But the trail becomes still stranger as Steve is drawn into a network of coincidence and towards a mysterious, presiding figure.

'A most remarkable novel – contemplative but intense, subversive yet melancholy – and sometimes you hear yourself laugh out loud'
Fay Weldon

'I couldn't put it down. This ingenious, maddening and provocative novel explodes like shrapnel in the mind. Highly recommended'
Wendy Perriam

'A comic tour de force'
GQ

'I loved it . . . marvellously fizzy and original – the funniest new novel I've read for months'
Deborah Moggach

'Nicholson achieves a focus-juggling act of considerable dexterity and walks off with a deliberate Tommy Cooper curtain I thought entirely satisfying'
The Guardian

'Nicholson pulls things together with such audacity that you feel like applauding'
Time Out

sceptre